Born to Run

ALSO BY JAMES GRIPPANDO

Last Call★

Lying with Strangers

When Darkness Falls★

Got the Look★

Hear No Evil★

Last to Die★

Beyond Suspicion★

A King's Ransom

Under Cover of Darkness

Found Money

The Abduction

The Informant

The Pardon★

And for young adults

Leapholes

★A Jack Swyteck Novel

Born to Run

A Novel of Suspense

James Grippando

An Imprint of HarperCollinsPublishers

BORN TO RUN. Copyright © 2008 by James Grippando. All rights reserved. Printed in the United States of America. No part of this book may be used or reproduced in any manner whatsoever without written permission except in the case of brief quotations embodied in critical articles and reviews. For information address HarperCollins Publishers, 10 East 53rd Street, New York, NY 10022.

HarperCollins books may be purchased for educational, business, or sales promotional use. For information please write: Special Markets Department, HarperCollins Publishers, 10 East 53rd Street, New York, NY 10022.

FIRST HARPERLUXE EDITION

HarperLuxe™ is a trademark of HarperCollins Publishers

Library of Congress Cataloging-in-Publication Data is available upon request.

ISBN: 978-0-06-171970-7

08 09 10 11 12 ID/RRD 10 9 8 7 6 5 4 3 2 1

For Tiffany . . . and tramps like us

Born to Run

September 1960
Nicosia, Cyprus

Chapter 1

The Italians called him the Greek. The Greeks called him the Sicilian. He was from Nicosia. It was a funny coincidence that the largest city in his native Cyprus shared a name with a city in Sicily—the birthplace of his bride.

"Sofia," he whispered in the darkness.

His wife of eleven months lay sleeping beneath a clingy cotton sheet, the gentle curve of her hip a silhouette in the shadows of night. A late-summer heat wave had sent them to bed naked, and like true newlyweds, they'd made the best of it. Cyprus was the mythological birthplace of Aphrodite, the goddess of love, who couldn't have held a candle to Sofia. She was a classic Italian beauty, a strong and passionate woman with dark hair, captivating eyes, and flawless olive skin.

The Greek felt lucky to have her, and he marveled that she loved him enough to leave her family and run all the way to Cyprus with him.

He only wished he could stop running.

"Sofia, did you hear that?"

Her head didn't move from the pillow.

The Greek slowly slid out of bed, crossed the room in silence, and went to the open window. The lace curtains were motionless in the warm night air. He crooked his finger and parted the panels just enough to check the quiet street from his second-story apartment.

The cloak of night could hide centuries of decay, and Nicosia was beautiful in the moonlight. Flanked by the Pentadaktylos, the five-finger mountain, Nicosia was one of the oldest cities in the world, the geographic heart of an island paradise in the eastern Mediterranean. Behind thick sandstone walls, Cypriots had defended themselves from a host of invaders and occupiers dating back at least to the Byzantine Empire. The mid-twentieth century had proved to be another violent chapter, with five years of armed struggle finally bringing an end to more than eighty years of British rule. The Greek had taken no stake in that fight—which was why *real* Greeks called him the Sicilian (or worse)—but he'd grown accustomed to noisy nights, even gunshots.

It was purely instinct, but tonight the Greek felt another type of raid coming—one that had absolutely nothing to do with Greeks, Turks, or any of the country's traditional ethnic divisions. He stood quietly at the lone window in their one-room apartment and listened. He was certain that he had heard something, and it took more than a cat on the roof to wake him from sleep after sex.

He walked around to the other side of the bed and sat on the edge of the lumpy mattress.

"Sofia, wake up."

She grumbled and propped herself up on one elbow. Even at 3:00 A.M. she was beautiful, but she immediately sensed his concern.

"What is it?" she said.

He didn't answer. He sat and listened for that noise again. There it was—a thumping that came from the first floor of their building.

"They're coming!" he said in an urgent whisper. He sprang from the bed and quickly pulled on his underwear.

"Who's coming?" said Sofia.

He pulled on his pants. The thumping noise was louder, like a herd of stallions charging up the stairs.

"It's me they want, not you."

"Who? *Who?*"

"Listen to me. Don't tell them I was here. Just say—tell them I left you."

He kissed her before she could protest.

The loud bang on the door was definitely not a knock. Someone had put a shoulder into it. They were busting their way in. The Greek couldn't find his shoes or his shirt, and there was no time to grab anything—except his gun in the top dresser drawer. He dived through the open window and out onto the balcony as the chain lock ripped from the frame and the apartment door crashed open.

He heard his wife scream.

"Sofia!" he shouted—which accomplished nothing, except to give himself away.

"Out the window!" a man yelled from inside the apartment.

The Greek could only run for it. He grabbed the rain gutter and pulled himself up to the second-story roof. His first step loosened an old barrel tile, and it crashed onto the street below. As he regained his footing, the Greek glanced back to see the lead man climbing up onto the roof behind him.

He was wearing a police uniform.

The Greek didn't hesitate to shoot, the sound of Sofia's scream replaying in his mind. The return gunfire told him that he'd missed—and the bullet ripped through his hand. He cried out in pain and dismay as his revolver flew from his grasp, slid down the roof, and landed in the gutter. Another shot shattered the clay roofing tiles at his feet.

The Greek kept running.

The slope of the roof changed from pitched to flat. He gained speed and jumped across the alley—the canyon between buildings—and landed on the neighbor's roof. A quick glance over his shoulder didn't slow him down a bit. Two—no, three—men in uniform were in pursuit. The Greek ran faster, his heart pounding in his chest. Beat after beat, the blood pumped from his wounded hand, leaving a crimson trail across the rooftops. He couldn't stop running. At any moment, he expected a bullet in the back. They were close enough to take him out.

He leaped across another alley, and this time it took his breath away. The ground had gone from two stories to four stories below him. The buildings on his street had the same roofline, but they were built on the slope of a hill, each one of increasing height.

Too high to jump.

He raced across the rooftop, but the footfalls behind him grew louder. His hand didn't hurt—too much adrenaline to feel pain—but the loss of blood was making him dizzy. No way could he outrun these guys.

He had to find a safe place to jump down and hide. The roof pitched upward, however, and the only way down from here was through the men with the guns. He climbed even higher, all the way to the crest, where the roof flattened into a wide expanse. It was a big building, like a warehouse. No, a hotel. The Mykonos Hotel—the last building on the block. No rooftop beyond it. No more alleys to jump.

Nowhere to run.

He went all the way to the edge, and his heart was in his throat. Six stories up.

Shit!

"Turn around!"

The voice confirmed his fears. The man was speaking Italian. There was no point in resisting. The Greek turned to face justice.

The chase had left the men breathing just as heavily as the Greek, but their faces bore the unmistakable smirk of victory.

"On your knees," the man said. His gun was aimed at the Greek's chest.

Again, the Greek obliged. He was too dizzy and exhausted to resist, even if he'd wanted to put up a fight.

The two bigger men stepped toward him. One grabbed his right arm; the other, his left. The Greek was no longer standing under his own power. His feet raked across the rooftop as the men carried him to the building's edge.

"What did you do to Sofia?"

The man with the gun went to him.

"What does it matter?" he said, and he spat in the Greek's face.

"What do you want?"

The man shrugged. "Nothing."

With a wave of his hand, the two bigger men tightened their grip, and the Greek felt his feet leave the rooftop.

It all happened in a flash, but the next few seconds seemed like an eternity, as the Greek was airborne, flying up into the night at first, the stars seemingly within his reach. Then gravity took over, and just as quickly he was a meteor tumbling out of control, spiraling down, down, down—headfirst, feetfirst, headfirst.

He didn't hear himself scream, or the Sicilians laughing, as his body collided with the cobblestone below.

Forty-six years later

Chapter 2

They looked dead—except for the eyes.

Sleek and dark saurian bodies lay perfectly still, concealed in a flat pool of water that was black as ink. The heavy air of night stirred not a bit—damp heat, no breeze to speak of, sweetened by the perfume-like scent of surrounding water lilies. The surest signs of life were in the chorus of sounds from unseen creatures of the night: the rhythmic belch of bullfrogs, the predawn squawk of egrets and osprey, the steady hum of insects. At any moment, however, that peaceful pulse of nature could spike into tachycardia. The eyes of a bull gator lurking in the marshland said it all— primeval red dots caught in the sweep of a handheld spotlight. There was hunger in that eerie, ruby shine. And with good reason:

Nighttime was feeding time in the Florida Everglades.

Phil Grayson wasn't precisely in the Everglades—gator hunting wasn't permitted there in December—but this guided hunt on adjacent private land was the next best thing. Grayson stood tall in the twenty-foot wooden rowboat, his gaze fixed on the telltale eye-shine in the darkness. His love of hunting dated back to BB guns and doves on telephone wires, and when Grandpa gave him a Harrington & Richardson single-shot rifle for his eighth birthday, he considered himself a true outdoorsman, even if he wasn't allowed to shoot without his dad looking over his shoulder. Over the next forty-six years, that passion continued to grow—from quail in Texas and duck in Arkansas to Montana deer and Canadian moose.

Gator hunting, however, was new to him. In fact, this cool autumn night in south Florida was his very first stab at conquering the king of Florida's freshwaters.

Grayson had spent two days exploring the nearby Everglades, which was not at all the dismal swamp he had imagined. To the north, Lake Okeechobee gathered water from rain-filled rivers and streams. Tea-colored water flowed for a hundred miles, south to the tip of mainland Florida and west to the Gulf of Mexico, much as spilled milk spreads across the kitchen table. All across these millions of watery acres grew the tall reeds of saw grass, a rare species of swamp sedge that has flourished here for over four thousand years. This legendary "river of grass" divided the east coast of Florida from the west, an utter North American anomaly where visitors found exotic reptiles, manatees, and rainbow-colored tree snails, roseate spoonbills and ghost orchids, towering royal palms and gumbo-limbos. Here, biblical clouds of mosquitoes could blacken a white canoe within seconds, and oceans of stars filled a night sky untouched by city lights. Grayson had traveled all over the world and never seen any place like it.

"Twelve footer, I'm bettin'," his gator guide said in an old-Florida drawl. "That's sumptin' special."

There were two boats in their hunting party, each in its own channel, each hunter with his own guide. Grayson's guide was a retired county sheriff named McFay, who took his gator hunting seriously. He rarely smiled, and when he did, his crooked teeth showed the stains of chewed tobacco. He reminded Grayson of the redneck version of Captain Ahab. No peg leg, but his left ring finger was missing, lost to the snap of a mammoth jaw and three thousand pounds of pressure per square inch. Grayson wondered if it was the same giant that had left an inch-deep bite mark—and a tooth—in the side of the boat.

McFay switched off the electric trolling motor. It was barely big enough to push along two men in a rowboat, but the quiet hum didn't scare away gators the way gas-powered engines did. McFay was a stickler for details, which was why he insisted on a wooden boat over noisy aluminum. The glare of a spotlight was the one hindrance to the hunt that he could put up with. Not even the craziest of gator cowboys relied solely on moonlight

Grayson released the bale on his rod. He could feel the power, and with good reason. His saltwater fishing gear could have whipped a hammerhead. Rod thick as his thumb. Microfiber line testing 150 pounds. Treble hooks in size 14/0.

"Get good 'n' ready before you cast," the guide said. "When there's a hook up, that line's gonna pop like a rifle shot."

"Bring it on," said Grayson.

Once an endangered species, the Florida alligator had grown in population to a robust million-plus—one for every eighteen people in Florida. Firearms were nonetheless illegal in gator hunting, except for the handheld .44 bang stick that delivered a death blow directly to the brain. Experienced hunters used a variety of weapons to snag their prey, from crossbows to snares, harpoons to slings. McFay was partial to a saltwater rod and reel, which allowed him to catch and release small gators.

Over eleven feet and—*bang*—lights out.

Grayson cast his line into the darkness. With a sniper's precision, he placed it just a few yards away from the glowing red dots at the surface. It was dead-center of the narrow channel that cut through razor-sharp reeds of ten-foot saw grass. Feeling for tension, he slowly retrieved the line, not sure what to expect. Clearly, however, that was no largemouth bass peering back at him through the night. Out there—all around him—was an unending fight for survival that bordered on prehistoric. He had witnessed that fight with his own eyes, and in most dramatic fashion, right before sundown. Grayson was visiting Florida on official business, trying to learn more about the latest threat to the Everglades—pythons. In the first five years of the new century, more than a million had been imported by the United States for commercial sale. Nearly half of them went to Miami. An alarming number of those were now thriving in the Everglades, growing to over twenty feet in length and rivaling gators for the top of the food chain.

Grayson felt the hook drag. With the angler's touch, he worked the line and set it firmly.

A growl in the pitch darkness made the hairs stand up on the back of his neck. The noise that followed was like a bus dropping into a lake. Line screamed off the big spinning reel as something truly gigantic thrashed amid the water lettuce, lily pads, and pickerel weed.

"Coming right at the boat!" McFay yelled.

"Under the boat!" Grayson shouted back.

Bubbles and mud boiled up from below as Grayson worked the bent double rod around the bow.

"Out on starboard side!" said McFay.

The mighty tail slammed the wooden hull as the gator motored away. McFay popped from his seat to help his client screw down the drag, and off they went on a gator-powered sleigh ride in a twenty-foot boat.

"Bigger 'n twelve feet!" shouted McFay. "Hold on!"

Grayson's arm suddenly felt numb. Sweat ran from his brow.

"I . . . can't," he said weakly.

The tingling gave way to a sharp pain in his chest that shot all the way up to his jaw. The fishing rod slipped from his hands and sailed over the bow. Grayson lost his balance and tumbled backward.

"McFay!" he called, but he was beyond his guide's grasp. In the blink of an eye he went over the side, headfirst into the marsh.

Suddenly, spotlights shone from virtually every direction. It was as if someone had flipped a giant switch, the way the channel lit up. Voices called to him. Grayson was kicking, flailing, and screaming for help, but it was nothing compared to the noises around him—ominous splashes, echoes of the one he'd heard upon hooking that bull gator. Two more, five more, ten more.

Gators!

They were fleeing the barrage of bright lights.

Or maybe it was the Secret Service agents diving in to rescue him.

The life jacket should have kept him afloat, but he felt himself sinking into the muck. Or being dragged down. The pain in his chest was now crushing, and he struggled to overcome it, but his mind was swirling. His body felt stiff and unresponsive. His only choice, it seemed, was to respect nature, to become one with black water, to be the third and weakest leg in a bizarre and deadly triangle. One angry gator. Untold pythons.

And Phillip Grayson—the vice president of the United States.

"Sir, give me your hand!" he heard a man shout.

But he couldn't lift his arm. He couldn't turn his head to look. He couldn't move his mouth to speak.

Vice President Grayson couldn't even breathe.

There was that intense brightness again—the emergency spotlights, or some other kind of light. And then everything was black.

Chapter 3

It was the big one. The other side of the mountain. The downward slope. Half dead. Four-oh.

Forty.

Jack Swyteck was born on December 7, exactly twenty-five years after the attack on Pearl Harbor. He'd been stepping on land mines ever since.

"I can't afford this," said Jack.

He and his best friend, Theo Knight, were in the chrome-and-glass showroom at Classic Cars of Miami, standing beside a fully restored 1968 Mustang GT-390 Fastback. Jack was on his heels, reeling from sticker shock.

"You can't afford *not* to do this," said Theo.

"I have no desire to make a big deal out of forty."

"Dude, I said it before: 'There's two kinds of people in this world—risk takers and shit takers. Someday, you gotta decide which you're gonna be when you grow up. And today is that day."

The Mustang's Highland Green finish gleamed beneath the halogen lights. Jack could hardly wait to see it in the south Florida sun.

It had been four years since Jack's beloved 1966 Mustang convertible with pony interior had gone up in flames at the hands of some pissed-off Colombians who had their own special way of getting his attention. Theo was at Jack's side as the wrecker towed the burned-out shell away—just as he'd been there for Jack's divorce, Jack's run for his life in Côte d'Ivoire, and everything in between. Theo was just a teenager when they'd first met, the youngest inmate on Florida's death row. It took years of legal maneuvering and last-minute appeals, but Jack finally proved Theo's innocence. Becoming the best of friends with a badass from Miami's toughest African American gang had not been part of Jack's plans, but Theo had vowed to pay his lawyer back.

Sometimes, Jack wished he would call it even already.

"You don't think this smacks of a midlife crisis?" said Jack.

"Dude, your whole life is a crisis."

The car salesman returned with the keys in hand. Jack's girlfriend, Andie, was with him. She was smiling—a good sign.

Jack had met FBI agent Andie Henning under the toughest of circumstances: she was tracking a serial kidnapper with his sights on Jack's girlfriend. She was now officially Jack's longest steady since his divorce. Even more important—for present purposes, anyway—any woman trained in hostage negotiation had to be able to cut one hell of a deal on a used car.

"Here's your number," she said, as she handed him a slip of paper.

Jack checked it. "Nice work," he said.

"Don't say I never did anything for you."

"So, let's see the Mustang run, shall we?" said the salesman.

Andie glanced at the cramped, fold-down backseat and said, "You boys have fun."

"You're not coming?" said Jack.

"I have a haircut appointment. I think it's time for that short, professional look, don't you?"

Jack was speechless. He loved Andie's hair—long and raven black. With her amazing green eyes and high, Native American cheekbones, it made her a captivating, exotic beauty.

"You're going to cut off your hair?" he said with trepidation.

"Naturally. It's what women do when they—wait a minute. I'm sorry. *You're* turning forty, not me. Whew, what a relief."

"Very funny."

"Love you," she said.

The L word had entered their relationship in August. Having watched it slowly evaporate from the vocabulary of his first marriage, Jack didn't take it lightly.

"Love you too."

He kissed her good-bye, and it was just Jack, Theo, and their own little piece of automobile history.

Theo snatched the keys from the salesman. "Let's roll," he said.

With the push of a button, the salesman opened the showroom door, and then he climbed in the backseat. Theo settled behind the custom leather-grip steering wheel as if the car were made for him.

"Shouldn't *I* be driving?" said Jack.

Theo glared. "I'm in the bed naked, about to have sex with Beyoncé Knowles, and you're telling me to move over so you can take a nap?"

"What?"

"It's a *test drive*, Swyteck. We ain't just kickin' the tires here."

It was one of the things Jack loved about Theo. He could hurl insults to your face and still make you laugh.

Jack rode shotgun and, with Theo's turn of the key, smiled at the sound of a perfectly tuned V8. He felt the vibe as the car rolled slowly out of the showroom, and Jack lowered his window. It was one of those mornings that screamed "convertible"—seventy-two degrees, blue skies, not a cloud in sight—but for every perfect December day in Miami there was hell to pay in August. One leaky canvas top on a vintage automobile with crappy air-conditioning was enough in Jack's lifetime.

The showroom garage door closed automatically behind them, and Theo burned rubber out of the parking lot.

"Easy on the new tires," said the salesman.

"Sorry," said Jack, as if it were his fault.

Theo didn't apologize. He just beat it up U.S. 1.

The salesman made his pitch over the roar of the engine.

"This baby isn't quite show quality," he said, "but it's a dead ringer for the modified Mustang Steve McQueen drove in the *Bullitt* movie. Highland Green paint. Black interior. Three-ninety big block engine pushing four hundred horsepower. I've met dozens of Mustang know-it-alls who swear it was a Shelby flying over the hills of San Francisco in the famous chase scene, but it was a fastback, just like this one. Which is a good thing for you. A restored Shelby in this condition would set you back well into six figures."

Theo downshifted and stopped at the red light. A couple of fit young women clad in running shorts and breathable tank tops were jogging in place at the curb, waiting for the walk signal. Theo revved the engine as they passed in the crosswalk. The Latina with long legs smiled and waved. Jack waved back.

Theo grabbed Jack's arm with enough force to break it.

"Never wave at chicks."

"Oh, come on. Andie is not going to get upset over that."

"Got nothin' to do with Andie. Mustang Rule Number One: You don't wave at chicks. Period."

"But she waved at me," said Jack.

"Don't matter. You just look, nod kind of cool-like, and say *Wassup?*"

"How is she supposed to hear me if I'm sitting inside a car?"

"She can see your lips move."

"She can also see me wave."

"If she sees your lips move, her mind hears *'Wassup?'* If she sees you wave, she hears 'Hey there, Lieutenant Dan: it's me, Forrest. Forrest Gump!' So, don't wave. *Ever.* Got it?"

"Got it."

The light changed and the Mustang launched like a rocket. Jack switched on the radio.

The salesman leaned forward and said, "The sound system is obviously not original, but you've still got your AM dial if you want that 1960s experience."

Jack tried to find music, but the AM band was mostly Spanish talk radio. At the left end of the dial, an English-language news station caught his attention. The reporter had a decided urgency to his tone:

"—is no official word yet, but Associated Press is reporting that Vice President Grayson was unconscious when emergency responders airlifted him from a private refuge near Everglades National Park and transported him to Jackson Memorial Hospital in Miami."

"Music," said Theo.

"No, wait."

"Mustang Rule Number Two," said Theo, but Jack cut him off.

"I'm serious. Shut up."

The reporter on the scene continued: "The vice president spent all day Friday in the Everglades with a special blue-ribbon commission that is studying twenty-first-century threats to the ecosystem. This morning he was on a guided hunting trip on privately owned land when, approximately thirty minutes before sunrise, something went terribly wrong. Of course, it is widely known that Vice President Grayson has a history of heart trouble. He suffered two heart attacks in his forties, and two years ago he spent his fifty-second birthday in the hospital with chest pains. We can only speculate as to whether today's emergency was health related or some kind of accident. At this point, information is scarce. The hospital has released no comment, except to confirm that the vice president is there. And this area of western Miami-Dade County where the incident occurred is very isolated, as you might well imagine. We're told that the other members of the vice president's hunting party are being transported back to a private residence in Key Largo, where Vice President Grayson was staying with friends. We're not sure how many hunters were in the party, but we hope to talk to them and bring additional details to you just as soon as we can."

The anchorman in the studio interrupted to promise "more on this breaking story in sixty seconds," and the station cut to a commercial.

Theo stopped at another red light.

"Wow," said Jack. "Sounds pretty grim."

Theo checked his sunglasses in the rearview mirror. "Your old man still buddy-buddy with the president of vice?"

"I'd say so," said Jack. "He was on that hunting trip."

Chapter 4

J ack was standing at his father's side as they watched the landing of Air Force One.

Jack had just signed the papers for his new Mustang when Harry called to tell him that the hunting party—sans vice president—was being transported by yacht from Everglades National Park to Ocean Reef Club. The exclusive Key Largo resort had its own airstrip, and Jack had driven down from Miami at nearly the speed of Air Force One. Steve McQueen would have been proud.

"It was all so surreal," said Harry, his voice barely audible over the roar of jet engines at the other end of the runway. "Phil's boat was in another part of the channel, but I knew from the burst of spotlights and all the shouting that something had gone wrong. It was a

Secret Service frenzy. My guide tried to motor us over there, but an agent jumped onto our boat, cranked up the outboard, and took us in the complete opposite direction. I felt like I was in JFK's limo speeding off to the hospital—without Phil."

"You think he'll survive?"

"They won't tell us if he's alive, if he's dead, if it was his heart—nothing."

"Did the Secret Service take your statement yet?"

"Yeah. I don't know what their agenda is, but they made me feel like I needed a lawyer."

One thing all criminal defense lawyers knew: if you think you need one, you probably do.

The last time Jack had visited Ocean Reef, he was fifteen years old and zipping around the club's two thousand acres with friends on a golf cart. Even back then, a vacation home there had been well beyond the financial reach of the Swyteck family. Today, it was barely within the reach of Donald Trump. Ocean Reef was a perfect place for a vice president to vacation. The club was surrounded on three sides by water, and on the fourth by protected lands under federal and state ownership. Forty-five security guards, continuous camera surveillance, and monitored water access made it an exclusive playground for people of privilege. Jack had passed a mile-long line of media vans on the entrance road, but not one got past the guardhouse. Every local station and several national networks had a microwave dish hoisted high into the air—tower after tower of modern communications systems that rose like a wintry forest from the mangroves and turquoise waters of the fragile keys environs. Helicopters were kept at bay for the landing of Air Force One, but Jack could see them hovering on the horizon, well beyond the championship golf course, the town houses that sold for over a million dollars, the new waterfront homes that sold for ten times that much, and the marina filled with yachts—many of which came at a price that made the homes seem cheap.

Two Secret Service agents pulled up in a customized golf cart that looked like a miniature Bentley. Jack said hello. They said, "Get in."

"Where are we going?" said Jack.

"The president wants to see you in his office."

"On the plane?"

"No, at the Tiki Bar."

A Secret Service agent with a sense of humor—now that was something Jack hadn't expected. The cart took them straight to the Jetway, and the door opened at the top of the stairs.

Jack felt a little rush of adrenaline, momentarily forgetting the circumstances of his first meeting with the president. It wasn't the familiar Air Force One—the runway at Ocean Reef wasn't long enough to accommodate a Boeing 747—but the smaller C-32 had an aura of its own. His father looked somber enough for both of them as the Secret Service led them aboard. Olivia Thompson, the president's blond, thirty-nine-year-old chief of staff, greeted them inside. A quick turn up the corridor took them to the state room. Thompson knocked, opened the door, and announced the Swytecks' arrival in a respectful tone.

"Welcome, Governor," said the president, as he rose to greet him.

They shook hands firmly, and then Harry introduced his son.

Another round of handshaking and good wishes followed, but the president's signature smile came across as a bit weary to Jack. Perhaps the news was bad about Grayson. Perhaps it was the cumulative weight of his first two years in the White House. Jack had seen photographic face progressions of past presidents, showing how the office aged them from one year to the next. By that standard, President Keyes was faring well. His skin was as youthful as could be expected for a man in his fifties, and he didn't have Lincoln's worry lines or Nixon's jowls. His transformation was more subtle— with the exception of the hair, which had been steadily receding since inauguration day. He was a handsome man, nonetheless, and he might have done well to throw in the towel and shave his head, like a Bruce Willis or a Yul Brynner. Keyes, however, seemed to be on track for the comb-over, preferring to hide as long as possible the Gorbachev-like birthmark at his vanishing hair line.

Jack and Harry took the seats facing the president, and the chief of staff stood quietly to the side.

"How is—"

"Harry," the president said before he could ask about Grayson, "how long have you and I known each other?"

Harry had to think about it. "I'm sure we shook hands long before this, but the first real sit-down-and-get-to-know-each-other conversation I can recall was at the national governors' conference in Milwaukee."

"And I recall taking an immediate liking to you."

"Thank you, sir."

"Much the same way I felt about Sunny Phil."

Sunny Phil was the nickname Harry had given his friend for his "always sunny" disposition. "He hated that name," Harry said, smiling.

"But it fit."

"Yes. As long as I've known him."

"You boys go way back," said the president. "Both of you All-Southeastern Conference athletes in college, I understand."

"Well, different decades, and definitely with different loyalties. He was a Georgia Bulldog. I was a Florida Gator."

The mention of a "gator" just hours after the vice president had been plucked from the Everglades triggered a moment of awkward silence. The president dug into the bowl of cashews on the tray table, then thought better of it. He had the body of a man who exercised and watched his weight.

"I'm sorry to tell you this, Harry. But Phil Grayson has passed."

Jack felt goose bumps, and instinctively he took his father's hand. It was shaking. Harry started to speak, then stopped to gather his composure. He was normally not one to express emotions, but it was as if the events of this overwhelming day—hunting alligators, battling the Everglades, working through a friend's medical emergency, and now his death—had struck him down. For the first time in his life, the sixty-four-year-old former governor truly looked old to his son.

"Sorry," said Harry, reeling in his emotions. "How's Marilyn?"

"Twenty-eight years of marriage. About what you'd expect."

Jack said, "Are you okay, Dad?"

Harry nodded.

The president said, "The White House will release a statement in about twenty minutes. I'll make a public television address from the East Wing this evening. I'll order flags to fly at half-staff for thirty days. It's appropriate that we mourn as a nation. But I don't want that period of mourning to turn into national anxiety over Phil's replacement. The Twenty-fifth Amendment to the Constitution doesn't say how quickly I have to move, but I plan to make an announcement on a vice presidential designate as soon as possible."

Jack bristled. Talk of a replacement so soon after death was a bit unseemly. But most everything about Washington struck Jack that way.

"That's wise," said Harry. "As you know, I'm retired from politics, but if I can be of any help formulating a short list, I'd be honored."

The president cast a half smile in the chief of staff's direction. "Didn't I tell you Harry's the most humble guy around?"

"You did, sir," she said.

The president said, "You're a good man, Harry. You were certainly a huge help in delivering Florida for the Keyes-Grayson ticket in the last election."

"That was my pleasure, sir."

"Hard to believe we're less than two years away from another election. Florida will be a key state again."

"It's the political story of the twenty-first century: Florida, Florida, Florida."

"You're one of the most popular governors that crazy state has ever had. If it weren't for term limits, I would have put my money on a third term for you."

"Thank you for saying that, but I have no regrets about moving on."

"Well, you have certainly kept moving. As you should. You're a young man."

"Not as young as you, sir, and getting older every day."

"Hell, you're not even eligible for Medicare yet. The bipartisan leadership role you've played in disaster relief efforts since your exit from politics has been nothing short of amazing."

"It's fulfilling work."

"Not to mention high-profile. Everyone from Floridians and their hurricanes to Californians and their earthquakes has taken notice." The president leaned forward in his chair, looking Harry in the eye. "*Voters* have taken note."

"Sir—"

"The work you and Phil were doing in the Everglades shows your commitment to the environment. And who knows more about dealing with the burdens of immigration and illegal aliens than a former governor of Florida? Another hot-button issue."

"Sir, I'm retired, and I—"

The president silenced him with a slow but firm shake of his head.

"I'm not taking no for an answer, Harry. I went through this short-listing exercise a year ago when Phil had his heart surgery. My list hasn't changed since then. I want Governor Swyteck to be my new vice president."

"Whoa—" said Jack. It was purely a reflex.

"Double whoa," said Harry.

Chapter 5

Washington was dressed in black. Flags were flying at half-staff. The country was in an official period of national mourning.

It had nothing to do with Jack approaching forty.

"The nation has lost a great and faithful servant," President Keyes said in a televised address from the White House, "and I have lost a dear friend."

William Grayson was the eighth U.S. vice president to die in office, only the second since the passing of President McKinley's would-be successor in 1899—and the first to be chomped by an alligator. The official cause of death was myocardial infarction, which gave his loved ones the comfort of believing that he'd probably never felt the removal of his right foot and ankle.

Funeral services began the following Monday on Capitol Hill, where Grayson's body lay in state in a flag-draped oak casket atop the Lincoln catafalque. Family, friends outside the Beltway, and a short list of dignitaries assembled on Thursday to pay their final respects in the vice president's hometown of Madison, Georgia. The flu kept Mrs. Swyteck from traveling, so Harry brought Jack.

"Name, please," the Secret Service agent said.

Jack and his father were standing where the taxi had dropped them, outside an iron gate at the entrance to a long and winding brick driveway.

Madison was the historic Georgia town that Union general William Tecumseh Sherman had refused to burn in his march to the sea. The Graysons lived in one of the surviving antebellum mansions, and it was mildly ironic that Phil Grayson became the first vice president to die in office since James Sherman, a relative of the scorched-earth general who had spared the Grayson home. It was a handsome Greek revival–style mansion with a sloping front lawn that was a leafy blanket of kudzu beneath a forest of oaks, magnolias, and dogwood trees. Jack imagined that in spring it would have been a colorful setting, but today's skies were fittingly gray, and a cool mist in the air was turning colder by the minute. Jack had heard that north Georgia could be balmy even in December, but there must have been some kind of meteorological law against it whenever a thin-blooded Floridian showed up with no coat or umbrella.

"Jack and Harry Swyteck," his father said.

The agent checked the printed guest list and then double-checked by radio communication. The gate opened, and a black Town Car took them up the driveway to the front door. An attendant escorted them inside. An old friend immediately pulled Harry into a circle of guests, and Jack let him go it alone, opting out of the "this is my son" tour.

The first thing Jack noticed was not the period antiques or priceless artwork, but the fragrance. The interior French doors that connected the foyer, parlor, and living rooms had been opened to create the effect of one continuous room that ran the length of the house, and it was a bower of southern smilax, green palms, white roses, and chrysanthemums.

The second thing he noticed was the tall brunette across the room. She was downright stunning, even dressed in conservative funeral attire, but her eyes showed signs of fatigue, as if broadcasting to the world that she was Phil Grayson's daughter.

Jack's cell vibrated in his pocket. He checked the number. Theo—the guy had a sixth sense for interesting women. Jack stepped outside onto the porch to take the call.

"Dude, how's it going?" said Theo.

Bar noises from Sparky's Tavern were in the background, and Jack knew instantly that this was another one of those pointless calls that Theo made from work just to pass the time.

"It's about what you'd expect," said Jack.

"That bad, huh? Any babes?"

"Theo, I'm at a *funeral.*"

"That sounds like a yes to me. Who is she?"

It was one of Theo's favorite games—getting men in committed relationships to admit that they could identify every beautiful woman in any room they ever entered, whether it was a wedding or a funeral. Jack could never fool him, so he just gave it up.

"All right. You got me. Grayson's daughter is a knockout."

"You gonna get her number?"

"*No.*"

"Jack, Jack. You disappoint me."

"First of all, I'm dating Andie. So why are we even having this conversation?"

"Because you're not married, and you automatically assume that a gorgeous woman is off-limits. That's wrong."

"Look, even if I wasn't seeing Andie, and even if this wasn't Phil Grayson's funeral, she's in her twenties and I'm, you know"—Jack could barely say it—"hours away from forty."

"Dude, you don't understand. Every man her age has been addicted to Internet porn since high school and truly believes that the only conceivable way to pleasure a woman is to lay back and let her give him a blow job. You could be the Clark Gable to an entire generation of Sara Lees."

"Sara Lee is a pound cake, moron. The actress was Vivien Leigh."

"No—Tara Lee, wasn't it?"

"No, Tara was the plantation that Scarlett—"

"Forget Clark Gable. You're Steve McQueen with a new Mustang."

"Right. I gotta go."

"Loser."

"Pound cake."

Jack closed his flip phone and tucked it into his pocket. The mist had turned to a light drizzle, and Jack took a moment on the covered porch to listen to raindrops falling on kudzu. A door opened at the far end of the long porch. It was the vice president's widow stepping out for air. Jack didn't want to intrude on her quiet moment. He could scarcely imagine what the past five days had been like for her—the phone call from the Everglades, the emergency flight down from

Washington, the rush to a Miami hospital, the news of her husband's death. And that was only the beginning. From there it was nonstop public appearances that left no time for private grief.

Jack remained at the porch rail, about fifty feet away from Marilyn Grayson. She dug into her pocketbook, foraged for a cigarette, and lit it. The patter of falling rain was almost hypnotic, and she was deep in thought, standing beside a pair of white rocking chairs, one of which had gone permanently still. Finally, she returned from wherever her mental journey had taken her, crushed out her cigarette in the ashtray beside the rocking chair, and walked over to thank Jack for coming.

It was strange to finally meet someone you'd seen thousands of times before, but only on television. Invariably, they were taller or shorter, wider or thinner, meaner or friendlier than even your high-definition television had led you to believe.

"You're Harry Swyteck's son, aren't you?"

"I am," said Jack as he approached. "Agnes is sorry she couldn't make it, but my father and I thought my coming might show how sorry the entire Swyteck family is for your loss."

"Thank you. It means a lot that you came to our home to tell me that."

She fell quiet and looked across the lawn toward a stand of fir and pecan trees. Jack got the distinct impression that the former Second Lady was positively tired of small talk, tired of all the ceremonies. She also seemed to appreciate the fact that Jack didn't mind the momentary silence—didn't feel compelled to spoil it with words that were just words.

"Do you think your father is going to take the job?" she said.

Jack was taken aback. No public announcement had been made, but of course she would have known about the impending nomination.

"Honestly, I think it's all up to Agnes. No one was happier about his retirement than she was."

"I can fully understand that," she said, "though I can't imagine a successor who would have pleased Phil more."

"That's very kind of you to say."

"But your father needs to go into this with eyes open."

"Not to worry," said Jack. "My father's a good man, but he's also a seasoned politician."

She turned to face him squarely, her voice lowering. "I will never say this directly to your father. From now on, I can't say *anything* to him that I don't want divulged in his public confirmation hearing. So I will tell it to you: I have serious questions about Phil's death."

Jack struggled for words, not wanting to insult her intelligence. "Mrs. Grayson, your husband had a heart attack."

"That's what *they* say."

She said the word *they* the way conspiracy theorists said it.

"You have reason to doubt that?" said Jack.

She considered it, then seemed to think twice about elaborating. "I know what you're thinking. I'm grief-stricken, my judgment clouded. But I've a feeling that, with the direction your father is headed, you might have some questions, too. If you do," she said, as she reached inside her pocketbook and removed her card, "call me."

She handed it to Jack, who had no idea how to respond.

"As I say," she continued, "I have serious questions. And I intend to get answers."

She stepped away, and Jack watched in stunned silence as she went back inside the house, ever gracious toward her guests.

White House correspondents were also invited, while the rest watched on a monitor from the press room in the West Wing.

Chloe watched from her living room, alone.

"My fellow Americans," the president said into the camera. "A little less than one week ago this country suffered a terrible loss."

Chloe was no longer among Washington's elite, no longer on anyone's list of rising journalistic stars. As a college student at Columbia she'd dreamed of becoming a White House correspondent. Snagging a coveted White House internship with the Keyes administration in the spring of her senior year had made that long-term career goal seem entirely achievable. Chloe had certainly shown the required dedication. Some interns arrived at 9:00 A.M., went to lunch at noon, and headed out to see the sights at 5:00 P.M. Chloe was there before 8:00 A.M., took lunch in the cafeteria when she could get it, and left when the rest of the office staff left, usually around 8:00 P.M. Her assignment was to the White House press office, where she knew a late night lay ahead whenever the speechwriters came back from a briefing with their Chinese food orders ready. Chloe never complained. She quickly learned that the good stuff happened after 6:00 P.M. Sometimes, the bad stuff did, too—bad enough to get her fired. Some said that her career and her life in general had gone down-hill since then.

Chloe would have said it was more like falling off a cliff.

"Upon Vice President Grayson's death, I immediately met with the Speaker of the House and Senate majority leader and asked members of both houses of Congress to submit the names of possible nominees for the vice presidency."

Chloe poked at her dinner, a bowl of microwave popcorn and a tangerine. She was already too thin, down to one hundred pounds of anger and bitterness, and the mere sound of President Keyes' voice was enough to kill what little appetite she had. Her office had been in the Old Executive Office Building, next door to the White House, but before getting fired she'd earned herself a blue pass, which afforded access to all non-residential parts of the White House. She was one of the lucky interns who'd actually gotten face time with the chief executive, and even though she would never forget what President Keyes looked like, the snowy image on her television screen made it difficult to discern his likeness as he delivered tonight's message from the East Room. The audio was fine, but the picture sucked. Her cable had been disconnected for nonpayment, and she was relying on rabbit ears.

"I also sought and received suggestions from my cabinet, staff, and other sources outside Congress."

To be fair, Chloe's loss of the White House gig had been only the start of her troubles—the first in a series of dominoes that had kicked her into the journalistic gutter. Two years ago she would have turned up her nose at a newspaper that didn't require its reporters to corroborate information from an anonymous source. Now, she worked for a rag that paid its sources in cash—*lots* of cash.

"I indicated just two qualifications for the job," the president told his television audience. "First, that the nominee be capable of serving as president; and second, that he or she be able to work with members of both parties in Congress and be capable of confirmation by both houses."

Chloe pushed the bowl of popcorn aside and brought up her e-mails on her laptop. Lucky for her, the downstairs neighbor had unsecured Internet. Chloe's Wi-Fi piggybacked onto it just fine, free of charge.

"In response to my request, the White House received hundreds of recommendations, including some very thoughtful suggestions from fifth and sixth graders at the Adams School in Lexington, Massachusetts."

Chloe scoffed. Nice line about the middle schools, but Chloe was losing interest in the rhetoric. She scrolled down on the LCD screen to the most recent e-mail from her source. She'd been going back and forth with him for at least two weeks now, ever since her editor had put her on the assignment.

"I studied each of these recommendations, and yesterday afternoon I returned to the White House with my mind made up."

Chloe reread the e-mail. It would be one hell of a story—her biggest about a White House she'd been attacking since her abrupt dismissal. There was just one hitch: she had to convince her editor to pay for it. More money than they'd ever paid before. Much more.

"Two hundred fifty thousand," the e-mail read. "Final offer."

"My fellow Americans, it is my pleasure to tell you that my nominee to be your next vice president of the United States is my good friend, one of the most fair-minded men I have ever met, the former governor of Florida, Harry Swyteck."

Chloe switched off the television. It was time for something truly newsworthy.

She picked up the telephone, took a deep breath, and started to dial her editor. Then she hung up. She knew the answer would be a firm NO. "Find out if there's a story," her editor had told her, "and if it's as big as this joker claims it is, pay him twenty grand—not a dime more."

Twenty thousand dollars. Her editor was an idiot. This story was too big to let a dolt like him screw it up. She'd made that mistake before, putting her trust in people far less capable than herself. Never again. It was time for her to take charge of her own life, play by her rules—not someone else's.

She banged out a short reply to her source's e-mail and hit SEND.

"Let's meet," was all it said.

Chapter 7

"Some party, huh?" said Jack.

"Sure," said Andie, "if you call a press party without *Playgirl* a party."

They were standing before the magnificently decorated Douglas fir in the White House Blue Room. Andie was gorgeous in her red dress, even if there were two other women wearing the same design.

Tonight's party for six hundred members of the press marked the halfway point of a presidential Iditarod of holiday receptions and dinners at the Executive Mansion. As always, the president and First Lady were fully committed to a two-hour block of handshakes, posed photographs, and thirty-second conversations that would test the superhuman strength of their smile muscles. It was a veritable Who's Who in White

House press coverage, and Jack's unofficial business was to keep his ears open and find out who his father's friends and enemies were in advance of his congressional hearings. Jack looked off toward the Cross Hall, where guests were streaming through a forest of red poinsettias toward the State Dining Room. The sense of history here was inspiring, but Jack could see in their ambitious eyes that it was mostly about proximity to power. Some would have sacrificed a vital organ for the promise of an invitation to next year's party, and no matter how blasé the regulars pretended to be about it, they would for months find a way to work into every conversation a sentence beginning with the words "When I was at the White House Christmas Party. . . ."

"Happy Birthday," said Andie, raising her glass.

Jack raised his. "Not a bad way to celebrate my fortieth, even if it is a couple of days late."

"I still wish you would let me and Theo throw you a party."

"No. Absolutely not. No party."

"Crab cake?" asked the server.

"No, thank you," said Jack.

Not that the food wasn't tempting. The White House chef had cooked up everything from chicken-fried tenderloin (good with gravy) to marzipan. Even the gingerbread replica of the White House looked good enough to eat. The whole experience struck Jack as somewhere between magical and over the top, from the boughs and lights twinkling in the East Room to the Marine Band playing Christmas songs by the grand piano in the foyer.

"Would you mind snapping our picture?" said a young man with a British accent.

"We just got engaged," said his fiancée, flashing her ring.

"Mazel tov," said Andie. It wasn't a term Jack had heard her use often, but it seemed to pop from her mouth instinctively, as if the Christmas overload had struck an ecumenical funny bone in her body.

Jack snapped their photo, and Andie moved closer as the lovebirds walked away, arm in arm, the crystal ornaments on the tree glistening like the 2-karat diamond on the bride-to-be's finger. Holidays were notorious turning points in relationships, and Jack wondered how many women at tonight's party would get diamonds this season, how many would throw their arms around their man and say yes, and how many had their stomach in knots just thinking about it. He wasn't anywhere near ready to pop the question, but he wondered if Andie was on the latter end of that continuum.

"Quite the ring," said Andie.

Jack's cell rang, and they both laughed at the mechanical play on word.

Jack checked the number. He didn't recognize it.

"You're not going to answer that, are you?" said Andie.

"Aw, come on. I've never taken a phone call in the White House."

Jack hit Talk and said hello, but no one was there.

"Still never taken a call in the White House," he said.

It rang again. This time it was an e-mail. Again, Jack didn't recognize the sender, but the subject line was enough to give him the creeps.

"What's up?" said Andie.

Jack's first reaction was to delete it, and his second was to open it up and read the entire message. He did neither. Jack wasn't entitled to his own Secret Service protection, but they had warned him about this, and he knew the protocol.

"Jack?"

He heard her, but he didn't answer. He took her hand, and they didn't stop walking until they approached the south portico, where the lighting was better.

"Something wrong?" said Andie.

He showed her the screen, and they read the message together.

I can make your father president. No bullshit. Meet me.

Suddenly the fact that they were standing in the White House mansion, just a short walk away from the Oval Office, was even more surreal.

"It's officially started," said Andie.

"What?" said Jack.

"The wackos have arrived."

Paulette Sparks staked out a strategic position in the State Dining Room beneath the watchful eye of Abraham Lincoln. Harry Swyteck didn't know it, but for the past ten minutes, he'd been in Paulette's journalistic crosshairs. He hadn't moved in over an hour, a steady stream of reporters plying the nominee.

"Good luck getting near him."

Paulette looked away from her target just long enough to respond to her friend.

"Watch me."

"You really are working tonight, aren't you?"

"Isn't *everybody*?"

Paulette covered the White House for CNN International, and by all accounts a soon-to-be-announced transfer would land her on the fast track toward White House correspondent—one of the youngest in the press corps. Seven years earlier she'd been an engineering student at Northwestern University. Much to the dismay of her honors physics professor, Paulette burned one of her electives in broadcast journalism—and loved it. She changed her major and never looked back. Internships more than class work led to a job as a general correspondent with a network affiliate, and she was quickly promoted to Washington. A "going home" piece she did on Vietnam—the village where her American GI father had met Paulette's mother before the fall of Saigon—won her a Peabody Award and triggered a slew of job offers that took her national. Her hard-hitting but poised and professional style during a ten-month assignment to the Keyes–Grayson campaign earned her even more respect and credibility—not to mention an invitation to the White House Christmas party.

"One more glass of holiday cheer should loosen the governor's tongue," said Paulette. "And then I move in."

Her friend smiled. "You can always tell the first-timers. They're the ones who don't know the White House eggnog has even more kick than calories."

Paulette's BlackBerry vibrated. She would have liked to ignore the thing, but her day never ended, and she was hopelessly addicted. The number on the display screen was a bit of a shocker, one she hadn't seen in almost ten months. It was her younger sister.

Paulette followed a server into the pantry, away from the noise of the crowd, and took the call.

"Chloe, is that you?"

"Paulette! Listen to me!"

The frantic tone concerned her. It sounded like the bad old days. "Calm down, okay? Just breathe in and out. Did you take something?"

"No—*no!*"

The call was breaking up. Paulette could only imagine where her sister was calling from. The last time they'd spoken, Chloe was on the verge of passing out in the backseat of a taxi at 3:00 A.M., no money to pay the fare. She only called when she was in real trouble. Seven years apart, Chloe the offspring of their father's second marriage, they had never been as close as Paulette would have liked. Still, it had been heart-breaking to watch Chloe's decline after getting fired from her White House internship for suspected substance abuse. Chloe denied any drug use, of course, and she refused rehab. Paulette had done her best to help her land on her feet, but it was no easy task when Chloe hated her for being everything she would never be.

"Are you in trouble?" said Paulette. "I'm at the White House party, but just let me know if I need to come get you."

"No, you don't—just . . . *listen!*"

She sounded out of breath, on the verge of hyper-
ventilation.

"Chloe, what are you doing?"

"Working. A story. A really big one."

"I'm worried about you."

There was no reply.

"Chloe, are you still there?"

Paulette heard a scream.

"Chloe!"

The line was silent.

"Shit!" said Paulette, as she punched 911.

Chapter 8

C hloe tucked her cell into the pocket of her blue
jeans, angry at herself for the way the call had
gone. Paulette was such a bitch. She zipped up her
jacket and started walking.

Chloe had agreed to meet her source at the covered
bus stop on Georgia Avenue at ten o'clock. It would
have been a pleasant walk past Howard University
in daylight, but nighttime made it a long, cold mile.
Her breath was steaming and her hands were freez-
ing. Driving, however, was out of the question. She'd
lost her license after the DUI conviction, and her old
Sebring had been collecting white pocks of bird shit in
the alley behind her apartment since June.

Did you take something, Chloe?

It had taken her sister all of ten seconds to accuse
Chloe of drug use. Chloe couldn't even brag to perfect

Paulette without her heart racing and throat tightening. It was pointless trying to explain that she was about to break the biggest story in the country—bigger than anything "Paulette Sparks reporting live from the White House" had ever dreamed of. And *of course* Paulette had to tell Chloe—the fallen intern—that she was at the White House Christmas party. What a joke. The stupid member of the Sparks family—the one who was way too dumb for print journalism—was drinking eggnog with the president and First Lady. It was enough to make Chloe gag. She wanted to scream. Again.

Get control, girl.

Screaming in Paulette's ear had been a big mistake. She was probably on the phone right now telling their father how Chloe had snapped again. *But so what?* Chloe's source was about to make her—not Paulette— the Washington reporter on the move.

The blinking bank marquee at the corner said it was 9:57 P.M. and twenty degrees Fahrenheit. The wind made it feel colder. Chloe pulled her jacket tighter. Gloves would have helped, but she'd lost her only pair on the subway yesterday. She blew on her hands to warm them and—*whoa*—even she could smell the vodka. It seemed weird that something so odorless in the bottle could stink so badly on the breath, but alcohol was alcohol. She'd learned that lesson when she lost her internship at the White House, too. She dug a mint from her pocket and popped it into her mouth. Cool. Just like Chloe. Way cool.

Definitely too cool for this fool.

The wind gusted as Chloe reached the bus stop. The covered shelter was protected on three sides with Plexiglas, which provided welcome relief from the cold. Down the street, the traffic light changed from red to green. A cluster of cars rolled past the bus stop, and then the street was quiet again. Chloe took a seat on the wooden bench, folded her arms tightly, and looked out toward the empty street.

Nineteen degrees according to the bank marquee. The temperature was literally dropping by the minute, and the minutes were passing like frozen molasses. She'd agreed to meet her source at the bus stop, thinking it would be a safe, public place with plenty of people around. She hadn't planned on an unusually brisk cold front keeping everyone but her off the street.

At exactly 10:00 P.M., her cell rang.

"This is Chloe."

"Hello, Chloe," the man said. "It's me."

It was the first time she'd heard his voice. Until now, they'd communicated only by e-mail and the accent threw her. The *h* in *hello* sounded more like the German *ch* in *Ich* or *Nacht.*

Chloe said, "I'm here, just like I said I would be. Where are you?"

"Watching."

An uneasy feeling came over her, as if she were suddenly in a fishbowl.

"You owe me," he said.

"I know, but it's—here's the thing about that," she said, unable to steady her voice. It was so much easier to play it cool by e-mail. She was quaking like a school-girl in the principal's office.

Pull yourself together, damn it!

He said, "Don't get cheap on me," but it took Chloe a moment to realize that *tsip* was *cheap.*

"We have to talk."

"Talk, my ass," he said. "I done enough talking."

She swallowed hard. "You need to be patient."

"No," he said. "You work for a rag sheet. The rag sheet pays its source."

Rag sit? What is that accent?

"I e-mailed you copies of the wire-transfer instruc-tions. Didn't you see?"

"You think I'm stupid, Chloe?"

Her heart sank. She'd thought the documents were convincing fakes. "Transferring that much money to an offshore account takes time," she said.

"You bitch, I see what you're doing. Make me think the money is right around the corner, get me to give up the story for free, bit by bit. I could have sold this story to any of the tabloids. I picked yours."

"It was the right choice."

"Until your editor put a newbie on the assignment. A story like this, I expected him to take it straight up to the owner. Guess your boss only wants pictures of celebrity party girls in short skirts and no underpants."

"A White House story is a more complicated negotiation. I have to flesh out the gist of it, at least, and then I can get the money."

"And I believed that crap at first. You seemed smart. Hungry. Primed to stick it to President Keyes, after the way they fired your ass from the White House. But you know what, Chloe? I don't think you intend to pay me a dime. It's like you changed on me. What happened—all of a sudden you decided you don't like being a checkbook journalist?"

She didn't dare tell him how true that was. What was the point in landing a story this big if the world—led by Princess Paulette—was going to accuse her of sleazy tactics?

And, of course, a quarter million dollars was simply *way* over budget.

"Please," she said, "just—"

"Shut up!"

Chloe gripped the phone, afraid that he was going to hang up. Suddenly, his tone took on an even sharper edge.

"Do you have any clue who you're dealing with? *Do you?*"

"Just calm down, all right?"

"I calm down when people pay. And if they don't pay, I *make them* pay."

Chloe froze, unaware of the approaching car on the street.

"We can work this out," she said.

"I already told you too much," he said. "I know better than to trust a reporter. You aren't going to pay. Period."

"Let's be reasonable adults here."

He didn't answer.

"Hello?" she said, but the line was silent.

Her source was gone—and so was her story of the century.

Chloe closed her flip phone and held her head in her hands, staring down at the sidewalk—until she noticed a car pull up to the bus stop.

The night was suddenly a blur, and everything seemed to happen at once. Instinct took over, warning her that the same car had passed by the bus stop just a few minutes earlier, that someone had been circling the Plexiglas fishbowl, that the driver's side window was open despite the cold night air, that the silhouette behind the wheel was the face of her informant, that she was staring into a marksman's tunnel of death. She braced herself for the flash of gunpowder in the darkness, the crack of a pistol, the sound of her own scream—but there was none of that. Or perhaps she'd simply blinked and missed that final split second of her young life.

Chloe felt the hot explosion between her eyes— and nothing more—as the car pulled away. Her body slumped forward and dropped, face-first, onto the sidewalk.

Chapter 9

J ack and Andie went straight from the White House
Christmas party to the FBI Headquarters.

Initially, Jack had agreed with Andie's gut reaction:
the message was from some wacko who'd gotten hold
of Jack's cell number. That all changed when Andie
forwarded it to Stan White, the assistant special agent
in charge (ASAC) of the Washington field office.
White immediately summoned Jack for a debriefing,
and Andie came along. Something about that message made the FBI treat it as a serious and credible
threat.

Jack and Andie were seated on one side of the conference table. Around the table with them were the
ASAC, two supervisory special agents from the FBI, a
criminal profiler from the FBI Academy in Quantico,

and two special agents from the Secret Service presidential protection detail. Each had a printed copy of the message:

"Congratulations to your old man. How would he like to be president? I can make it happen, guaranteed. Meet me. Monday. Two P.M. Wait outside the mall-side entrance to the National Museum of Natural History. Alone."

"Clearly he's talking about assassination," said White. "How else could someone 'guarantee' that a vice presidential nominee will become president?"

White was in his fifth year as the Washington ASAC, bumping right up against the FBI's mandatory retirement age of fifty-five. He struck Jack as the anti-G-man. Had they allowed smoking in the building, he probably would have lit up. If neckties were optional for a man of his position, he wouldn't have owned one.

White glanced toward the profiler, inviting her comments.

"Very similar to the previous message," she said.

"Previous message?" said Jack. "I didn't get a previous message."

"No, you didn't," said White. "Someone else did."

"Who?"

"That's a detail the FBI can't share with you."

"Do you have a suspect?" said Jack.

"We've constructed a profile," said the ASAC. He glanced again at the profiler, as if to say *"Give him a little."*

"In general terms," she said, "a self-deluded loner who fancies himself an assassin who works for hire."

Jack said, "Why would he contact me instead of my father directly?"

Another agent jumped in. "Between a lawyer and a politician, maybe he thought the lawyer was more open to murder for hire."

That brought a few smiles from law enforcement—even Andie.

"Traitor," Jack said beneath his breath.

"Sorry," said Andie.

White said, "More likely, he fears that every communication to Harry is being screened by law enforcement. You're a criminal defense lawyer with privileged communications. Surely someone like you isn't going to allow law enforcement to monitor his incoming e-mails."

"He had to know I'd run to the FBI. He's probably just a nut who gets off by broadcasting his intentions. I saw plenty of that doing death penalty work."

"I don't think he's broadcasting anything," said the profiler. "He's negotiating."

"Let me get this straight," said Jack. "You truly think that this guy wants to meet with me tomorrow morning outside the Smithsonian and talk about killing the president for money?"

"We did say '*self-deluded* loner,'" said White.

Jack said, "So if I show up at two P.M. tomorrow, he'll be there?"

The ASAC shrugged. "One way to find out."

"Wait a minute," said Andie. "I've been quiet because of my relationship with Jack, but this is starting to sound dangerous."

"What Andie's trying to say is that I'm a great catch but I make lousy bait."

"Cut the cornball, Jack, or I'll switch sides."

The ASAC raised a hand, as if to step between prizefighters. "Let's break this down. One, we have a threat against the president. Two, we believe it's credible."

"For reasons you won't share with me," said Jack.

"Three," said the ASAC, "we know where he'll be and when he's going to be there. The Washington Mall, especially around the Smithsonian, is a very public place at two o'clock in the afternoon. All we need is Jack to hang out in the crowd and wait for him."

"No," said Andie.

"I suppose you're right," said White. "It takes a pretty courageous civilian to step up and help the FBI apprehend a would-be presidential assassin."

"I'm courageous," said Jack.

"No you're not," said Andie.

"I date you."

The ASAC raised a hand again. "We're not going to take chances here, Jack. You'll wear a Kevlar overcoat. Undercover agents will be posted all around. You'll be linked to the command center by surveillance electronics."

"I'll do it," he said.

"What?" said Andie.

"But I want Andie talking me through it. Appearances notwithstanding, she's probably the least likely to get me killed."

"You sure about this?" said Andie.

"You mean about doing this, or the part about you not getting me killed?"

"Both."

"I'm sure."

"Good man," said White. "It's a go."

Chapter 10

It was Paulette's first visit to her sister's apartment.

The phone call had come Sunday at 3:12 A.M. As a White House correspondent, Paulette was accustomed to breaking news and ringing telephones at all hours of the night. The detective's tone of voice, however, made it immediately clear that this call had nothing to do with world peace, a terrorist bombing, or the latest Washington scandal. She drove straight from her Georgetown town house to the medical examiner's office, and in a split second, she knew: "That's Chloe," she'd told the assistant ME.

Seven hours later, Paulette still felt numb.

The sun had yet to poke through the gray morning sky, and last night's nip had yet to burn off. The apartment door was open, but Paulette watched from the outside, behind a taut line of yellow police tape. Inside, a photographer captured the efficiency apartment exactly the way Chloe had left it, from the notebook computer on the loveseat to the can of diet soda on the table. Investigators searched for drops of blood, evidence of a struggle, indicators of a violent boyfriend, or any other details that might tell Chloe's story.

"I'm very sorry for your loss," said Detective Edwards, "but I can't let you come inside just yet."

"I promise not to touch anything."

He was sympathetic, but firm. "Ms. Sparks, how many years do you think I've been working homicides in this city?"

She could have guessed "too many." A long career was written all over his face—the jaded look in his eyes, the worry lines that seemed chiseled in stone. It spoke of too many crimes unsolved, too little satisfaction in the occasional service of justice.

"Twenty?" she said.

"More. So I totally understand when loved ones want to help. But it's best to let the professionals do their job. Even though this isn't where the crime took place, I've seen crucial evidence turn up at a victim's home. Sadly, I've also seen crucial evidence contaminated by the victim's family."

"Okay, I'll wait," she said, but it was hardly her nature to stand aside. She remained in the doorway, watching.

Chloe's efficiency apartment was tiny even by LaDroit Park neighborhood standards. A Murphy bed and loveseat on one wall. A table, two chairs, and a small television on the other. There was a small stove right next to her closet, and a small alcove in the back apparently doubled as the dressing and cooking area. In the very back was the bathroom. The only window was in the corner, and it looked directly at the alley. Paint was peeling from the ceiling. Several brown stains and a distinct musty odor told of leaky pipes from the apartment above. An investigator was on hands and knees, searching the old sculptured green carpet with a flashlight. It struck Paulette that he could easily have found something buried in those fibers from two or even three decades removed.

Paulette said, "What are you hoping to find?"

"Luck," said Detective Edwards.

He was drifting across the room like an art lover in the Louvre, slowly and methodically observing and absorbing everything. He stopped at the back wall in front of a framed photograph. There were no other paintings or photographs on any of the walls, but Paulette was too far away to see who was in it.

Detective Edwards said, "Your sister knew the vice president?"

"Is that who's in the photo?"

"Yup," said Edwards. "Looks to be in his office. Signed, too: *For Chloe, warm regards, Phillip Grayson.*"

"Chloe was a White House intern. They assigned her to the vice president."

He glanced around the shabby apartment. "What happened?"

"Chloe did something very stupid. Went out one night and partied till dawn, showed up at work the next morning still stinking of vodka and with a joint in her purse. Fired on the spot."

"Drugs," he said, as he jotted down his thought on a notepad. "Might explain what she was doing on the street alone last night. Might also explain why she got shot."

Paulette didn't argue. "May I see the photo?"

Edwards took it off the wall and brought it to her. Seeing Chloe in the proudest moment of her life brought on an unexpected wave of emotions—sadness, anger, a terrible sense of waste. There was guilt, as well. Not that she felt responsible for Chloe's death. Her feelings stemmed from the simple fact that she and Chloe had been born seven years apart to different mothers and had never lived in the same house together. It was classic half-sister guilt—the knowledge that their father had always wanted "the girls" to be closer, the awkward feeling that she should have felt sadder than she did about the death of her father's other daughter.

"Were you two close?" said Edwards.

The question only added to Paulette's pain—and confusion. "I tried reaching out to her so many times. Chloe wanted help from no one. Her decision to work for the *Inquiring Star* made it clear that she especially didn't want help from me."

"When was the last time you two saw each other?"

"We hadn't spoken in months. Until she called last night."

"What was that about?"

"Hard to say, exactly. It was totally unexpected. And she was very scattered. I feared she was on drugs again."

"The toxicology report will answer that for us. What did the two of you talk about?"

"It was very bizarre. As best I can tell, Chloe was calling to tell me that she was working on a big story. To brag, I guess."

"Brag?"

Paulette breathed a heavy sigh. "Chloe and I had a complicated relationship. I'm sure she knew that

I was at the White House press party last night. It's sad, but with everything that happened to her since the internship, the thought of me at the White House probably made her a little crazy. My guess is that she had something to drink—or worse—and then picked up the phone to tell me that while I was wasting my time drinking eggnog at some big-shot party, she was out getting the biggest story of the year."

"Did she say what the story was about?"

"No. Honestly, I doubt there was even a story."

He drifted in the direction of Chloe's computer. It was on the loveseat next to an open bag of popcorn. The LCD screen was black, but when he moved the mouse, Paulette could see it brighten. For Paulette, it was an odd feeling—to think that the detective was now viewing the very same thing—possibly the last thing—that Chloe had looked at before going out and getting shot.

The photographer announced that he was finished, and Paulette stepped aside to let him out the door.

"Can I come in now?" she asked Edwards.

The detective was fixated on Chloe's computer.

"Detective?" said Paulette.

He looked up. The crime scene investigators had finished with the carpet and had moved to the kitchen area.

"Come on over here," said Edwards. "Take a look at this."

Paulette ducked beneath the tape and crossed the room. Displayed on Chloe's computer screen was the inbox to her e-mail, the typical collection of information: sender, date received, subject.

Edwards said, "Do you recognize any of these senders?"

Paulette took a closer look. There was the usual smattering of obvious spam—collectively, important messages for men with erectile dysfunction who needed to lose weight and borrow money fast. Paulette was only halfway down the list when another visitor knocked on the door frame.

"FBI," the woman said with authority. "Step away from the computer."

"What?" said Detective Edwards.

"Supervisory Special Agent Lloyd," she said, as she stepped beneath the police tape and flashed a badge. Then he showed Edwards her papers. "We're here to exercise a search warrant."

"Since when does the FBI investigate homicides?" said Edwards.

"Could you step aside, please? I need the computer."

Paulette watched the two law enforcement officers square their shoulders and stiffen their jaws, a sure sign of an ensuing state/federal jurisdictional squabble. The computer was obviously a significant piece of a larger puzzle that she hadn't even begun to understand. Paulette studied the screen, but she couldn't possibly commit Chloe's inbox to memory. She snatched her iPhone from her purse and quickly snapped a photograph of the screen.

"What are you doing?" Agent Lloyd said sharply.

"Nothing," said Paulette.

"Did you just take a photograph?"

"Gotta go. See ya."

Paulette was under the tape and out the door faster than the FBI agent could say J. Edgar Hoover. She didn't slow down until she was beyond the courtyard gate and outside on the sidewalk. A gust of cold wind nearly slammed her against her car, but it didn't faze her. She stopped and pulled up the photograph on her iPhone. It was a little blurry, but the zoom made it legible.

More spam. A few messages looked legitimate, but nothing of moment—until she spotted the third one from the bottom. It had been delivered yesterday afternoon. The sender was unrecognizable, an apparently random selection of numbers and letters rather than a coherent screen name. The subject line was what caught her attention. It read more like the opening lines of a full message than a "re" line. In fact, it was too long to fit in the allocated space, so Chloe's inbox had cut it off with an ellipsis:

I can bring down Keyes. No bullshit. Meet me at . . .

Paulette felt chills, and it had nothing to do with the December cold front. Even ten minutes earlier, the message would not have hit her with this impact, but the FBI's sudden interest in Chloe's computer changed the picture entirely. Last night's unexpected phone call—Chloe's last words to Paulette, perhaps her last words ever spoken to anyone—had just taken a quantum leap in credibility.

It looked like Chloe had a meeting with a source.

She really was on to a story.

A big one.

Chapter 11

Jack exited the subway at Smithsonian Station and started walking along the National Mall toward the Capitol. He was following the instructions contained in his anonymous e-mail exactly. More important, he was doing it all under FBI surveillance.

"We see you," said Andie, her voice transmitting through Jack's tiny earpiece. "Move to the far left of the walkway if you can hear me clearly."

Jack drifted left, comforted to know that he wasn't going it alone.

It was an overcast Monday afternoon, the gray-white skies as cool and washed out as the surrounding sea of stone buildings and marble monuments. Jack stopped at the foot of the museum steps, his back to Madison Drive and the mall. He wasn't looking to be a hero—especially a dead one. The National Mall was a busy place in the middle of the afternoon. Jack was fairly certain, however, that he was the only visitor wearing an FBI-issued Kevlar overcoat and FBI surveillance electronics.

"I'm here," he said for Andie's benefit.

"Don't talk unless you have to," she said, her voice in his earpiece. "If he sees your lips moving, he'll know you're wired."

Jack stood and waited, glancing about nervously at strangers coming and going from the museum. The block-long, granite-faced building was a classic design, and the fact that Jack actually recognized it as Beaux-Arts style was yet another disturbing sign that he was indeed forty. His last visit to the Smithsonian had been as a teenager, one of several bonding trips that Harry Swyteck had arranged in hopes of dealing with the rough spots in their relationship the same way he had always dealt with them: by pretending they didn't exist. The trip was nonetheless memorable, not because the Hope Diamond had turned out to be much smaller than Jack had expected, but because the burning question of the day was whether to commit suicide or homicide before his old man could drag him to every last one of the museum's 126 million specimens.

Jack's cell rang, and the display flashed "Out of Area," no incoming number. Jack answered it, and the instructions came quickly:

"Go inside to the rotunda. Walk around the stuffed elephant and come back outside."

The call ended before Jack could respond. It seemed like a pointless exercise, until Jack realized that the museums probably had metal detectors. It was a clever way for his caller to find out if he was armed. He wasn't—but he did worry that his wire would be detected, screwing up everything.

Andie's voice was suddenly in his ear, as if she could read his mind. "Don't worry about the metal detectors. The museum only has enough staff to turn them on at random intervals. Your caller obviously doesn't know that."

Jack was only partially assuaged. It somehow seemed way too predictable that the terrorist with a bazooka would get through security, but the good citizen trying to thwart a possible presidential assassination would be stopped.

Jack climbed the granite stairs and entered through the revolving door. The rotunda was as impressive as he'd remembered it, though some things had changed. The simulated habitat around the eight-ton African bull elephant in the center appeared more natural. And in the post-9/11 world, there were of course metal detectors. As Andie had predicted, however, Jack breezed right past them without setting off alarms. The security guards didn't pick up his FBI-issued surveillance equipment or Kevlar overcoat either. He paused to check out the elephant—he suddenly wondered if his caller was a Republican—and then he circled around and exited to the mall side of the museum.

Jack stopped at the top of the stairs, expecting the phone to ring at any moment. He heard only traffic noises from Madison Drive and the whistle of the wind through barren tree branches on the mall. A young mother pushed a stroller along the walkway. A man on the bench had his nose buried in the newspaper. At the base of the stairs, a docent was giving a brief history lesson to a group of tourists. Jack wondered if his caller had lost his nerve. It was starting to feel like a hoax, until he heard the voice from behind.

"This is for you."

Before Jack could speak—before he could even turn around and see what the guy had in his hand—an entire team of undercover FBI agents sprang into action. The man reading the newspaper, the mother pushing the stroller, the docent and his tourists—every single one of them rushed forward, guns drawn.

"Drop your weapon!"

"I don't have no weapon!"

"Drop it!"

The man shrieked and jumped on Jack, causing them both to tumble down the granite steps. Jack braced himself for a gunshot from the attacker or even a barrage of firepower from the FBI. Rather than pummeling Jack or trying to hurt him, however, the man was clutching him out of sheer terror. Andie's voice was in Jack's ear, but she was drowned out by his attacker's panicky screams and a chorus of commands from undercover agents. One agent finally managed to pry Jack away from the wrestling match. It took three or four agents to bring the man under control.

"Don't move!" they told him.

"I didn't do nothing!" the man shouted back, and he started rattling off something in Spanish.

Another agent helped Jack to the bench, and it took him another moment to realize that it was Andie. She'd rushed over from the hidden command center on the mall.

"Are you all right?" she asked.

"Yeah, fine."

"You did great."

"If you say so."

Jack watched the team of agents lift the man to his feet. He was wearing an old navy peacoat, tattered blue jeans, and tennis shoes that didn't match. His hair was bundled up in a lumpy, matted mess beneath a knit cap. It was hard to tell when he'd last shaved and bathed, but it wasn't in the last week or probably even in the last month. His hands were cuffed behind his back, and he was no longer fighting back, but he wouldn't shut up.

"Muggles! Harry, I'm surrounded by muggles!"

He was talking to Harry Potter, Jack realized, not Harry Swyteck. The rant continued as the FBI took him away.

Jack looked at Andie, and she back at him. For a moment, it seemed like a standoff to see who would speak first. Finally, she broke the silence.

"Strange world out there, isn't it?"

"Stranger than it appears, muggle."

"What do you mean?"

Jack glanced toward the base of the stairs, where a pair of agents was struggling to stuff their suspect into the back of an FBI sedan.

"That accent," said Jack. "He's obviously Hispanic. The guy who spoke to me on the telephone had some kind of accent, but it was totally different."

"You're saying they're different people?"

Jack took another look. One of the agents was cursing and wiping his hands on the grass. The guy had apparently soiled his pants to make the job of law enforcement that much more unpleasant.

"I'd bet my life on it," said Jack.

A crime-scene photographer approached. A team of specialists had already cordoned off the entrance to the museum with police tape and was collecting evidence.

"Agent Henning," the photographer said. "Thought you might want to see this."

"What is it?" said Andie.

"We bagged and tagged the original evidence. This is a photo of what was inside the envelope he was carrying."

Jack didn't ask for permission to see it. He peered over Andie's shoulder and checked out the image on the digital camera's LCD display.

It was a photograph of a handwritten message.

I told you to come alone, it read.

Before Jack could say anything, Andie turned and ran down the steps. Jack followed. They caught up with the sedan just before it pulled away. She flung open the door.

"Who gave you this?"

The man's eyes were like saucers. "That's what I been trying to tell you! Some old man paid me fifty bucks, told me to walk up to the guy at the top of the steps and say, 'This is for you.'"

"What did he look like?"

"A muggle! He looked like a muggle!"

Andie told the driver, "Take him to headquarters. Set up for questioning."

The driver nodded. Andie closed the door, and the car pulled away.

"You believe him?" said Jack.

"I do," she said, as her gaze drifted toward the mall, as if she sensed that they were still being watched. "We just caught ourselves a decoy."

Chapter 12

It was almost midnight when Jack and Andie finally sat down for dinner with Harry Swyteck. The hotel's main dining room was closed, so they took a table in the bar, where the bartender and two lonely businessmen were watching the news on television. It was one of those dark, cherry-paneled rooms with coffered ceilings and red velvet draperies that made Jack think of nineteenth-century robber barons feasting on caviar and smoking cigars while trying to decide which congressman to buy next. As they settled into leather wing chairs, Harry seemed glad to be away from the constant hound of the media, and Jack was equally pleased to see Secret Service agents at a nearby table. Protection had kicked in with the nomination, but after a day like today, not even Andie—an FBI agent—could hazard a guess as to how many agents were assigned to the nominee.

"My apologies," said the waiter. "But our bar menu is quite limited at this hour."

"In that case, three cognacs," said Harry.

Harry's Senate confirmation hearing was scheduled to commence in ten days, but that announcement had been lost in the day's events. The FBI had given Jack strict orders not to speak to the media about the ongoing investigation, but that wasn't enough to keep the networks from making him a central part of the night's lead story—which was playing out again on the TV behind the bar:

"A tense scene unfolded outside the Smithsonian this afternoon, as undercover agents from the FBI overpowered and arrested a man in connection with what White House sources are calling 'a serious and credible threat against President Keyes.' With more on the story, including an exclusive report on the key role of Harry Swyteck's son in today's arrest, is White House reporter Paulette Sparks—"

The bartender hit the remote, switching from cable news to ESPN.

Harry said, "How is it that every news station on the planet has the same *exclusive* report?"

"Politically correct journalism," said Andie. "The inclusive exclusive."

Harry glanced at the hockey game on the TV screen, but today's headlines were still clearly on his mind. "So, how does it feel to be a hero, son?"

Jack shook his head. "This was supposed to be your show, not mine."

"Well, from now on, it's a two-man show."

"What do you mean?"

"It was the president's suggestion, and I think it's a good one. For the congressional hearings, he would like to see you seated beside me as my lead counsel."

"Are you serious?"

"Dead serious. What do you think of that, Andie?"

"I think . . . that's up to Jack."

"I don't know a thing about congressional hearings."

"No worries. You'll have teams of the best lawyers in America backing you up."

"So unlike Ollie North's lawyer, I guess I *am* a potted plant."

"Not at all. Look, I'm not going to pretend that there isn't a public relations component to this decision. Plenty of ink was spilled in the press about our disagreements when I was governor, and making you my lawyer is a very public way of putting those issues to bed once and for all. Beyond that, you're my son, and you're a great lawyer. Why shouldn't you represent me?"

The waiter brought their cognac, but just the sight of it had Harry yawning uncontrollably.

"I'm beat," said Harry. "I'll leave you two alone and enjoy this in my room. The plan is to do congressional role-playing tomorrow and get me ready for the hot seat. So don't stay up too late, Jack."

"I didn't say yes," said Jack.

"You will. Sleep on it. I'll meet you in the lobby at nine."

They said good night, and the Secret Service agents followed Harry to the lobby. Jack cast his gaze toward Andie. Even at this late hour, she was the proverbial sight for sore eyes. Jack liked her in sweaters, and he didn't often see her wearing them in Miami.

She said, "Sounds like you won't be flying back to Miami with me tomorrow."

Jack swirled his cognac in the glass. "I should at least see what this is all about."

"You're going to end up moving to Washington. I can see it."

"No way. I love Miami."

"Is that the reason you won't leave? You love *Miami*?"

"You know it's more than that."

"Jack, we need to talk."

He gulped. Those seemingly innocuous words killed with quiet efficiency—the death by lethal injection of relationships.

Best defense is a good offense.

"Suppose I do move up here after my father becomes vice president. What would you do?"

"You mean, would I move up here with you?"

"Yeah. Maybe not now, but say it's six months from now and things are still going strong between us."

"Let's not do this."

"Just hypothetically," said Jack.

"I don't like hypotheticals."

"Then have another drink."

"Jack, stop. Have you given a moment's thought as to how hard this is for me?"

"How hard what is?"

"The whole son-of-the-vice-president Washington scene. Tonight alone, I must have gotten fifty phone calls from people telling me that you were all over the national news."

"Today was a bizarre day."

"It's going to be one bizarre day after another."

"Until the confirmation hearings are over."

Her reaction was one of complete incredulity. "Do you really think that's the way it works? Your father becomes vice president, and your life goes back to the way it was?"

"Absolutely. My father was governor, remember? That didn't stop me from living my life the way I wanted to."

"Tallahassee is not Washington. And what about me?"

"How do you mean?"

"I've worked really hard to build my career. How do you think my colleagues at the bureau are going to treat me knowing that I'm dating the vice president's son? What kind of assignments will I get? Who would even want to work with me when, in their minds, I could pick up the phone and get everyone from the cleaning lady to the director of the FBI fired if I wanted to?"

Jack paused. It embarrassed him to realize that he hadn't seen her side of things. "We'll work through it. We love each other, right?"

"It's not a question of how much we care for each other."

Another gulp. Bad sign when "love" turned into "care."

Jack said, "Do you honestly think any of this is going to change us?"

"Don't you?"

"No."

"That's what really scares me, Jack. You don't even see it coming."

He tried to catch her eye, but she wouldn't look at him directly. His brain was working overtime, searching for the magic words. They didn't seem to exist.

"I'm sorry," she said. "I didn't mean to get into all this tonight."

"No, I think it's a good thing."

She rose and grabbed her coat. "I'm going to bed."

"Right behind you," he said, rising.

His BlackBerry chimed, signaling a "new" voice mail message that was actually four hours old. Jack was getting crappy wireless service in Washington. Jack listened as he and Andie walked toward the elevators.

"This call is for Jack Swyteck. Paulette Sparks from CNN International."

She paused for more than just a moment. Jack might have hung up on another reporter, but he would have recognized Paulette as an important Washington player and a television personality even before his father's nomination.

"I'd like to meet with you," she said. "Tonight, if possible. Or first thing tomorrow. There's something I need to discuss with you. It's important."

There was another pause, and Jack sensed that it wasn't just for effect. The silence between thoughts and halting cadence were very unlike her confident on-air delivery. It only intrigued Jack further.

"This is not another reporter hounding you and your father for the Washington scoop. In fact, this will be totally off the record."

One more pause.

"It's . . . personal, you might say. Call me. Please."

The message ended, and Jack tucked away his phone, thinking.

"Who was that?" said Andie.

"A reporter."

"As Ronald Reagan once said, 'There you go again.'"

"No, this sounded different. She says it's personal."

"Funny," said Andie, as the elevator door opened.

"What?" said Jack.

Andie stepped inside. "I didn't think *anything* in Washington was personal."

Chapter 13

At 6:00 A.M. Jack walked Andie down to the cab stand in front of the hotel.

"Now remember, Jack. When you go up Capitol Hill without your Jill, don't fall down and break your crown."

"Very funny," he said, then kissed her good-bye. She had an early flight and, as she'd predicted, Jack wasn't going back with her.

Jack hadn't slept well last night. He wasn't really worried about that team of Washington lawyers. He'd dealt with those types before.

The call from Paulette Sparks was on his mind.

Jack walked back upstairs, showered, and dressed. He figured 7:00 A.M. was a civilized hour to return Paulette's call, given the urgency she had seemed to attach to their meeting.

"Thanks for calling," she said. "Can you meet me at the Pennsylvania Avenue Caribou Coffee at seven-thirty?"

His meeting with the lawyers wasn't until nine-thirty. "What's this about?"

"Can't discuss it on the phone. We have to meet."

She made it sound as though they really did *have* to meet.

"Sure, I'll see you there," he said.

Jack did his best to be on time, but he had so much on his mind that he walked right past the coffee shop without even realizing it. Paulette was on her second cup by the time he doubled back and apologized for being late, but she thanked him just for showing up. Either she was the nicest journalist he'd ever met, or she *really* wanted something from him.

"I enjoy your coverage of the White House," he said.

"Thank you. Let's hope that doesn't change."

She was smiling when she said it, showing Jack a warmth that seemed more genuine than her television personality. She was prettier in real life, too. Less makeup.

"I saw the e-mail you got on Sunday," said Paulette.

"Really? That hasn't been made public."

"I'm a Washington reporter. I see lots of things that haven't been made public."

"I'm sorry, but I can't discuss it with you."

"That's fine. I've already promised the FBI that I wouldn't go on the air with it."

"A journalist with self-restraint is a good thing," said Jack, "at least until the FBI has a better handle on the threat against the president."

"Nor do I want to jeopardize the investigation into my sister's murder."

Jack paused. "I'm sorry. I didn't realize. When did that happen?"

"Saturday night. She was shot at a bus stop here in the district a few hours before you got your e-mail."

"Are you saying there's a connection?"

She took her iPhone from her purse, pulled up an image on the screen, and slid the phone across the table to him. "You tell me."

"What is this?"

"It's a picture I took of Chloe's e-mail inbox on Sunday morning, right before the FBI came to her apartment with a warrant and took away her computer. Look at the subject line for the message third from the bottom."

Jack didn't have his e-mail memorized, but Chloe's message—*"I can bring down Keyes. No Bullshit. Meet me at . . ."*—was so similar to his message—*"I can make your father president. No bullshit. Meet me"*—that it triggered perfect recollection.

"Eerie, isn't it?" said Paulette.

"What did the full message say?"

"The FBI won't show it to me, and I'm still working on a source to leak it."

"I'm not your source."

"Don't need one yet. When I do, I'll let you know. You'll come around."

Jack wasn't sure if she was kidding, serious, or somewhere in between. He took another look at the photograph.

"I need some context here. Why would your sister get an e-mail like this?"

She began with a sigh, and Jack listened to the compressed version of what he knew was a much longer story. Juxtaposed with Chloe's most recent job at the *Inquiring Star*, her work for Vice President Grayson as a White House intern jumped out most for him.

"Why did she get fired?"

"They said she got caught with a joint in her purse."

"You sound skeptical."

"Chloe always denied it was hers. Claimed somebody planted it on her. I didn't believe her. Now, I'm not so sure."

"What changed?"

"As I'm sure you can imagine, Chloe was kind of an embarrassment for me around the White House."

"Because she got fired?"

"That. And the rumors."

"What rumors?"

Paulette smiled thinly. "We're here."

"Here—where?"

"That place I mentioned earlier. Where you trust me enough to be my source."

"Your source on what?"

"These threats, if more come in. The investigation, if there are any breaks into who sent the e-mail you already received."

"And why would I be your source?"

"Because I'm not coming to you as a journalist. I just want to find out what happened to my sister. And because I can tell you things that you couldn't possibly have learned in just two days at the White House. All you have to do is trust me."

"I don't even know you. I can't promise you anything."

"Tough guy, huh? That's okay. I'll tell you a few things anyway. After all, sharing knowledge is power."

"I think the actual saying goes, 'Knowledge is power.'"

"Not in Washington. Here, the real power is in deniability. If I share knowledge with you, I take away your deniability. It's the ultimate power play."

Jack took a second to process that one. Andie's words were suddenly tumbling around in the back of his mind: *You don't even see it coming, Jack.*

"Okay, I'm listening," he said. "I guess."

Paulette said, "Last month, a friend in the White House told me that Chloe was trying to get in touch with the vice president. It got to the point where Grayson's chief of staff called me into her office to see if I could put a stop to it, before the FBI stepped in."

"The FBI? She was a journalist who used to work for the vice president. She has every right to try to contact him."

"Contact, yes. Stalk, no."

"Your sister was stalking the vice president?"

"Depends on your definition of stalking. Chloe had some history that worked against her."

"You mean getting fired?"

"Other issues." She drank some coffee, then continued. "The protocol for White House interns is strict: how to dress, where they're allowed to go, and most important, how to act when the 'principals' are present."

"She violated that?"

"The White House is the only place where the president is not a celebrity. Interns aren't supposed to hang out in halls that they expect the president or vice president to walk through, or park themselves outside rooms where they may be meeting. Chloe was one of the few interns who earned a blue pass, which gave her access to the West Wing. Frankly, I think she became a little starstruck. Chloe started to, shall we say—hover— around Grayson."

"What happened?"

"Well, she ended up getting fired."

"For drugs."

"That's what they say," said Paulette.

"Again, you sound skeptical."

"I can't help it. I'm a journalist," she said, her tone turning more serious. "And because this is my sister we're talking about."

"I think I'm beginning to understand you," he said. "But I really don't see where this is leading."

"It comes down to this e-mail," she said, holding her iPhone. "I'm guessing that it wasn't the first communication between Chloe and her source. Why else would the FBI have shown up at her apartment with a warrant to get her computer? So let's say the give-and-take between Chloe and her source went back a few weeks, maybe longer. If you read Chloe's e-mail—the promise of a story that will bring down Keyes—in tandem with the message you got—an offer to make your father president—it makes you stop and think. Maybe there was a reason Chloe was trying so hard to reach the vice president. Maybe she was trying to convey the same information."

"About an assassination attempt?"

"*No.* Don't you get it? The key word here is not 'threat.' It's *information.* Chloe had *information* that could bring down Keyes and make Grayson president. Your source has *information* that could still bring down Keyes and make your father president. That's why the FBI won't let me see the full e-mail that Chloe received."

"Wow" was all Jack could say.

"So?" said Paulette. "Are we there yet?"

Jack was about to ask *where,* but she had that look on her face again, and he knew she was talking about trust. "Are you proposing some kind of partnership?"

"The FBI is not going to tell me anything. Mark my word: they are not going to tell you anything, either. I have sources. You'll have yours. If we cooperate, I might just find out what happened to my sister. And you might find out what your father is walking into— before it's too late."

"That makes some sense."

"It will make even more sense if you're free for about another hour."

Jack checked his watch. He had time. "Free for what?"

"I have a meeting, and you're welcome to tag along."

"Who's it with?"

"Someone who is now terrified to talk to anyone, thanks to the strong arm of the FBI. He may be the only man alive who can identify the person who sent you that e-mail."

"Are you talking about that homeless guy who hand-delivered the message to me yesterday?"

"You got it."

"The FBI wouldn't even tell *me* his name. How did you find him?"

"Sources."

"Must be nice to have them," said Jack.

"Good boy," she said, smiling thinly. "You're learning."

Chapter 14

A scenic walk down Pennsylvania Avenue took Jack and Paulette to Lafayette Park, a seven-acre public green space directly north of the White House. At the southeast entrance they were greeted by a statue of Marquis Gilbert de Lafayette, a French hero of the American Revolutionary War and France's "pay-it-forward" answer to World War II and the liberation of Paris. A block north was St. John's Episcopal Church, the unofficial chapel to the White House since James Madison staked out pew 54 almost two centuries ago.

"They call this the church of presidents," said Paulette, as they approached.

Four homeless men were resting on the front steps, two of them either sleeping or passed out.

"These must be the vice presidents," said Jack.

She smiled and said, "Are you making fun of your father or my church?"

"You go to church?"

"Does that surprise you?"

"Only because most of the Washington reporters I've met so far think they *are* God."

"And I suppose monster egos would be something completely new to you, being a trial lawyer and all."

"Touché," said Jack.

As they climbed the granite stairs, the sun poked through the clouds and brought a springlike glow to the golden cupola and exterior walls of yellow stucco. The morning air was still quite cold, however, and Jack wondered how many nights these homeless men had spent shivering outside church doors just a block away from the White House.

"I started coming here when I was assigned to White House coverage," said Paulette, "though, to be honest, on my first visit I was just curious to see who might be here. That's how I found Juan."

"Juan?"

"My source."

"*Princesa,*" the man said, rising from the top step. "*Como estás?*"

"*Muy bien, gracias.*"

Jack shot Paulette another look of surprise. "You speak Spanish?"

"Not really. But Juan doesn't seem to care."

Jack was suddenly reminded of the embarrassment it caused his *abuela* to have lady friends compare her grandson's Spanish to Speedy Gonzalez's English.

Paulette made the introductions, but instead of shaking Jack's hand, Juan hugged Paulette and said, "She's beautiful, no?"

It was apparent to Jack that Juan wasn't just a source.

"Sit," he said, inviting them to take a place on the church step. *"Mi casa es su casa."*

Juan's smile was short on teeth but not on sincerity. He wore a Washington Redskins cap, black mittens, and Easter-egg-blue golf slacks that the embarrassed wife of a lawyer must have thrown into the Salvation Army box. Juan was a large man with a nonthreatening manner, and the scar on his forehead made Jack guess that he was probably one of those gentle giants who got provoked into bar fights by short, drunk guys with Napoleon complexes.

Paulette said, "Juan and I have been sitting next to each other every Sunday for about six months now."

"We met at La Casa," said Juan.

"La Casa is a homeless shelter," she said, "mostly Hispanic men. I volunteer down there."

Jack tried not to look too surprised, but Paulette was turning out to be very unlike the person he had expected. And yet she hardly knew her sister.

The world is a weird place.

"Got good news for you," said Juan.

"You found our man?" said Paulette.

"Sí."

"Can you take us to him?" said Jack.

"No."

"Why not?" said Paulette.

"He is hiding."

"From who?" she said.

"Todo el mundo." The whole world.

Jack said, "My guess is that he knows the FBI is using him as bait. That's why the bureau released him—to see if the man who hired him as a decoy comes looking for him again."

Paulette didn't disagree. "Did you talk to him, Juan?"

"Claro. Turns out he's a friend *de un amigo* of a friend."

Jack calculated that as a friend, once-Hispanic and twice-gringo removed. "Did he tell you anything about the man who hired him to meet me outside the museum?"

"Un viejo."

"How old of an old man?" said Jack.

"In a wheelchair."

"A wheelchair?"

"Sí. A chair. With wheels. *Tu sabes?* Or you no speak English?"

Paulette swallowed her laughter.

"Yes," said Jack, "I know what a wheelchair is."

"Did your homeless friend tell you anything else about the man?" said Paulette.

"He like Anthony Hopkins."

"He's like Anthony Hopkins?" she said. "Or he likes Anthony Hopkins?"

"He is him. That character in the movie."

"You mean he's a Hannibal Lecter?"

"No. The other one." Juan started dancing, arms up over his head, humming to the tune of Zorba's famous Sirtaki.

"You mean Anthony *Quinn,*" said Paulette.

"Sí, sí. El Griego."

The Greek.

A volunteer from a local shelter passed by with cups of hot coffee. Juan called to her and was about to bolt. Jack needed to get to his morning meeting anyway, so with Juan's assurance that he wasn't forgetting to tell them anything, Jack and Paulette bid him good-bye and walked back toward the White House. At the corner, facing the Executive Mansion, Jack and Paulette exchanged glances.

"What do you think?" said Jack.

"I think the man who sent that e-mail to you also sent that e-mail to Chloe. I think if we find out what was actually inside Chloe's e-mail, we'll find out why he shot her."

"But that was your theory even before we talked to Juan."

"Right. A theory. Now I'm convinced it's fact."

"How'd you make that leap?"

"It makes perfect sense that the shooter would be in a wheelchair."

"Why?"

"Something broke down between him and Chloe. He needed to eliminate her and deal with you instead. He instructed her to walk to a bus stop where he could drive by, make the hit from his car, and make a quick escape. A clean job and a clean getaway for an old man who can't walk."

Jack considered it. "That actually makes some sense."

"Of course it does. You factor in the way the FBI has shut down the flow of information to both you and me, and it makes even more sense. The guy has *something* on President Keyes. Maybe he told it to Chloe, and she didn't pay him for it. He killed her before she could go public and make his secret worthless. Now he's looking to sell the same information to you—with the promise that, if your father is confirmed as vice president, it will make him president."

"I don't follow that last part. If he has some dirt on the president, why not just blackmail him or his supporters? Why come to me, the son of the vice presidential nominee?"

"I haven't figured that one out yet. But this much I can compute: right now the FBI is pulling out all the stops looking for an old Greek man in a wheelchair. We should be, too."

"How many of those can there be in Washington?"

"No idea," she said.

"Me neither," said Jack. "But something tells me we're going to find out."

Chapter 15

J ack was surrounded by lawyers.

He counted thirteen in all. They were gathered in the walnut-paneled courtroom on the ninth floor of the law offices of Carter and Brooke, the high-powered law firm that would be the Washington muscle behind Jack and Harry at the confirmation hearings. It was a moot courtroom, used primarily for dress rehearsals of important trials, and Jack could only imagine what kind of corporate skulduggery had been tested here. *Yes, ladies and gentlemen of the jury, my client did routinely fly its crop dusters while the migrant workers were in the tomato fields, but surely those company-issued sombreros offered more than enough protection from any cancer-causing pesticides.* Theories abandoned, cases settled, egotistical corporate executives convinced not to testify at the real trial only after being shredded by their own lawyers in mock cross-examination.

Today was the mock grilling of Harry Swyteck, as eight-hundred-dollar-an-hour lawyers played the role of congressional representatives and White House chief of staff Olivia Thompson ran the show.

"For the last time," she said, groaning. "Please frame your responses to avoid open disagreement with the administration. President Keyes supports a complete ban on assault weapons."

"I don't," said Harry. "I'm against any law that pushes us closer to becoming a nation where only criminals have guns."

"Dad's right," said Jack. "Imagine if this country had laws against obscenity. Only prostitutes could have sex."

And so the tap dance began—and it continued well beyond dinnertime.

Daylight was short in December, and it felt much later than 7:30 P.M. as the limo carried Jack and his father back across town. The driver dropped Harry first for dinner with Agnes at a Moroccan restaurant. Jack was dead tired, but if he returned to the hotel and hit the sack now, his eyes would probably pop open at 3:00 A.M., and he'd be left staring at the ceiling until sunrise.

"Could you take me toward Massachusetts Avenue?" he told the driver.

"Sure. Whereabout?"

Jack removed a business card from his wallet. "Number One Observatory Circle."

"The vice presidential mansion?"

"Yes."

"Right away, sir."

Jack knew from the news coverage that the late vice president's widow was in town packing up the Grayson family possessions. Jack had not spoken to Marilyn Grayson since the postburial gathering at her home in Georgia. He'd kept her business card, however, and in light of the past several days' events, her unsettling words to him about the circumstances of her husband's death seemed almost prophetic: *With the direction your father is headed, you might have some questions too. If you do, call me.*

He dialed from the backseat of the limo, the tinted windows turning even blacker as they sped away from the lights of downtown, through the nighttime in Dumbarton Oaks Park. The call went to her cell, and when she answered, he introduced himself as "Harry Swyteck's son Jack."

"How nice to hear from you again, Harry Swyteck's son Jack."

Perhaps he was reading too much into her joke, but it felt like a friendly warning never to fall into the trap of giving up your own identity in this town—a reminder that he was Jack Swyteck first, not someone's son.

"I'm sorry to bother you, but I've been thinking about the conversation we had at your home, and I have—"

"Questions?" she said. "So soon?"

"I'm afraid so."

"When would you like to talk?"

"I'm actually in your neighborhood right now, if that's not too short notice."

"I'd be pleased to have the company. I'll tell the Secret Service to let you in."

Built originally for the superintendent of the naval observatory, the Vice Presidential Mansion had all the hallmarks of late-nineteenth-century Queen Anne architecture, from its signature round turret to the broad veranda wrapping the ground floor. Jack was cleared at the gate, and the limo took him up the long driveway to the entrance. Marilyn Grayson greeted him at the door, and Jack stepped into a foyer that was large enough for a piano and its own fireplace. It was filled with corrugated boxes.

"Excuse the mess," said Mrs. Grayson. "We've been packing all day."

She led him directly across the foyer to the first-floor library. A portrait of the first vice president stared down from over the fireplace. Jack thought that Mr. Adams looked to be on the verge of sneezing. The bookcase and end tables were already devoid of family photos and other personal touches, and not a Christmas decoration was in sight.

She was as gracious as Jack had found her in Georgia, and even though the mourning period was not yet over, she looked more rested and relaxed than on their first visit. She asked about Harry, and Jack kept up his end of the pleasantries by asking about her daughter, who at that moment entered the room, as if on cue, still quite striking even in blue jeans, a sweatshirt, and no makeup.

"You remember Elizabeth?" said Mrs. Grayson.

"We met briefly," said Jack.

Elizabeth wiped her palms in her sweatshirt and then shook Jack's hand. "Excuse the way I look," she said. "We're in a packing mode."

"Totally understand," said Jack. "Moving is never pleasant, and I'm very sorry for the circumstances of yours."

"Yeah, it pretty much sucks."

"*Elizabeth,*" her mother said.

"Mother, please. That word no longer has the sexual connotation that your generation thinks it does. Right, Jack?"

Jack fumbled for a response. "I think I'm kind of the transition generation on that one."

"Cute," Elizabeth said, smiling. "How long are you in town?"

"As long as it takes to get my father through the confirmation process."

"I'll be here helping Mother another week or so. We should have lunch. I can fill you in on all the secrets."

"Secrets?"

"The kitchen and the dining room are on separate floors. The ghost dresses in buckskin, but he's been spotted only by the Mondale children. That kind of thing."

"I'm sure Jack is quite busy," said Mrs. Grayson.

"He looks old enough to decide for himself."

"Indeed. Which is precisely—" Mrs. Grayson stopped herself this time, as if to steer away from a sore subject.

"Mother thinks I'm asking you on a date, which scares her. My ex-fiancé was in his forties. She didn't approve."

"Forties?" said Jack. "Heavens to Murgatroyd."

"So, lunch?" said Elizabeth.

Jack didn't even want to test Theo's theory that this Georgia beauty had thus far in life dated only Generation Y porn addicts and desperately needed her own personal Clark Gable. And then, of course, there was Andie.

"I think—"

"If you say no, I'm going to short sheet the beds before your father moves in."

"Well, if you put it that way."

"Good. I'll call you," she said.

She smiled and left Jack and Mrs. Grayson in private. The former Second Lady settled into the armchair, and Jack took the chair opposite her.

"That Elizabeth," said Mrs. Grayson with a shake of her head, "she certainly has her father's spirit."

"That's a good thing, I'm sure," said Jack.

The widow didn't answer.

"How can I help you, Jack?"

He wasn't sure where to begin. "It's been a strange week."

"I've been following it all in the news," she said.

The news. If that was her only source, she knew nothing about Sunday's e-mail from the man who claimed to be able to make Harry Swyteck president. That wasn't Jack's focus anyway. "When you say you've been 'following it all,' does that include the death of Chloe Sparks?"

"Who?" she said.

"You've never heard of her?"

She shrugged. "Should I know her?"

"Last year she was a White House intern assigned to the vice president. She was fired for—"

"Ah, yes. The druggy."

"She was murdered Saturday night."

Mrs. Grayson paused to absorb the news. "I hadn't heard about that."

"From what I've gathered on the Internet, it was much bigger news in her hometown of Chicago than it was here. What little media attention it got in Washington was couched in terms of Chloe being the younger stepsister of White House reporter Paulette Sparks."

"How awful for Paulette. I've always thought she was such a class act. And her sister—well, what a terrible downward spiral for a young person with so much promise."

"She was a reporter for the *Inquiring Star* when she was shot."

Her arms folded in a defensive posture. No one among Washington's elite escaped the *Inquiring Star*. "Now that you mention it, I think I had heard that somewhere."

"Chloe was having discussions with an anonymous source who claimed to have information that could bring down President Keyes."

"Now *that* sounds like something I would have heard on the news."

"It's not public information. I heard it from Paulette Sparks. She also told me that Chloe was trying to communicate with the vice president—trying so hard that the FBI contacted Paulette about possible stalking issues. Do you know anything about that?"

"No."

Jack paused, expecting her to say more. But she was finished.

"You don't seem to believe me," she said.

"I do. But honestly, I came here expecting you to say that Chloe's anonymous source and her attempts to contact the vice president had everything to do with the questions you have about your husband's death."

"Well, I didn't know about those things, so they obviously could not have raised any questions in my mind, could they?"

She seemed to be closing that door pretty tightly. "Obviously not."

"But I'll make a deal with you, Harry Swyteck's son Jack. I will tell you what makes me question Phil's death, if you'll tell me what the FBI doesn't seem to want anyone to know: What caused you and the FBI to arrange that meeting with a homeless man outside the museum on Sunday morning?"

Jack paused. Telling her about the anonymous e-mail was no small step, even if Paulette Sparks—a member of the media—did already know about it.

She said, "Naturally all of this remains between us. You have my word on it."

Jack was still considering it. She was a curious woman, the widow Grayson. But for reasons he could not fully explain—perhaps it was the way she had reached out to him at the funeral—he trusted her.

"You've got yourself a deal," said Jack, and then he fell silent.

"I'm listening," she said.

"Former Second Ladies first. Please."

She smiled thinly, as if she liked his style. And then she told him.

Chapter 16

"With or without training wheels, dude?" said Theo.

Theo Knight was the last person Jack had expected to run into at the hotel bar at the end of the day. A flight of tequila shots was set up before him. "Training wheels" were lemon and salt.

"I'm not doing tequila tonight," said Jack. "And what the hell are you doing in D.C.?"

"Interview."

"For what?"

"Secretary of Education. I'm big on educational programs. Head Start. Wipe No Child's Behind. All the big ones."

"It's Leave No Child Behind, Einstein. Seriously, what are you doing here?"

"Your father's lawyers want to talk to me."

Shit, I am a potted plant. "Nobody told me about that."

"Said they're afraid something might come up about the settlement money you got from the state of Florida to pay me back for the four years I spent on death row."

Jack processed it: it took an act of the state legislature to get compensation for wrongful conviction. Harry's signature had approved the settlement that made it possible for Theo to buy Sparky's Tavern.

"So," said Theo, "with or without?"

"I'm meeting with about a dozen lawyers and the White House chief of staff first thing tomorrow morning."

"Definitely without," said Theo. He slid the brimming shot glass in front of Jack.

"Did you not hear me?" said Jack. "No tequila."

"Dude, what did we do when your ex-wife turned into a fruitcake?"

"Tequila."

"When your girlfriend Mia dyed her hair, changed her name, and left town?"

"Tequila."

"When Réné chose relief work in Africa over a love life in Miami?"

"Tequila."

"Exactly. We're talking tradition here. You can't break tradition."

"You're talking as if Andie dumped me."

"Well, she's going to—if you don't get rid of this really nasty case of Washington-itis."

"You talked to her?"

"Yeah. She likes Miami fuckup Jack. Not Capitol suck-up Jack."

"You make me sound pathetic."

"You are pathetic."

Jack raised his glass. "I'll drink to that."

They belted back their shots together.

"Smooooth," said Theo.

Jack winced, as if he were drinking gasoline. "I hope we're not starting with the good stuff," said Jack, and he belted back another shot. He slammed the empty glass on the bar and added, "Vice President Grayson had ED."

It was a perfectly timed non sequitur that had Theo coughing on his tequila. "You mean . . . the guy . . . couldn't—"

"Is there another kind of ED?"

"I don't know. What do politicians get—*electile* dysfunction?"

"Stop being an idiot. He had ED."

"How do you know this?"

"His widow told me."

"When?"

"Right after his daughter asked me out to lunch."

"You shittin' me?"

"No."

"Dude, you gotta let me come on that date. A mother-daughter thing is like my biggest fantasy."

"First off, it's not a date. She wants to tell me what it's like when your father is vice president."

"Sounds better than a date," said Theo, as he slipped into an affected Elizabeth Grayson voice. "Oh, Jack, I've been so lonely. Greta Garbo lonely. Farmer's daughter lonely. Lonelygirl15 on the Internet lonely. Kiss me, you fool. Kiss me right now!"

The pucker was enough to make the businessman at the other end of the bar get up and leave.

Jack said, "And even if it was a date, Marilyn Grayson is fifty-one years old."

"Damn. Old enough to be your . . . sister."

"Shut up and listen. There was a perfectly legitimate reason for her to tell me about her husband's condition."

"I'm listening."

"In addition to ED, Phil Grayson had atherosclerosis."

"I dare you to say that after one more shot."

"Focus. The thing is, you can't take any of the ED medications if you have atherosclerosis. What's the big warning you hear on all the TV commercials for ED medication?"

"If you have an erection lasting more than four hours, call your girlfriend's girlfriends."

"That's not the warning I'm talking about. You can't take the drug if you have atherosclerosis. It can cause a fatal drop in blood pressure and a heart attack."

"And this is important because . . .?"

"The toxicology report from Vice President Grayson's autopsy hasn't been made public yet. But it will be released soon, which is why, I'm sure, Marilyn Grayson was so candid with me. The whole world will know this in a few weeks. It will disclose that the vice president had taken an unusually high dosage of ED medication a few hours before his death."

"But the man died on a hunting trip with your dad."

"So what does that tell you?"

"Your dad's gay?"

"*No*, numb nuts."

"Then Grayson probably had a honey on Miami Beach. Big deal. Doesn't everybody?"

"That's one interpretation," said Jack. "Marilyn Grayson has another."

"*Two* honies in Miami Beach? Maybe a mother-daughter combo." Theo belted back another shot. "Lucky bastard."

"Will you give that up already?" said Jack. "It comes down to two possibilities. One is that Grayson took a pill to have sex with a woman who was not his wife, knowing that the medicine could very well send him into cardiac arrest and kill him."

"He wouldn't be the first guy with a weak heart to take that risk."

"True. But what if he wasn't cheating on his wife?"

"Then why would he take the little blue pill?"

"What if someone gave it to him—without him knowing it?"

"You mean dissolved it in his food or slipped it into a drink?"

"Exactly."

The proverbial lightbulb glowed over Theo's head. "Dude, that's it."

"What's it?"

"I swear that must be what Trina's been doing to me. I'll be walking around on three legs all afternoon, wondering where the hell Mr. Happy came from, and then Trina shows up at the bar all rarin' to—"

"Stop. This isn't about you."

"Sorry."

"I'm saying, what if someone knew that the vice president had atherosclerosis and pumped him full of pills for reasons other than having sex?"

"What other reason?"

"To *kill* him, genius. That's why Marilyn Grayson has questions about her husband's death."

"Whoa," said Theo. "The Viagra Assassination. It's like *Desperate Housewives* meets *24*."

"Except it's not a Kennedy- or Lincoln-like assassination. This assassin didn't want people to suspect foul play."

"So the question is, who wanted Phil Grayson dead, and who wanted it done in a way that didn't look like murder."

"I may know someone who can help me answer that—someone who hasn't been telling me everything so far."

"Does she have a hot mother?"

"No," said Jack, turning very serious. "A dead sister."

Chapter 17

Jack returned to his hotel room by 10:30 P.M. With the aid of Theo's tequila, he was well on his way to dreamland—until the telephone phone rang at 10:47 P.M.

"Go to bed, Theo," he answered, groaning.

There was a pause on the other end of the line. "Jack?"

It was a woman's voice.

"Andie?" he said, even though it didn't really sound like her.

"No, this is Elizabeth Grayson."

He sat up quickly. Head rush—*tequila*!

Sorry," she said, "I woke you, didn't I?"

"It's okay, I had to get up to answer the phone anyway."

She laughed, assuming that it was a joke, and only then did Jack appreciate that he'd had more than one shot too many. *Theo, I'm going to kill you.*

Elizabeth said, "Mother told me what the two of you talked about and—well, I wouldn't do this if it weren't important. I'm in the hotel lobby right now. Can you come down? We need to talk."

Jack was suddenly feeling wide awake; this was the second time in two days that a woman had dropped the *"we-need-to-talk"* bomb.

"Uh, sure. Give me five minutes."

He jumped out of bed and pulled on a pair of jeans and a sweater. A splash of cold water brought color back to his face, but he couldn't do much about the blood-shot eyes. He made it downstairs with thirty seconds to spare. Elizabeth was waiting on the couch near the grand piano. She apologized again for dragging him out of bed, which meant that he probably looked even worse than he felt. A waitress came from the coffee shop, and they ordered a couple of decafs. When they were alone again, Elizabeth said, "I suppose you're wondering what's so urgent that I raced over here at this hour."

"Not at all," said Jack.

She looked at him curiously, and he smiled.

"Okay," said Jack, "maybe just a little."

She smiled back, then noticed his distraction.

"Who are you looking for?" she said.

Jack had been not-so-discreet in scanning the lobby. "Are we alone, or is there Secret Service lurking about somewhere?"

"We're alone. I'm the child of a *former* vice president now, so I don't get Secret Service protection. Even children of former presidents only get it till age sixteen. You'll learn all about that."

"Got it," said Jack. "I'm sorry. You were saying?"

Elizabeth drew a breath, then began. "My poor mother. She refuses to believe her husband could have cheated on her, and she simply can't comprehend that he would have risked his life with ED medication to pull it off."

"Are you saying that's what he did?"

"I have two words for you: Chloe Sparks."

"She was at least thirty years younger than him," he said, suddenly realizing that he was sounding more like forty with each passing day.

"Thirty-one. That's why the very idea of me dating older men strikes such a sour note with my mother, even if that isn't entirely logical."

Jack recalled the awkward moment when Elizabeth had invited him to lunch.

"Anyway," said Elizabeth, "Chloe Sparks was a tramp. From day one of her internship, she was determined to bed someone in the White House. She aimed high, and my father was stupid enough to bite."

"Was this a onetime thing or ongoing?"

"Ongoing."

"How do you know?"

"I'm Phil Grayson's daughter, for Pete's sake. It was disgusting the way he looked at Chloe. I could see it all over their faces."

"That's your proof? You could see it on their faces?"

"Don't minimize what I'm telling you. I don't need DNA on a cocktail dress to know what was going on."

Their coffee arrived, and Jack allowed the waitress to retreat before continuing.

"So what you're telling me is . . . what?"

Elizabeth stirred a pack of sweetener into her cup. "A couple of things," she said. "One, the fact that ED medication was found in my father's blood at the time of his death tells me one thing only: he was a cheater."

"You don't share your mother's suspicions that someone who knew about his health problems gave it to him surreptitiously to induce a heart attack?"

"Not in the least. He did it to himself."

"This latest one—the one that did him in—was that with Chloe or someone else?"

"I don't know. And frankly, I don't care. Or let me put it another way: it has nothing to do with what I came here to tell you tonight."

"You mean there's more?"

She nodded. "There's something I wanted to clear up immediately. I'm concerned about the impression my mother may have given you about the role of President Keyes in all this."

"His role in what, exactly?"

"I'm sure you can imagine that I wasn't the only one who knew about my father's indiscretion. Some very powerful people jumped for joy when Chloe got nailed for drug possession and had to be fired."

"On some level I can understand their being happy. But weren't they afraid she'd go public with the affair? 'Kiss and tell' can be a pretty profitable game in today's world."

"That was the beauty of it. Once Chloe was labeled a twenty-two-year-old druggy, she had zero credibility. Her claims of sex with the vice president would have been dismissed as total fiction, or maybe even turned against her as stalking."

"It all seems pretty convenient," said Jack, thinking like a criminal defense lawyer, "the way Chloe was stupid enough to show up for work with drugs in her purse."

"It does, indeed," she said. "And that's why I felt the need to speak with you tonight."

"I'm still not sure I understand the urgency."

"Mother told me about the anonymous e-mail you got from someone claiming that he can bring down President Keyes. Naturally, I immediately started to wonder what information this person might have. There was only one thing I could think of: finally, someone was going to accuse the Keyes administration of framing and firing Chloe Sparks to put the kibosh on a potential sex scandal."

Jack thought about it. Lesser cover-ups had ended political careers. "Honestly, I don't know what information my source has. Maybe it's what you think it is."

"And if it is, I would hate to see your father withdraw his name and give up the chance of a lifetime based on a vicious rumor like that."

"You're sure it's just a rumor?"

"I'm here to tell you one thing with certainty: the administration had nothing to do with any drugs being planted on Chloe."

Jack considered her choice of words. "You make it sound as if they *were* planted," said Jack. "By someone."

She looked at him very seriously. "All I'm telling you is that the administration had nothing to do with it."

Even on too little sleep and too many shots, Jack realized exactly what she was saying. "I guess that leaves just one question," he said.

"What?"

"Were the drugs planted by the vice president's wife or by his daughter?"

She flashed a semblance of a smile, but it was a serious one. "I can give you one very good reason why you'll never know the answer to that question."

"I'm all ears."

She leaned closer, moving to the edge of the couch as she looked him straight in the eye. "Because this conversation never happened."

She rose from the couch and gathered her overcoat.

"Good night, Mr. Swyteck."

Jack watched as she turned away, crossed the lobby, and disappeared through the revolving door.

Chapter 18

A sweet, floral aroma rose from the White House coffee mug.

"Jamaica Mountain Grown," said President Keyes in a tortured Caribbean accent. "Cool runnin', mon. Harry? Frank? Join me?"

The president's relaxed demeanor belied the fact that this was no routine update from Secret Service Agent Frank Madera, former head of protection for Vice President Grayson. The meeting was called—rather, *demanded*—by Harry Swyteck, and the three men were in the Treaty Room, the president's personal office adjacent to the Lincoln bedroom in the White House residence. President Keyes sat in a big leather chair with his feet up on the Treaty Table, a magnificent Victorian desk originally used as a cabinet meeting table.

"Love some," said Agent Madera.

The president poured another cup from the French press. "Harry?"

"It's midnight, sir. One more cup of joe and I'll be awake till dawn."

"Oh, come on. I can get you any bean you want."

Coffee beans were to the Keyes administration what jelly beans had been to the Reagan White House. Harry could scarcely say no. "Sure, why not."

The president rang the kitchen on the intercom. "James, the governor wants a cup of joe."

"What shall it be this time, sir?"

He flashed a boyish grin, as if matching up beans with guests made his presidential day. "What's the one from Indonesia that those little tree-climbing marsupials can't digest and the bean pickers gather up off the ground after the critters crap them out?"

"Kopi Luwak, sir?"

"That's it. Send up a whole pot."

"Right away, sir."

He switched off the intercom. "You're going to love this, Harry. Has sort of an earthy body with a hint of chocolate. Unusual aroma, however."

"Imagine that."

"Some people call it crappy Luwak because—"

"Enough with the coffee," said Harry.

The tone took the president by surprise. "Maybe you'd prefer decaf," he said.

"Sorry, sir. But frankly I've been on edge ever since my son got that e-mail from someone who claims he can bring down the president."

"And as I told you, those things happen about once a week."

"I don't doubt that," said Harry. "But today I heard disturbing things about a former White House intern who recently turned up dead. In my eyes, this is critical. As I told you on the phone, I need some answers about Chloe Sparks."

"That's why I have Frank here," said the president. "He can tell you everything you need to know about her."

Harry's gaze shifted to Agent Madera.

A fifteen-year Secret Service veteran, Special Agent Frank Madera began his career in the Washington field office. People had been telling him since high school that he looked like a Secret Service agent—six feet two inches tall, athletic build, stoic but handsome facade—but he would have liked to think it was his exemplary work on complex counterfeiting investigations that had earned him a promotion to the presidential protection division. His first major assignment was to protect president-elect Keyes, and by inauguration day Madera found himself standing within arm's length of the new chief executive. He became the president's most trusted agent, which precipitated a few questions when, thirteen months into his first term, the president suddenly had him reassigned to the vice president.

"Fire away," said Agent Madera.

"Let's start with the reason you were reassigned to Phil's security detail."

"That woman—Chloe Sparks—was unstable. After she was fired for drug possession, we tagged her as a potential stalker."

The president interrupted, as if propelled to fill in the blanks. "Frank was seen as the best man to contain the threat."

"That sounds like a crock," said Harry.

"What did you just say?"

"Pardon my tone," said Harry, "but I need you to stop talking to me as if I were an idiot. I've heard enough to know that it had less to do with stalking and more to do with the vice president's libido."

The president's expression soured, but Harry's gaze was cutting across the room like a laser beam, breaking down the wall of misinformation.

"All right," said the president. "Phil was being Phil. Chloe Sparks made overtures to him—we called it stalking—but Phil didn't see her advances as, shall we say, unwelcome as we did. That's why Frank was reassigned to the vice president's detail. To stop Phil from meeting with her."

"I knew Phil as well as you did," said Harry. "Once he made up his mind, no one could stop him from doing what he wanted to do. Not even the president."

There was silence in the room, Harry's words wrapping around the president like the coldest of realities.

"I want the truth," said Harry, "or I'm withdrawing my name from consideration."

"Harry, come on now."

"I mean it," said Harry. "The truth about Chloe Sparks. Or I'm out."

He didn't appear to be bluffing. The president blinked.

"All right," he said with a sigh. "Frank, tell him."

"Sir?" he said, incredulous.

"You heard me. Tell the governor why you were reassigned to Vice President Grayson."

Agent Madera seemed uncomfortable with the task, but he never refused a direct order from the president—at least not in front of a third party. "It was my job to make sure that whatever the vice president did and however he did it, national security interests would not be compromised."

"That's a nice spin," said Harry. "But what does it mean?"

The president said, "You said it yourself, Harry. I couldn't stop Phil. But if we left it up to the vice president to pursue her, he was bound to end up like every other man who cheats on his wife. He'd get caught, eventually."

Harry said, "So Agent Madera became the Secret Service facilitator—like JFK and Marilyn Monroe?"

"When it comes to sex," the president said dryly, "few things are without precedent in Washington."

"Are you telling me that Chloe Sparks was with Phil Grayson on the night of his death?"

The Secret Service agent took the question, even though it was directed to the president. "The good news is that the answer to that question is no."

"Then why was he pumped full of ED medication?"

"How did you know that?"

"Jack told me," said Harry.

"Your son has been busy, I see."

"He has it on good authority that the toxicology report is going to show that Vice President Grayson was full of ED medication at the time of his death. So I want the whole truth: Was she with him in Florida?"

The president looked at his Secret Service agent and said, "Frank, the whole truth, for our distinguished nominee."

"Yes, sir," he said. "She was supposed to come, but it didn't work out. Too much media surrounding the vice president's visit to Florida, too many guests around who might see something they shouldn't see."

"But he took the ED medication anyway?" said Harry.

"It was a time-released dosage, good for thirty-six hours. I presume he wanted to be ready whenever she showed up."

Harry fell quiet again, but he seemed satisfied that he was finally getting the straight dope.

"So, how do we deal with this toxicology report?" he said.

"Fortunately," said the president, "the medical examiner doesn't plan to release it for another week."

"It will leak before then. We need a plan."

The president smiled. "I like the way you say *we*."

"I have no choice," said Harry. "The media will undoubtedly feast on this. Since I was with the vice president on the night he died, I am going to spend a lot of time answering questions about something that has very little to do with my qualifications to be vice president."

"Are you okay with that?"

Harry paused, thinking. It didn't take long. "Here's the way I see it. I can decline the nomination and be accused of having arranged for Phil to come to Florida and bed his former White House intern. Or I can accept the nomination, and be accused of the very same thing."

"You're a smart man, Harry Swyteck."

"Or a fool for having gotten back into this game."

"Do I take that to mean that you're in for the long haul?"

"Only if you can assure me that putting Agent Madera on the vice president was for national security reasons, as you said, and not simply to cover up a potential scandal."

"You have my word on that."

The two men looked each other in the eye, and the president searched for that certain body language that said lies were unacceptable—unless they were believable.

"Then I'm still in," said Harry. "With one caveat."

"Name it."

Harry turned deadly serious. "No more ticking time bombs like Chloe Sparks. No more secrets of any kind. Or not even Agent Madera will be able to stop me from kicking your ass."

The president smiled, even though Harry didn't.

"Fair enough, my friend."

They shook on it, the president applying his famous double touch, shaking with his right hand while applying his left to Harry's right shoulder.

The president said, "While we're on the subject of security, I feel we should talk more about this anonymous e-mail Jack received. You still seem concerned about that."

"Anyone who claims to have the power to bring down the president sounds like a nut case to me," said Harry. "With my son on the front line, concern is probably a good word."

"I can understand that. I know the FBI has given you assurances about Jack's safety, but in the world of personal protection, I trust no one more than Frank. I'd like to arrange for him to be assigned to you."

"I appreciate the gesture. But that's not really necessary."

"I insist. He has experience on the vice presidential side of things with Phil, so it's an easy transition. We'll make the reassignment first thing in the morning." The president took one last swallow of coffee. "You look tired, Harry. Go to bed."

"I am beat. Thank you, sir."

Harry said good night to both the president and the new special agent in charge of vice presidential protection, and then he left through the north door. Agent Madera remained behind with the president. Neither seemed eager to be the first to speak, each waiting for the other's reaction.

"You told him too much," said Madera.

"He'll be fine. Harry Swyteck wants to be vice president in a bad way. Much more than he lets on. Now that he's in the loop about Chloe Sparks and Phil Grayson, he has no choice but to toe the line."

"You trust him that much?"

"I do now that you're on his security detail."

"Nice touch, the way you couched it in terms of personal safety."

"I'm sure he sees through that. The only question is how *far* he can see."

President Keyes rose and stepped toward the window. Surrounding city lights gave the south lawn a warm glow on a cold December night. "Do you think . . ."

He stopped himself.

"Do I think what?" said Madera.

"I have this unsettling suspicion about his son."

"He does seem a bit too friendly with Paulette Sparks since coming to Washington."

"Not to mention Marilyn and Elizabeth Grayson."

"All on the heels of that e-mail."

The president leaned against the window frame, his back to Agent Madera as he spoke to his reflection in the pane of bullet-resistant glass. "It could be paranoia on my part. But I'm beginning to wonder if Jack has already figured out that Phil Grayson having sex with an intern has absolutely nothing to do with the power to bring down the Keyes administration."

"That would be our worst fear," said Madera.

He shook his head, speaking in a solemn voice. "You want to know my worst fear, Frank?"

Agent Madera did not respond.

President Keyes was a student of history, and in times of stress, snippets of White House history seemed to rise up from the floorboards to haunt him.

"Did you know that President Garfield was brought to this very room after he was shot in the summer of 1881?"

"Is that what keeps you up at night, assassination?"

"Of sorts," he said, turning to face him. "My worst fear is that the entire world is about to know what the Greek knows. And there's nothing I can do to stop it."

Chapter 19

The Greek was the last customer of the night at Mahoney's Pub. He walked past the empty booths and pulled up a stool at the Formica-topped bar.

"What'll it be, old man?"

The bartender was young, short, and skinny—the complete opposite of the Greek, who was an imposing figure even when seated.

"Shot and a beer," he said.

The beer was dinner. Or breakfast. Whatever worked at 1:00 A.M. for a guy with a huge problem on his mind and who couldn't sleep. Alcohol touched his lips only when the back pain flared up—something he'd dealt with for almost fifty years, ever since those thugs had thrown him off an apartment building in Nicosia to watch him splatter like a watermelon. The doctors had told him he was lucky to be alive, lucky not to be paralyzed. They obviously didn't know Demetri Pappas. Luck had nothing to do with it. *What doesn't kill you makes you stronger.* It was a cliché, but the Greek lived by it. Swimming in the Mediterranean Sea had whipped his body back into shape. A mile a day for over forty years. Then cycling. Seventy miles in a single day had been commonplace in his prime. Finally, he was ready to run. He'd finished eight marathons in his lifetime, and he was determined to run another before he hit seventy. He still smiled at reruns of that old TV show, *Ironside.* The Greek should have been that guy in the wheelchair. Instead, he was Iron*man.*

The bartender set him up. He downed the drinks quickly.

" 'Nother round."

The Greek's brain was buzzing, but he was still thinking clearly. He never let himself drink to the point of intoxication, never did anything to cloud his judgment. Especially when it was decision time.

Plan A was dead—literally. Chloe Sparks had totally conned him. He should have known that serious money from the *Inquiring Star* was out of the question when the editor had refused to negotiate and handed him off to a young reporter. Plan B had seemed like a better idea. What politician wouldn't pay a king's ransom to launch himself overnight from second-in-command to head of state? It certainly would have worked that way in Cyprus—and not just because Shakespeare had written of such false loyalty in *Othello*.

"Here's to you, Iago," he said, and then he downed the second round as quickly as it was poured.

The bartender switched off the glowing neon beer sign in the window. "Closing time, old man."

"How about a coffee?"

"There's a diner across the street."

The Greek grumbled, but he was angrier with himself than anyone. He should have known better than to put his trust in the likes of Jack Swyteck—a lawyer *and* the son of a politician. *Swyteck*—what the hell kind of a name was that, anyway? Must have been another one of those hatchet jobs by immigration officials at Ellis Island. The Greek had once known a Jozef Swatek from Galicia. Or was it Prague? Could have been Russia.

Fucking Russians.

The Greek tipped back his beer glass and found one more swallow. Plan C would be the charm—as soon as he figured out what it was.

The bar was empty, and the bartender looked ready to head home. "Twenty-four bucks," he said.

The Greek checked his wallet. Four singles. He was twenty dollars short. *Two hundred fifty thousand and twenty dollars short, to be exact.*

"You take an IOU here?"

"This ain't no charity."

"World keeps getting crueler every day, don't it?"

The bartender started wiping down the Formica. "Tell me something I don't know, pal."

The Greek snatched the towel, giving the bartender a start.

"What the hell, old man?"

With a quickness that belied his age, the Greek brought his hand up from his lap and rested it on the bar top. It was wrapped in the towel.

"I'm telling you something you don't know."

The bartender glanced uneasily at the towel. "What you got wrapped up in there?"

"Could be just my hand. Could be my hand holding a bobcat."

"A bobcat?"

The Greek turned deadly serious, working extra hard to speak with no accent. "I mean the Beretta model 21A semiautomatic twenty-two-caliber pistol fully loaded with forty-grain lead, round-nosed, standard-velocity subsonic ammunition. Weighs less than a pound, easily concealed in the palm of a man's hand. Wrapped in a towel like this one, the muzzle blast is reduced to something less than a cap gun. Much less. On the street, it's called a bobcat. You didn't know that, did you?"

The Greek delivered his patented stare, a penetrating laser that could have burned through men of steel, much less a skinny bartender who looked barely old enough to drink. To most folks, the Greek was another one of those sixty-something-year-old marvels who could have lifted weights with Chuck Norris and out-boxed Sly Stallone. An unlucky few, however, learned *why* he stayed fit—though it had been a very long time since he'd killed a man over twenty bucks.

"There's two hundred dollars in the cash register," said the bartender, his voice quaking. "Grab it and go."

"Don't shit your pants, okay? This ain't a robbery. I'm good with the drinks. Just put them on my tab, junior." *Dzunior.*

"Forget about it. They're on me."

The Greek slid off his bar stool. "I'm gonna pay you for the drinks. I got some money coming in."

"Sure, whatever. Just be cool and walk your bobcat right on out of here."

He started toward the door, but an almost unbearable shooting pain in his right leg brought him to a halt. Sciatica from the L5 vertebra felt as if someone had taken a hot knife and sliced him open from hip to heel. It got that way only when he was under serious stress—and these last two weeks had been as serious as it gets.

He closed his eyes for a moment, the way his Zen muscular therapist had taught him. She'd given him various techniques, starting with a descriptive name for his pain that would make it seem weaker than his will to defeat it. He tried "Useless Pain in the Ass," but that was too cumbersome. He settled on "Politico," a shorter but synonymous term.

The Greek swallowed the pain and walked out the front door.

The cold night air cut to the bone, which only exacerbated his back pain. It was possible that the bartender would dial 911, but if he did, so what? As much trouble as the Greek had gotten himself into on the outside, he was probably safer in jail.

He stopped at the pedestrian crossing on the street corner. A taxi pulled up before he could even get his hand out of his coat pocket to flag him down. It was a van. The side door slid open, and the Greek climbed up into the middle seat.

"Motel Six," he said, as he closed the door. "Just outside the Beltway."

The driver nodded and pulled away, and before the Greek could react, a leather strap came up and over his head from behind. He grabbed it instinctively, trying to pry it from his neck, and it loosened just enough for him to breathe.

"Move and you die," the man said. He was in the luggage area behind the middle seat. His accent was definitely Russian.

Shit, not again.

The Greek struggled to speak. "That you, Vlad?"

"It ain't your momma."

It was definitely Vladimir. He gave the Greek another centimeter of slack on the strap, and the words came easier.

"I'm no good to you dead," said the Greek.

"No damn good alive."

"I can't raise a quarter million dollars overnight."

"Should have thought of that before you started skimming from us."

The Greek drew a breath. In the old days, a casino manager could pocket ten grand a month from the counting room and the Sicilians would look the other way, almost expecting their local boys to grab a little "walking-around money." All that changed when the Russians took over Cyprus. Skimming in the classic sense—hiding your own money from the government—was still cool. But hiding money from the *Mafiya* was almost certain death, if you got caught. And the Greek had been caught red-handed.

"I'll double what I owe," said the Greek. "Five hundred thousand. Give me two weeks."

The taxi rounded a corner, and in the rearview mirror the Greek caught a glimpse of the man behind the pistol. He appeared to be smiling.

"One week," said Vladimir. "Call it professional courtesy."

The taxi stopped, and the Russian leaned closer to whisper into his ear: "If I come back, it won't be pretty, and it won't be quick. Half a million in one week. Or you'll wish to God I'd finished you off tonight."

The driver hopped out and opened the door. Vladimir pushed the Greek out into the street, and the taxi sped away as he picked himself up from the pavement. He walked to the curb and cinched up his coat.

Half a million dollars. In one week. It didn't seem feasible, not with two strikes named Sparks and Swyteck already against him. At this stage of the game, his only real choice was to go back to Keyes' people. The Greek had sold his secret way too cheap the first time around anyway. They might pay again if he threatened to go public.

Or kill me.

He buried his hands in his pocket and walked slowly into the night. Yeah, they might kill him this time. But one thing was certain.

It beat letting the Russians do the job.

Chapter 20

The winds shifted overnight, and by morning the grip of winter had lifted from the Capitol. Jack and his father decided to go for a jog in the National Mall before breakfast. They weren't alone by a long shot. It didn't take springtime and cherry blossoms to bring out the joggers by the hundreds, more stress than sweat oozing from their pores. Harry, however, became winded in less than ten minutes. He found rest on a park bench near the World War II Memorial.

"I ran two miles every morning when I was in the governor's mansion," said Harry, shaking his head. "Your old man isn't what he used to be."

This was one of those moments when the good son was supposed to step up and say something like

Nonsense, you're in great shape. But Jack was thinking other thoughts.

"Dad, there are some things I need to tell you."

Harry reached down and tried to touch his toes but made it only to his knees. "Okay," he said, groaning. "I'm listening."

"I'm starting to wonder about this whole thing."

"My being vice president?"

"It's more about how the job came open in the first place."

Jack sat on the bench beside him. A group of college students ran by. Jack could almost smell last night's frat party in the air. He let them pass, then continued.

"I've been hearing some disturbing things lately. Did you know that Grayson was cheating on his wife?"

Harry looked as if he'd just sucked a lemon. "What does that have to do with anything? Let the man rest in peace. And who told you that, anyway?"

"His daughter."

"You talked to Elizabeth about her father's sex life?"

"Well—yes, actually. His widow, too."

"You've been hanging around Theo too much."

"It's not what it sounds like. This is serious."

"Seriously weird."

"Dad, just listen."

"No, I really don't want to hear this. You of all people should know better than to put rumors inside my head. I'm about to face off against two congressional committees, and there are members of those committees who never miss an opportunity to embarrass the president. The less I know about anything that doesn't deal with my own qualifications for the job, the better."

"This isn't about you being qualified. I've been talking with Paulette Sparks about this—"

"Damn, Jack. Why would you do that?"

"She's been helping me sort this out."

"She's a Washington reporter. She's not helping you."

"Paulette thinks Grayson may have been murdered."

"That's it, I'm outta here," he said as he sprang from the bench.

Jack went after him, jogging at his side. "Why won't you listen to this?"

"Why won't you stop talking?"

"This is important."

"This is poppycock."

"How do you know?"

"Because I live in the real world, Jack. You should try visiting there some time."

"A fifty-year-old man cheats on his wife, and both he and his young lover end up dead. For a criminal defense lawyer, that is the real world."

Harry stopped abruptly. "I'm trying to pull you up out of that cesspool, Jack. I'm giving you a shot at the big leagues. Don't blow it."

"A shot? I didn't ask for a shot."

"As your father, I'm asking you to stop talking with Paulette Sparks."

"As your lawyer, I'm telling you to open your eyes."

"As my lawyer, you should have known better than to put your trust in a reporter in the first place."

"What are you going to do, fire me?"

Another runner passed them. It gave Harry time to reflect, but he still didn't pull any punches. "Yeah," he said, grunting. "I think I am."

Jack stopped running. "What?"

Harry continued several paces down the path, then turned to look Jack in the eye. "I need a lawyer who really wants this job. Ever since you got here, all you've done is play detective. That's not helping me."

Fired by my own father? Jack didn't know what to say. "Okay. If that's the way you want it."

"If this keeps up, we'll end up not speaking to each other, and it'll be the bad old days all over again. That's what I *don't* want."

"So . . . I should go back to Miami?"

"I think it's best this way. Now, come on, let's start back."

"You go ahead. I don't much feel like it."

"Suit yourself."

Jack watched in silence as his father turned and merged into a long line of joggers that was headed in the general direction of the White House.

Chapter 21

Paulette Sparks returned to Washington on Tuesday night. Chloe's funeral had left her completely drained.

She wondered if her father would ever recover.

Paulette's relationship with Chloe's mother had never amounted to much, but it killed her to see their father suffer. Chloe had caused him so much heartache in her teenage years—drinking and driving, hitting the party scene, not coming home at night. Paulette resented her for that, but it was nothing compared to Chloe's resentment toward her. As the older sister, Paulette had done everything before Chloe. Chloe was riding a bike when Paulette learned to drive. Chloe was in middle school when Paulette started college. At the funeral, Paulette recalled an argument they'd had years earlier, when just by coincidence Chloe's acceptance to journalism school was completely overshadowed by Paulette's landing a job with CNN.

"I hope you die before I do, too!" Chloe had screamed at her.

Her sister hadn't gotten her wish.

"Seventh Street," Paulette told the taxi driver.

"Where?"

It was a dark and drizzly night at Reagan International Airport, and the only sound in the car was the *wump-wump* of the windshield wipers.

"Columbia Bowling Alley. You know it?"

"Yeah. Do you?"

"Sure," she said.

"Funny," said the driver. "You don't look the bowling type."

"Looks can be deceiving."

"I hear you. But you know, if you're going to the alley looking to soothe the beast, I could probably help you find whatever you—"

"I'm not looking for drugs. I'm going bowling."

"Okay, sure. If you say so, lady."

Paulette was only half lying. No, she wasn't looking for drugs. But she wasn't going bowling. She was on a mission. Instinctively, she reached inside her purse and touched the envelope, just to make sure it was still there. It was.

Chloe's letter had landed in their father's mailbox on the morning of her burial. The poor man had nearly fainted. He gave it to Paulette to read it to him. The very idea of getting a letter from a daughter he had just laid beneath the earth was too painful for him to handle. Chloe had mailed it just one day before her death. The timing was not mere coincidence.

Paulette opened the envelope and read it one more time in the backseat of the taxi, the dim reading lamp giving her barely enough light:

Dear Dad,

I can't remember the last time I snail-mailed a handwritten letter to you, but don't be alarmed. This is good news. Mostly good news. I am working on the biggest story of my life right now. This one goes all the way to the White House.

I've been dealing with a confidential source for a couple weeks now. He hasn't told me everything, but I know enough to understand that this could be dangerous stuff. That's why I'm writing you this letter.

I have been making copies of all my notes on this story. In case something happens to me—I'm not saying it will, but just in case it does—I want you to know where they are. Take the key that's in this envelope. It's to locker number 23 at Columbia Lanes Bowling Alley on 7th Street. You'll find everything in the locker.

I know you probably think this sounds crazy or even paranoid. If you're sharing it with Paulette, she's probably rolling her eyes right now. But this is serious stuff, Dad. It's going to be big. Bigger than anything you can imagine. You are going to be so proud of me.

Love, Chloe

The taxi stopped at the curb in front of the bowling alley. The orange neon sign on the door said they were "PEN," the letter "O" burned out. Paulette paid the driver and stepped onto the sidewalk. She tried to put one foot in front of the other, but something stopped her. The cold night air hit her in the face, unleashing swarms of butterflies in her stomach.

Not until that moment—as she stared at the entrance to the Columbia bowling alley—had Paulette even considered the possibility that the locker might hold some kind of journalistic treasure. She'd promised her father to check it out and take whatever was inside the locker to the police. Knowing Chloe, she expected the locker to be empty. The girl just wasn't well.

Two men with bowling bags passed her on the sidewalk, and Paulette followed them inside. It was a league night, lots of men dressed in baby blue shirts with short sleeves and their names stitched onto the pocket. Paulette was strangely reminded of her midwestern roots—the winter days of Ping-Pong after school in the basement and bowling on weekends. Chloe used to throw a fit when their father told her to use the bumpers to keep the ball out of the gutters. She had always insisted on competing straight up with her older sister.

Paulette walked past the counter toward the women's lounge. The lockers were in a separate room adjacent to the bathroom. She double checked the number on the key and found locker 23 in the second row. She stepped toward it, inserted the key, and turned the handle. It opened. The butterflies returned; the locker wasn't empty.

You never cease to surprise me, little sister.

Paulette took the expandable folder from the locker and went to the wooden bench in the center of the room. She untied the string and peeked inside. It contained notes, just as Chloe had explained in her letter. Some were handwritten. Others were typed. Paulette was certain that the handwritten notes would be utterly unintelligible. She took a closer look at the typewritten pages, which were stapled together and better organized. They appeared to be a rough draft of an article.

The first line was a grabber: *When should a president no longer be president?*

Paulette almost smiled. She read on.

> *In dark times, this country has asked that question before. The Keyes presidency, however, presents an entirely unique question in American history: When should a president never have become president in the first place?*

Paulette's adrenaline was pumping. She kept reading—couldn't *stop* reading. By the fourth paragraph she *had* to put it down and catch her breath. She went right back to it, read some more, and instinctively brought the papers to her chest, as if to prevent her pounding heart from exploding.

My God, Chloe.

A wave of paranoia suddenly came over her—a taste of what her sister must have felt at the end of her life—and Paulette checked over her shoulder to see if anyone was watching. No one else was in the room. She gathered up the papers, stuffed them back into the file, and closed up the locker. Chloe's notes were hers now. This story was too important to sit on the shelf inside some locker in a bowling alley. Someone had to run with this. She would do it for Chloe—maybe even give her a posthumous co-byline. All Paulette had to do was verify a few facts.

And then one way or another, this story would rock the White House to its political core.

Without question, Sofia was the love of his life. Forty years hadn't changed his feelings toward her. That one night in Cyprus, however, had changed everything else.

The express ride from a hotel rooftop without an elevator had left him unconscious for days and had landed him in traction for weeks. The sterile smell of white hospital linens was forever imbedded in his brain, and sometimes he could still feel the itch beneath the body cast. Sofia had taken him home in a wheelchair, but his life as an invalid was finished at their doorstep. Despite Sofia's protestations, he had insisted on walking up the stairs to their second-story apartment under his own power. It took him almost ninety minutes, and the irony was not lost on him that this was his first journey up those steps since the Sicilians had rushed upstairs to throw him off the roof. He was exhausted, as much from the pain as from the effort. At the top, Sofia had taken him in her arms, and he made a promise to her and to himself. He would make himself stronger than ever, he would refuse to live his life on painkillers, and he would once again make sweet love to Sofia the way a man should make love to a beautiful woman. He'd started slowly with her, bringing his sense of touch back to life by exploring the curve of her neck, the soft wave of her long black hair, the smoothness of her skin. When he was ready for more, however, she pulled away. At first he thought it was the battered state of his body that had turned her off, the scars from the many surgeries that had put his broken bones back together.

"It's not you," she'd told him, and the way she looked away in shame, he knew immediately.

"The Sicilians. Did they—"

A weak, almost imperceptible nod of the head confirmed it.

Eight months later, his body was well on the mend. But the marriage was officially over.

The Greek had checked on her over the years, just out of curiosity, to see how she was doing. She'd married an American and moved to New York, where they opened Angelo's Italian Bakery and worked side by side for more than three decades. The Greek respected her right to move on, even though his need to see her had at times been overwhelming. Every so often, he would give in and watch her from a distance—a glimpse of Sofia walking to the bus or raking leaves in the front yard. The Greek didn't think of it as stalking, but Sofia never even knew he was there—except once. Two years earlier, he'd allowed himself to be seen. He was standing on the sidewalk in front of her house as she stepped outside to the mailbox. So many years had passed, but there is a way a man stands, a way he looks at a woman that endures over time and identifies him like a fingerprint. They didn't say a word to each other, but their eyes met and held, and the silence between them spoke volumes. The feeling had been unlike any the Greek had ever felt, and the spell was broken only when Sofia's husband called to her from inside the house. Even then, she hadn't turned away immediately—but finally she did, and she disappeared inside the house. That minute or so between them wasn't much in terms of time. But it had been enough to convince the Greek that the connection was still there, that his "once in a lifetime" was her "once in a lifetime," too, even if she had settled down and remarried.

The Greek hadn't returned since then. On some level, however, his memories of Sofia were at least part of the reason he'd kept himself in such amazing physical shape. The Russians breathing down his neck made him want to see her one last time. An Internet search at the library, just to see if she was still living in the same place, had turned up an obituary. Sofia's husband was dead—and at that moment, the light had switched on.

Plan C was hatched.

The Greek would visit Sofia. He would tell her how he felt. And unless those eyes had lied to him two years earlier, she would help him. She would believe in him this time, forgetting or at least forgiving him for the fact that he was a man whose actions never lived up to the tenderness of his words or intentions. Sofia was his last hope.

The bells on the door tinkled as he entered Angelo's Bakery. Four P.M. was the end of another eleven-hour day for a baker. Sofia was behind the counter cleaning when she looked up and saw him.

"*Ciao*, Sofia," he said softly.

She froze with recognition. Or maybe it was disbelief. She averted her eyes, staring down at the bread crumbs she'd swept into a neat pile on the floor, as if afraid to look at him.

"It can't be," she said.

"You know it is."

She still wouldn't look at him. He stepped toward the counter. She was just three feet away, and even in the twilight of her life, her beauty pulled him closer, triggering the memories. For a very brief moment, Sofia was nineteen again, his body was strong, and they could wrestle till dawn bringing each other pleasure.

"You are such a beautiful woman," he said.

Sofia nervously brushed back a wisp of hair from her face.

"Why have you come here?" she said.

"I need you."

"You lie."

"It's true," he said. "Right now, I need you more than ever."

"For what?"

He leaned forward, getting as close to her as he could without crawling over the counter. "Sofia, this time they are going to kill me."

She was silent for a moment, then slowly raised her eyes to meet his. "You should have been dead a long time ago."

"That's true. But I'm still here."

"Who is it this time? The Sicilians again?"

"The Russians."

"Why are they going to kill you?"

"Does it matter?"

She put the broom aside. "I suppose not."

"I need money," he said.

"How much?"

"Half a million dollars."

She laughed without heart. "Good luck."

"Luck has nothing to do with it," he said. "I have a plan."

Sofia didn't answer.

The Greek fell silent, too, but it was calculated. Even after all these years, he knew that if he just shut his mouth long enough, she would eventually look at him, their gaze would meet, and then he would have her.

Finally, he caught her eye, and before she could speak, the Greek made his plea.

"Sofia, only you can help me."

"I don't want to help you."

"You can't mean that."

"I've lived a simple life all these years. I'm not the girl you married."

"Yes, you are," he said. "Please. I'll be dead in a week if you don't help me. You're the only person in the world I can count on."

Her eyes narrowed, and for a moment he thought she was angry at him. But the anger seemed directed toward herself, perhaps for not being stronger.

"What kind of plan are you talking about?" she said.

"Very simple," he said. "I pulled this off once before, and it worked like a charm. Just follow my instructions."

"Why not do it all over again yourself?"

"Sofia, what did I always say about parties?"

She seemed confused for a moment, but then it came to her, and the memory almost made her smile. "Never throw the same one twice."

"Exactly. I've already thrown this party. It was a beauty, but now I need a new host."

"What do I have to do?"

"Take a dirty little secret," he said, "and sell it."

"What secret?"

The Greek smiled thinly, then pulled up a chair at one of the little round breakfast tables. "It's a long story, *amore mio.* Come sit down. And listen."

Chapter 23

J ack was glad to be back in Miami. Sort of.

His old boss from the Freedom Institute had stepped in to keep Jack from committing malpractice while he was in Washington, but day one was payback. Jack's secretary was out sick, the landlord was hounding him for last month's rent, and Jack was walking into arraignment with a screwball for a new client. The man was a frustrated understudy in a local production of *The Full Monty*, and the charge was reckless endangerment for slipping his rival a near-fatal dose of ED medication before curtain time. The courthouse jokesters immediately dubbed it the "standing ovation case." Jack thought of Vice President Grayson and the cause of his heart attack, and he took it as a sign: on anyone's list of *locos*, Miami was still *Numero Uno*.

How could I ever leave this place?

Luckily, at the end of the day, there was Key Biscayne. Paradise found.

The scenic drive across the causeway in his fastback Mustang was positively therapeutic. The office towers and high-rise condominiums of downtown Miami were behind him. Pelicans soared above the palm trees. Windsurfers and kite surfers enjoyed one last run before sunset, gliding across the blue-green waters that separated the mainland from the key. It was the same group of guys every day. They lived in bathing suits, drove open-air jeeps, drank beer out of coolers, and hung with bikini-clad women on the beach. Jack wondered what they did for a living. He wanted their job.

Jack went straight to the refrigerator and cracked open a cold one. He was about the plop himself into the armchair when the doorbell rang.

"Who is it?"

"Dr. Ruth," said Andie. "Here to give you tips on sex after forty."

Jack opened the door. She was wearing an FBI trench coat, but it wasn't raining, and it wasn't even a particularly cool evening.

"Do these tips come with an instructional video?"

"No," said Andie, her eyebrow arching in a seductive curve. "But we could make one."

She slowly opened her coat, and Jack's pulse quickened. Then it dropped.

"You're not naked," he said.

"What?"

"For a second there, I thought you were naked under your coat."

She smiled. "Sorry, you're not in the White House anymore."

"No," he said. "Not even close. That's over."

She laughed, then turned serious. "Seriously?"

"My dad thought it was . . . not working out."

"He *fired* you?"

"Well, he didn't really fire—"

She laughed again.

"Why is that funny?"

She tried to stop but couldn't.

"What are you laughing at?"

"It's just so . . . *you.*"

Jack turned and walked toward the kitchen. Andie followed. He started to pace, then stopped, giving her an assessing look as he planted his palms firmly on the countertop.

"What is that supposed to mean—it's so *me*?"

"Nothing. I'm sorry. Tell me what happened."

Andie removed her coat and took a seat on the bar stool. Jack got another beer from the refrigerator and poured it for her.

"I'm not exactly sure," said Jack. "I'm really worried that my dad is getting too caught up in this Washington bullshit."

"In what way?"

"Paulette Sparks thinks Grayson was murdered," he said.

Andie coughed on her beer. "Why does she think that?"

Jack paused. Sometimes he needed to be careful what he said to Andie, given her job. But he had to believe that the FBI already knew about Grayson's affair with Chloe Sparks, and the FBI definitely had the full e-mail—*I can bring down Keyes*—that Chloe received from her source. So Jack told her.

"Wow," she said. "You've been a busy boy."

"But when I tried to tell my father, he didn't want to hear any of it. That's when he fired me."

Andie took a moment to process that one. "Why would he react that way?"

"Honestly, I think he just doesn't want to be around anyone who is going to force him to dissect the night of Phil Grayson's death."

"Because Grayson was a friend, and it's a bad memory?"

"Possibly."

"Or because he knows what really happened?"

Jack's gaze tightened. "What *did* really happen?"

"I don't know. I'm just asking the question."

"Andie, I just laid out everything I know for you. If you can add something to the mix, I'd like to hear it. Especially if you're saying that my father is hiding something."

"I'm not saying that."

"Do you think Grayson was murdered?"

Andie shook her head, but it wasn't a denial. "I can't answer that."

"Why not?"

"Because if I do, you'll think I'm speaking for the FBI."

"Just tell me what *you* think."

She paused, then said, "I'd rather just help you analyze the facts."

"I'm all ears," said Jack.

"Grayson was cheating on his wife. He's dead. And now his girlfriend is dead, too. Who does that make you suspect?"

"I think Paulette would like to pin it on the president. She likes the vice presidential sex scandal and cover-up theory."

"Forget Paulette Sparks. You're the criminal defense lawyer. Two of the three players in a love triangle are dead. Who does it make *you* suspect?"

"I understand what you're saying, but—"

"But what?" said Andie. "Marilyn Grayson is beyond all suspicion?"

"It doesn't make sense. She was the first one to raise questions about her husband's death. We talked about it at the funeral, and when I followed up with her in Washington, it was Marilyn who suggested that someone surreptitiously slipped her husband ED medication to induce a heart attack."

"What better way to deflect suspicion from yourself than to be the first one to ask questions and suggest the modus operandi?"

"I see your point. But motive is one thing. Opportunity is another."

"There's the rub, Jack. Grayson came to Florida as your father's guest. Your father took him on a private hunting trip many miles away from a hospital. Your father was one of the last people to see Phil Grayson alive. Somewhere in there lies opportunity."

"Are you suggesting that he and Marilyn Grayson conspired to commit murder?"

"No. I'm simply telling you why people like Paulette Sparks who ask questions about Phil Grayson's death make your father so nervous."

Jack took a moment to read between the lines. Sometimes it was impossible to know when Andie was his girlfriend and when she was being an FBI agent.

"I think you're doing more than that," said Jack. "It's obvious that you've thought about this, or maybe you've heard scuttlebutt around the FBI. In your mind, my father is a suspect, isn't he?"

"Not necessarily."

"What does that mean?"

"Sometimes people with motive make people with opportunity unwitting accomplices. Maybe now your father realizes that he was used."

"And that's why he doesn't want to talk about it."

"Or why he's affirmatively covering it up."

Jack took a step back. He wanted to shoot down Andie's theory like a clay pigeon, but she was making too much sense.

"Jack, let's not talk about this anymore, okay? The reason I drove over here was to apologize for the way I wigged out on you in Washington. All that paranoia about Vice President Swyteck stifling my career. That wasn't my finest hour."

"It's totally okay. But don't shift gears on me. I really want to flesh out this stuff about my dad."

"I have a better idea. What do you say we drop this whole thing, I take off my clothes, put on my coat, and go ring your doorbell again?"

He didn't answer.

"Jack, did you hear what I just said?"

"I'm sorry. Somebody's at the door?"

"Exactly," she said, rising. "And what a funny coincidence."

"What?"

"Her name was opportunity," she said, as she pulled on her coat. "And you just missed it."

Chapter 24

At 10:00 P.M. Paulette Sparks drove to Club SI. Paulette was not a clubber, but she hadn't picked the meeting place. Her source had.

Paulette had stayed up all night Tuesday to decipher Chloe's notes. As best she could tell, Chloe and her source had spoken about a half dozen times. Each time, Chloe had managed to extract a few more details, all on the promise to pay "big money," though nothing ever changed hands—a good thing from Paulette's standpoint. Paulette and her network wouldn't touch a story built on checkbook journalism. By stringing her source along, Chloe had kept the story alive. Paulette could only speculate whether that same tactic had gotten her sister killed.

The story Chloe had cobbled together would have enticed any journalist. Potentially, it was bigger than anything *Paulette* had ever done. Chloe had collected most of the puzzle pieces, but in the end her story— the bombshell that would *"bring down Keyes"*—was based on a single source and built on inferences that bordered on conjecture. Paulette was confident that she could fill the holes. Step one was the corroboration of key facts. Paulette had spent the entire day following up leads and hunches, making phone calls, but all were dead ends. Except one.

Three little words—"Let's meet tonight"—had been music to Paulette's ears.

"Press," she said, as she flashed her credentials to the three-hundred-pound goon at the velvet rope. Club SI catered to the upscale twentysomething crowd, the kind of place that turned away unaccompanied women who weren't dressed like a cling-wrapped piece of sirloin. The promise of free publicity was Paulette's best shot at getting inside.

"You're good," he said.

She pushed through the door and stepped into the world of flashing lights, mirrored ceilings, and pounding music. The dance floor was packed, and people were lined up four- and five-deep for drinks at the bar. It was a much bigger crowd than she'd expected on a Wednesday night. And a much *different* crowd. Unbeknownst to her, Wednesday night was Goth night, and everything was black, except for the occasional multicolored hairstyle, which incorporated reds, purples, and some faded blond. Women wore black hoodies, black chokers, black armbands, and gossamer black halters with black leather flames licking their breasts. Black corsets were hot, as were black bustiers. Men wore everything from leather to tuxedo jackets, always with heavy chains. Man or woman, it was often hard to tell where the clothing stopped and the tattoos began. On the lighter side, there were dragons, fairies, or fantasy figures, but equally popular were the symbols of white witchcraft—a five-pointed star called the pentacle, and the "athame," a double-edged blade used in Wiccan rituals. Paulette remembered all that from Chloe's Goth days. "We're not the occult," Chloe would tell her, "we're highly intelligent creative types." Then she would lock herself in her bedroom and listen to her music—"Horror Show," by the Birthday Massacre, "Transylvanian Concubine" by Rasputina, or Zombie Girl's "We Are the Ones (Rotting Corpse)."

"Buy me a drink, Mama?"

Paulette turned. The guy standing next to her had jet-black hair, pasty white skin, and a silver ring in his pierced eyebrow. Paulette guessed he was about twenty-two, but she was hardly his "Mama."

"Kool-Aid stand is that way," she said.

He laughed and moved on, though the music was so loud that Paulette wondered if he'd even heard her. She tried to move forward, but the crowd was impenetrable. Paulette was losing patience. Her plan was starting to feel like an ill-conceived long shot, the product of too much enthusiasm and too little sleep. She knew her source wasn't in this crowd and wasn't coming any time soon. The joke was on Paulette. Send the ambitious bitch from CNN into Goth Night at Club SI. Ha, ha, ha, what a belly buster.

It was time to bail.

She zigged and zagged through the crowd and ducked out the exit. The transition from the stuffy, hot nightclub to the cold night air felt good on her face. Her ears continued to buzz as she started down the sidewalk, and her thoughts churned. She knew she was on to something, but she was being jerked around. She needed another angle to reach her target. Paulette wasn't too proud to ask for help. She pulled her cell from her purse and dialed Jack Swyteck.

Jack was in bed when his cell phone vibrated on the dresser. Quietly, so as not to wake Andie—she had given him a second "opportunity"—he slipped from beneath the covers, pulled on his boxer shorts, and grabbed the phone. The LCD read "Paulette Sparks."

He debated whether to answer, then ducked into the walk-in closet and closed the door so that he could take the call without waking Andie.

"Jack, hi, it's Paulette. Got a question for you."

"Paulette, I can't—"

"Has anyone mentioned anything to you about another e-mail like the one you and my sister got?"

The question left Jack silent. Finally, he said, "I'm sorry, I can't talk to you about that."

"You're breaking our deal. Remember: I agreed to tell you what I found out, but you had to tell me what you found out. We shook on it."

"That was then. I'm out of the loop now and back in Miami."

"I know, you got fired."

"Well, I wasn't really fired, but—"

"Jack, news travels fast in Washington. But it doesn't matter. This is a simple question: Have you heard anything about a third e-mail?"

"Why do you want to know?"

"After Chloe's funeral, I found some of her notes. She mentions that someone got an e-mail just like hers about a month before she did."

"Who?"

"She doesn't say. It's almost as if she was afraid to mention a certain person by name. But I have a strong hunch."

Jack took a seat atop the wicker clothes hamper. "I'd be curious to hear it."

"Does that mean our deal is back on?"

"I'm going to say yes. But you're on a roll here. Keep going."

"All right. Let me see if you think the way I do. You got your e-mail after Chloe got hers."

"Right."

"Somebody else got the same e-mail before Chloe got hers."

Jack hesitated. He knew that was true from information he'd gotten from the FBI, but he was reluctant to be as forthcoming with Paulette as he once had been. "Let's assume that's true for argument's sake."

"Fine. I'm thinking that Chloe was sandwiched between two bookends. And we all know what bookends do, right?"

"Hold up books?"

"They *match*, genius."

The closet was dark, but the figurative light suddenly went on. "So if the son of the future vice president got the e-mail after Chloe—"

"Then the daughter of the sitting vice president got it before Chloe did."

"And they both get the same offer," said Jack.

" 'I can make your father president.' "

The line was silent. It was as if, for each of them, hearing it aloud made it sound so logical.

Jack said, "What do we do about this?"

"I called Elizabeth Grayson today and asked her to meet me. I didn't tell her what it was about, but I don't think it would have mattered. The bitch sent me to a Goth bar and didn't show up. Obviously she has no intention of talking to me about anything. Probably still holds a grudge over my sister sleeping with her father. But didn't you mention that you had a lunch date with her?"

"Yeah. She offered to give me a few pointers about having a father who's vice president, but—"

"That's the perfect pretense."

"I don't know. The last time we talked, it was pretty awkward." He was thinking about her late-night visit to the hotel.

"Jack, you are our only shot. If you don't do this, all we can do is wait for the FBI to sort this out on their own terms and on their own schedule. By that time, your father could be part of an administration that is neck-deep in a congressional investigation. And time will only tell who is left holding the bag. Is that what you want?"

Jack considered it. She'd punched exactly the right button. He couldn't help but fear that his father was descending into the land of no return—especially after his conversation with Andie.

"Jack, is that what you want?"

"No," he said, gripping the phone tighter.

"So, you'll meet with Elizabeth?"

Suddenly, Jack was all too aware that the FBI was asleep in his bed. But it didn't change his mind.

"Yeah. I'll do it."

Chapter 25

Paulette was in her car when an idea came to her.

Tomorrow's schedule was busier than usual, starting at 6:00 A.M., when she and the congressional correspondent, the chief political consultant, and the senior legal analyst were slated to begin taping a four-part segment on the political and legal ins and outs of the Harry Swyteck nomination. Paulette should have driven straight home and gone to bed. Instead, she drove home, grabbed the key to Chloe's apartment, and hopped right back in her car.

There was no available parking on the street, so Paulette pulled around to the back alley and squeezed her car in between a Dumpster and a utility poll. She climbed out, and the car door closed with an empty thud. The quiet alley was dimly lit, a single yellow-tinted light glowing at the street entrance. While the cold night air had felt good upon stepping out of Club SI, it now made her cinch up her coat and walk quickly. The click of her heel echoed in the alley, and it made her stop and look around. The backs of the surrounding buildings were covered with burglar bars. Not another human being was in sight. The sounds of the city had seemed to evaporate. Urban quiet. It reminded Paulette of her first job as a crime-beat reporter—that eerie, ghost-town effect that marked high time for crime. Her gaze drifted toward Chloe's apartment building, and she could see the lone window in the corner with its second-story view of the alley. She thought for a moment of Chloe all alone, looking out her window toward trash cans and the backs of buildings. Then her thoughts turned to a stranger standing in this very spot, looking up toward Chloe.

Paulette shook off the image and started toward the rear entrance to the building.

The back door was locked, but Chloe's passkey still worked. Paulette pushed the door open and climbed the stairs to the second floor. The police tape was gone, and there was absolutely nothing about the door to Chloe's apartment to tell the world that a young woman had been murdered. Weird, but even though she'd attended the funeral and written the obituary, Paulette had a fleeting thought that if she knocked,

Chloe might answer. Murder was against the natural order of things, and it could play terrible tricks on the mind.

Paulette inserted the key. The tumblers clicked, the lock disengaged, and Paulette opened the door. She was about to switch on the light, but she stopped. From where she was standing, she could look all the way across the little efficiency and out the lone window in the corner. In the darkness, with the alley lit behind the building, she could actually see the very spot where she'd been standing and looking up toward Chloe's apartment just a few minutes earlier. She walked across the room in the dark and tried to pull the Venetian blinds shut. They were broken, however, and the slats wouldn't close all the way. It gave Paulette an eerie feeling. She wondered if it had ever occurred to Chloe that she was on permanent display.

Paulette went back and switched on the light. She would make this quick.

The forensic investigators had left the place reasonably undisturbed—nothing like the way they would have dissected an actual crime scene. The rent was paid through the end of the month, and one of the tasks on Paulette's to-do list was to sort through Chloe's belongings and clear things out. Tonight, however, her focus was on just one of Chloe's possessions. A prized possession. Her autographed photograph of Vice President Grayson.

The framed photograph was still hanging on the wall. Paulette crossed the room and took it down.

She hadn't studied it closely on her last visit, the morning after Chloe's death, when the homicide detective had brought it to her attention. Seeing it then had triggered only sadness. A seemingly unimportant detail, however, had lodged in her brain—and with all the recent talk of the vice president's daughter, her sadness had morphed into suspicion.

Elizabeth Grayson was in the photograph.

Paulette moved closer to the lamp for a better look. The pose seemed almost candid, or perhaps it was a staged pose that had broken down into something more casual. The vice president was seated on the corner of his desk. Chloe was standing next to him. Elizabeth was right beside Chloe. *Right* beside her—with her arm around Chloe's shoulder. The two women were smiling widely, heads tilted to the point where they were almost touching.

Paulette laid her hand atop the photograph and covered the vice president. With him out of the picture, the photograph told an entirely different story. There was nothing forced about the connection between the two women. Chloe and Elizabeth looked like old girlfriends, a couple of college-aged women cutting up and having a laugh in the White House.

Suddenly, the vice president's betrayal was of a whole new magnitude.

Shit, Chloe. How could you have done that to a friend?

Paulette put the photograph back on the wall and switched off the light. One last glance through the half-opened blinds rekindled that *I'm being watched* feeling, and she resolved to come back and clean out Chloe's apartment in the daytime. She locked the door on her way out, took the rear staircase to the back entrance, and started toward her car. She hadn't parked far away, but the night was turning colder, and the walk across the cracked concrete seemed longer than it was. Paulette didn't frighten easily, but she was eager to get out of there. She reached into her purse as she approached, disengaged the lock with the keyless remote, and opened the driver-side door. Her hand was actually shaking as she aimed the key at the ignition—and the tip had just touched the slot when she felt the plug of cold metal behind her right ear.

She froze.

"Don't make a sound," the man said. He was behind her in the backseat with his gun to her head.

"What do you want?" said Paulette.

There was silence. Enduring silence. The man couldn't or wouldn't tell her what he wanted. Paulette did not take that as a good sign. Suddenly his left hand was at her throat. She gasped, about to scream, but he shoved a bottle in her open mouth.

"Drink," he said.

Paulette couldn't have swallowed if she'd wanted to. The barrel of the gun pushed more firmly against her skull.

"I said *drink.*"

Paulette's heart raced with fear, but whatever was in the bottle had to be better than a bullet in the brain. She tilted her head back, and the warm liquid poured down her throat. It was bitter and a little salty, unlike anything she had ever tasted. She coughed through the last few swallows.

"All of it," he said.

She closed her eyes tightly and forced the rest down. When she finished, he took the bottle from her lips.

"Good girl," he said, though his voice seemed strangely distant, as if she were hearing only the tail end of an echo. "Now we wait. We wait. We . . . *waaaaaait.*"

Chapter 26

The scream woke Jack at dawn, and he shot bolt upright in the bed. The window shades were drawn and the room was still dark, but Jack immediately sensed that the other side of the bed was empty.

"Andie?" he said, but he didn't wait for a response. He heard something—*muted voices?*—and ran toward the kitchen.

"Whoa!" said Theo, shielding his eyes. "Forty-year-old naked man. Not pretty." Jack quickly wrapped himself in a towel from the hallway linen closet and entered the kitchen. Andie was standing at the counter, already dressed for work and making coffee.

"What was the screaming about?" said Jack.

"Oh, you mean Andie?" said Theo. *"There's a black man in the house, there's a black man in the house!"*

Andie swatted him. "I didn't say that. I just didn't expect someone to be standing in the kitchen."

Jack said, "What *are* you doing here, anyway?"

"Time to go fishin', dude. Dolphin are running."

Jack had a three-year lease on the most modest waterfront property on Key Biscayne, one of the original "Mackle houses" that were built mostly for World War II veterans who were brave enough to live in what was, at the time, little more than a mosquito-infested swamp. The house originally sold for twelve thousand dollars, and the current owner was renting it out to Jack until market appreciation added three more zeros to the land value—which wasn't far in the offing. It was basically a two-bedroom concrete shoe box, but it came with over one hundred feet of waterfront and a dock. Four years ago, Jack and Theo had gone boating, and by the end of the day, they were too tired to load the boat onto Theo's trailer. Jack said he could dock it overnight. It was still there.

"Coffee?" said Andie.

"Sure," said Theo.

"She was asking *me*," said Jack.

Andie poured a cup for each of them. Jack enjoyed the aroma before drinking. Theo gulped his, then said, "I hear President Keyes is a real coffee carouser."

"*Connoisseur*, Webster."

"Sorry, I don't speak Latin."

"It's French."

"Technically, it's English," said Andie, reading from the webpage on her iPhone. "Derived from old French. Originally from *cognōscere*, which is Latin."

"I was right!" said Theo.

"Whose side are you on?" Jack asked Andie.

Theo poured himself more coffee. The guy couldn't get enough of anything that was free.

"So," said Theo, "did you at least have coffee with the *prez* in the White House before you got canned?"

"I didn't get canned."

"That's what the paper said."

"Shit, it was in the newspaper?"

"Jack," said Andie, "you were fired, okay?"

"I repeat: Whose side are you on?"

She didn't answer. Her gaze was still fixed on the display screen of her iPhone, but she had turned very serious.

"Something wrong?" said Jack.

"I—" she started to say, then stopped. Jack knew she'd received one of those FBI e-mails that she couldn't tell him about.

She looked up and said, "Turn on the television."

Jack grabbed the remote and switched on the set. Andie took the control from him and tuned to CNN.

On-screen, a reporter was standing outside a three-story apartment building. The red banner with white letters at the bottom of the screen identified her as Heather Brown, and her location was listed as the LaDroit Park neighborhood of Washington, D.C.

"That's where Chloe Sparks lived," said Jack.

Andie raised a hand, telling him to listen.

The reporter continued: "It was in an alley directly behind this apartment building, at approximately four o'clock this morning, that police found a white sedan. Police have confirmed that the vehicle belongs to CNN reporter Paulette Sparks."

"Hey," said Theo, "isn't Paulette the reporter you—"

"Quiet!" Jack and Andie said in stereo.

The wind was kicking up in Washington, and the reporter fought to keep her hair out of her face. "CNN has also learned that the car's engine was running, but the lights were off, and the first officers on the scene did not see anyone behind the wheel. As the first officer approached, he saw what he described as a hose running from the exhaust pipe into the car through the rear window, which was opened just a crack."

"A hose?" said the anchor.

"Yes," said Brown. "A regular rubber garden hose. It was then that they shined their flashlights inside the vehicle and saw a body slumped over the console.

The door was locked, and police shattered the driver-side window. Paramedics were notified immediately, and the victim—described as a white female in her early thirties—was taken to George Washington Medical Center."

"Any report on her condition?"

"I don't have that information."

"Has the victim been positively identified yet?"

"I'm told that she has, but police are not releasing her name until her family can be contacted."

"Of course we don't want to speculate," said the anchor, "but Paulette Sparks is like family to many of us here. We are all deeply concerned. Our thoughts and prayers are with Paulette and the Sparks family right now."

The anchor switched gears to another breaking story. Jack switched off the television and looked at Andie.

The look on her face said it all, but she verbalized it anyway. "It's Paulette."

Jack glanced at Theo, then back at Andie. "Is she going to be all right?"

Andie drew a breath before answering.

"She's dead."

Chapter 27

Jack caught a mid-morning flight into Reagan National Airport and called his father as soon as the plane touched down. Harry had a full day of meetings at the White House, but he didn't have to guess what all the urgency was about. By lunchtime, Paulette's name had been released to the public, and the story was all over the news. The two men met in private in the only vacant office in the West Wing—Vice President Grayson's old office.

"Sounds like she killed herself," said Harry. The office was barely wide enough for the camelback sofa in the center of the room. Harry sat at the far end of it, near the window, and Jack was in the armchair beneath the brass chandelier.

Jack shook his head. "Not Paulette. No way."

"How can you be so sure?"

"First of all, she wasn't even close with her sister. This idea that she was so upset over Chloe's murder that she drove over to her apartment and took her own life just doesn't wash."

"It may seem far-fetched to you. But by definition, anyone who commits suicide has lost perspective."

"This was not a suicide," said Jack. "Paulette called me last night. She was not a woman on the verge of checking out. I could feel her energy, her excitement."

"About what?"

Jack told him about Chloe's notes and the reference to someone other than Jack and Paulette's sister getting an e-mail about bringing down the Keyes presidency.

"Where are those notes now?"

"I'll bet they're gone," said Jack. "And if they have disappeared, that's the nail in the coffin for the suicide theory, if you ask me."

"Have you reported this to the FBI?"

"I told Andie this morning."

Harry nodded, but not in agreement. He was simply thinking.

"What would you like me to do?" he said.

"Be honest with me," said Jack.

"Of course."

"The other day, when we were out jogging. When you, you know—"

"Fired you?"

"Well, you didn't really fire me."

"Yes, I did."

"Okay, all right. I got fired. F-I-R-E-D. Is everybody as happy as a pig in a pile of shit now?"

Harry glanced around the room. "Jack, it's only you and me here."

"Never mind. This is important, and I need you to be completely straight with me."

"I'm starting to resent the implication that I would be anything less than that."

"You're right," said Jack. "I'm sorry. Let me just put this to you, and we'll go from there. The other day, when I got f-f—"

"Fired."

"Yes. You were really upset with me for putting my trust in Paulette Sparks."

"I was upset with you for putting that level of trust in a Washington reporter. *Any* Washington reporter. It just so happened to be Paulette Sparks."

"And now it just so happens that she's dead."

Harry's mouth was agape. "Are you suggesting that *I*—"

"No," said Jack. "Not even when you were governor and signing death warrants for my clients did I call you a murderer to your face. That's not what this is about."

Harry checked his watch.

"Am I holding you up?" said Jack.

"I don't mean to be rude, but I have a meeting with the chief of staff in five minutes."

"Okay," said Jack. "Here's the thing. I told you how determined Paulette was to find out who sent me and her sister those e-mails about President Keyes. I also told you that she thought Vice President Grayson had been murdered."

"So?"

Jack narrowed his eyes, more like the way he would press a witness than speak to his father. "You're the *only* person I told."

Harry folded his arms—a defensive gesture, it seemed to Jack.

"I see," said Harry.

"So my question to you is this," said Jack. "Did you tell anyone what I told you?"

There was a knock at the door. The chief of staff poked her head into the office.

"The president is going to join us for our three o'clock," she said. "Let's not keep him waiting."

Harry nodded, as if to tell her that he needed just a moment more, and she closed the door.

"I have to go," said Harry, rising.

"I'd like an answer before you go anywhere," said Jack. "Did you tell anyone what I told you about Paulette?"

Harry took a deep breath, and he seemed to hold it for the longest time. Then he looked out the window, his gaze fixed so long that Jack, too, needed to turn and see what had caught his attention. There was nothing.

"Dad? Did you tell anyone?"

Harry started to shake his head, but then he shrugged and said, "I don't remember."

"You don't remember?"

"No. I truly don't. But if I had, don't you have to believe I would remember?"

"Honestly, I'm having trouble distinguishing between what I have to believe and what I want to believe."

Harry stepped toward him and laid a hand on Jack's shoulder. "Stop worrying, Jack. Or you're never going to make it to fifty."

An eerie feeling came over him. Jack knew that it wasn't a threat, but he wondered if it was more than just fatherly advice—perhaps some kind of warning.

Jack watched in silence as his father left the vice president's office for his meeting with President Keyes.

Andie had a four o'clock phone conference with the assistant special agent in charge of the Washington field office. She had been thinking about the call all day—and about Jack.

It wasn't that she didn't love Jack. Maybe he wasn't the smoothest guy she'd ever dated, and sometimes he drove her crazy, but there was cause for optimism. He tried to do the right thing—tried *really* hard. He still opened doors for her on dates. He paid the price to valet the car whenever she wore high heels. He told her she was beautiful, and not just to get in her pants. Not once did she have to tell him that a woman never wanted to hear the simultaneous sound of her man brushing his teeth and going to the bathroom. That alone made Jack a dream compared to her ex-fiancé in Seattle, though a groom who slept with the maid of honor didn't exactly set the standard for lifelong commitment.

No, it wasn't that she didn't love him. It was just that, at the moment, her loyalties were being tested.

"Agent Henning here," she said into the telephone.

The call was on an encrypted line, and it was just her and the Washington ASAC.

"Andie, what's on your mind?"

Andie had never met ASAC Stan White before the Sunday morning meeting at FBI headquarters about Jack's e-mail. It was White, however, who had authorized her to step in and lead Jack through his meeting with "the source" at the Smithsonian.

An intense assignment of that nature had a way of bonding agents together quickly, especially when they liked each other. White was a good man, and Andie could have easily seen herself working for someone like him.

Andie said, "You understand my relationship with Jack Swyteck."

"I do."

"Then you also must understand how difficult this is."

"Every agent has a personal life. In the end, it comes down to the fact that you swore an oath to the bureau."

"That I did," she said. It was framed and hanging on her office wall. The parts about allegiance and faithful discharge of duties seemed to be staring back at her.

"I have concerns about Jack's father," said Andie. "And not just because he's pushing Jack aside."

"It sounds like that's part of it," said White.

"Yes, but only because it's a symptom of a larger problem."

"All right. What kind of problem are we talking about?"

Andie debated how to say it, but directly seemed best. "Honestly, I smell a White House cover-up over the death of Phil Grayson. And I think Harry Swyteck is in it up to his eyeballs."

White was silent.

"Sir?"

"I'm still here," said White.

"The thing that makes me suspect Harry Swyteck's involvement is that—"

"I know what you're going to say."

Andie paused, surprised by the interruption. "You do?"

"Yes. And I don't disagree with you one bit. But . . ."

She waited, but again there was silence, as if the ASAC were mulling things over on the other end of the line.

"But what, sir?"

"If we're going to travel down this road, there is something you need to understand about Harry Swyteck."

She wasn't sure how to read his tone of voice. It was beyond serious.

"All right," she said. "I'm all ears."

Chapter 28

J ack kept his final promise to Paulette. He set up a meeting with Elizabeth Grayson that evening.

"I'm surprised you showed up," he said.

They were seated in a semiprivate booth in Cabanas restaurant at Georgetown Harbour. Elizabeth had plans to meet a friend there for dinner at eight, so she agreed to meet Jack for a drink at seven thirty. Cabanas was a bustling place with Aztec art on the walls, Mexican tequila at the bar, and enough twentysomething-year-old singles going at each other to make Jack at forty feel older than dirt. Outdoor dining by the fountain was popular in summer, but in December people drank their mango margaritas indoors. Elizabeth insisted that Jack try one, and he did, just to be polite. It was a running joke, however, the way people outside Florida thought that Miamians craved anything Mexican.

Without question, Miami had the Latin beat—Cuba, Brazil, Colombia, Argentina, and more—but trying to find a good Mexican restaurant in Miami was like trying to find good Japanese food in China.

Elizabeth smiled. "Why are you surprised? I said I would be here."

"True. But you also promised to meet Paulette Sparks at Club SI last night."

Her smile faded.

The waiter brought their margaritas—with salt for Jack, without for Elizabeth. She waited for the server to duck out beneath the long white draperies that shrouded their booth, then said, "How do you know about me and Paulette?"

"She called me late last night. We had a very interesting talk."

"That's such a meaningless word—*interesting*. The sinking of the *Titanic* was interesting. Sex is interesting. Even you're kind of interesting."

"This isn't about me."

She tasted her margarita. "No, you're right. It's about Paulette. Horrible news about her death. I feel terrible for her father. Losing two daughters in such a short period of time."

"It's even more tragic that Paulette died before she could really follow up on Chloe's story about President Keyes."

Elizabeth made a face. "I find it hard to believe that Chloe Sparks would have anything that a reporter of Paulette's stature would follow up on."

"That's what Paulette wanted to meet with you about."

"Me? What does any of this have to do with me?"

Jack put his margarita aside and leaned into the table, pressing his point. "Paulette had a theory. She thinks you got the same message I got. An anonymous e-mail from someone who claims to have the power to make your father president."

The mariachi band started to play, but not even the sudden blast of trumpets could make Elizabeth flinch.

"You're only about half right," she said.

"Which half do I have wrong?"

"I did get an e-mail about President Keyes. Something similar to what you got. But it didn't come straight from the source."

"How did you get it?"

"It was delivered by an old friend."

"Does this friend have a name?"

"Chloe Sparks."

Jack checked his surprise. "Okay, let me break this down. First of all, you're saying that Chloe Sparks was an 'old friend' of yours?"

"I should say *former* friend. I met all the White House interns assigned to my father. Most were ambitious ass-kissers, but Chloe was cool. I liked her. We started to hang out—dinners, movies, the clubs. We even came here a few times. Chloe liked to party. So do I."

Things were starting to click for Jack. "Let me guess: You and Chloe were out partying the night before she got fired from her internship for drug possession."

She tasted her drink again. "You add up two plus two pretty quickly."

"You planted drugs on her."

"That's what you say."

"That wasn't a very nice thing to do to a friend."

"Fucking my father wasn't a very nice thing for my friend to do to me."

Jack couldn't argue with that, but this was not the time to cut her any slack. "Obviously there were some hard feelings there."

"You think?" she said, scoffing.

"So how was it that, a year or so later, Chloe called to give you the message from her anonymous source about bringing down President Keyes?"

"That was out of the blue," said Elizabeth.

"How do you mean?"

"Chloe and I didn't speak after she got fired. At that point, she had probably figured out that I knew all about her and my father. I never told her that I had set her up, but I think she accepted the fact that she got what she deserved."

"That brings me back to the same question: Why did she call you about the message she got from her source?"

"I can only guess. In her head, I honestly think she believed that this would make up for what she had done, that things would be good between us. She told me that she was working on a huge story, and that the information from her confidential source could put my father in the White House."

"Did Chloe give you any specifics?"

"Just someone claiming to have the power to bring down President Keyes."

Elizabeth looked past Jack and waved. He turned around and saw a young woman checking her coat at the entrance.

"That's my friend," said Elizabeth.

"One more question before she gets here," said Jack.

"Better make it quick."

"When Chloe shared her message with you, what did you do with it?"

"Nothing."

"Nothing?"

"Nope. Not a thing. Because here's the deal," she said, as she leaned on her forearms and came closer, her glare cutting right through him. "My father didn't deserve to be president."

Her delivery was so cold that Jack actually felt it down his spine.

"Hey, girl," said Elizabeth as she rose to greet her friend.

Jack watched the two young women embrace, and he wondered if Elizabeth had used a similar maneuver to reach into Chloe's pocket or purse and plant the joint that had gotten her fired. The women launched into conversation, and Jack suddenly felt invisible.

"I'll see you around," he said, more than ready to leave.

Chapter 29

The Greek chose a sentimental spot for his Friday-morning meeting: Greek Taverna in the Old Post Office Pavilion.

Built in 1899, the pavilion's twelve-story tower had once made it Washington's tallest government building and first skyscraper. Its conversion to a shopping mall in 1978 helped to revitalize Pennsylvania Avenue between the Capitol and the White House, to the point that the shopping mall—with Abercrombie, Victoria's Secret, and Limited Too—was nearly as popular among tourists as the National Mall, no slight to Washington, Jefferson, and the Lincoln Memorial. The doors opened at 10:00 A.M., and by ten thirty the place was bustling with shoppers, diners, and people who just wanted to walk around and soak up the confluence of nineteenth-century architecture and twenty-first-century atmosphere. The Greek had chosen the pavilion for one reason only: a highly public place with hundreds of potential witnesses made it that much harder for someone to put a bullet in his head.

The hostess escorted him to a table outside the restaurant in the café area. He was still indoors, however, seated beneath the skylight in the mall's three-story atrium. The pavilion had three levels, and from his vantage point he could keep an eye on just about everyone, whether they strolled past the Taverna on the first level or looked down toward him from the upper levels. If the need arose, he could even make a run for it.

The thought triggered a memory, and as his gaze drifted up toward the skylight overhead, he could almost see himself falling from the rooftop to the stone floor below. He shook it off. That was the past. He had been young and stupid back then. He was in control now, not them.

Stay strong, he told himself. *You are stronger than ever.*

"Will it be just you, sir?" asked the server.

"No," said the Greek. "I'm meeting someone."

The server placed two mugs on the table and filled one with decaffeinated coffee, black. The Greek got a bottle of spring water as well, and when the server was gone, he pulled a sack full of tablets and capsules from his coat pocket. In it was literally everything from A to Z—as in vitamin A to zinc. He laid each supplement on the table in a neat row before him, methodically popped one at a time into his mouth, and washed it down with a sip of water. He'd been mega-dosing vitamins and minerals since his fiftieth birthday. No one knew for sure if it did any good, but it had been about five years since his last bout with the common cold, and the Greek was convinced that the supplements were at least in part responsible for his high stamina, quick reactions, and sharp mind. All were essential for his line of work, though his exact profession was open to some debate.

The Greek was not a hit man. He had never liked the label, never thought it applied to him. Yes, he had killed people. Yes, he had gotten paid to do it. But he was more like a sniper in wartime. His kills were highly personal, but they were essential to the overall mission. The Greek had never "offed" anyone unless it was absolutely essential. Sometimes, the assignments were easy. Most of the bastards on his list had deserved far worse. Other times, however, the jobs were more difficult. On occasion, it was necessary to kill someone you liked.

Maybe even someone you loved.

The Greek noticed a man with a beard, glasses, and a broad-rimmed hat coming toward him. He didn't recognize the man, but that seemed to be the point. A Secret Service agent couldn't be seen meeting someone with the Greek's past.

"How are you, Frank?" he said.

Agent Madera took a seat at the café table. "Don't use my name, idiot. And let's make this quick."

The Greek had rehearsed his pitch for an hour last night, and if he spoke slowly he could deliver it coolly and with almost no accent. Madera's edginess made him want to slow down even more, just to tweak the bastard.

"I know your boy's in trouble, and I can help."

"You don't know squat."

The Greek smiled thinly. "I know about the e-mail to Jack Swyteck. I know about the one to Chloe Sparks. I know much more than you think."

"Who do you think you're fooling? You know about those e-mails because you're the one who sent them."

"See, you're wrong already. I didn't send them. I sold you the goods on Keyes before the election, and I kept my end of the deal. I have not breathed a word to anyone. It's your secret now, not mine."

"Well, obviously someone else is in on it, too. And they are going to ruin a very good thing if this becomes public knowledge."

The server came by to offer coffee, but Madera waved him off, as if to say that he wasn't staying long.

"Like I told you," the Greek said. "I know who it is. And I can take care of that problem."

"Who is it?"

"Not so fast."

"You are so full of shit," said Madera, and he started to rise.

"Wait!"

The Greek immediately regretted his tone. A little too desperate.

Madera lowered himself back into his chair, intrigued.

"Okay," said the Greek. "I'll tell you who it is. But first we need to strike a deal: I'm the one who takes care of the problem."

"You mean really take care of it?"

The Greek unfolded the cloth napkin at his table and wrapped it around his fist. It was an allusion to his signature—the homemade suppressor, a towel wrapped around the .22-caliber Beretta.

"I mean permanently," he said.

"What's that going to cost us?"

"Five hundred thousand."

Madera scoffed. "You're out of your mind."

"That may sound high. But without me, you can't even identify the threat. Think of it as your half-million-dollar investment in preserving the status quo. I'm throwing in the disposal for free."

Madera considered it, and a decision came quickly. Almost too quickly.

"All right. Who is it?"

"Before I tell you, I want you to understand that I've set up a safety valve. If anything happens to me—even if I just mysteriously disappear—the truth about Keyes is going to be all over the newspapers."

"Who is it?" said Madera, refusing even to acknowledge the threat.

The Greek drew a breath, as if to underscore the difficulty of his position. And it was difficult. In fact, it was the most painful lie he'd ever told. He raised his coffee mug to his lips and spoke over it.

"It's my ex-wife, Sofia."

"You told me she didn't know anything."

"That was two years ago. Things change."

Madera showed no reaction, and the Greek tried to mask his own misgivings. He had gone to Sofia hoping to persuade her to meet with Madera and sell her silence. Over time, he probably could have convinced her to do it. But he didn't have time. Her refusal to help had left him no choice.

Madera said, "You're one lucky bastard. Not many men get paid half a million bucks to eliminate their ex."

"I'm giving you five days to get me the money. I want it wire-transferred to my account in Antigua. Here's the account number," he said, as he slid a business card across the tabletop.

Madera didn't take it.

The Greek nudged it forward. Madera still didn't reach for it. He didn't even look at it.

The Greek met his stare. "You're not going to pay, are you?"

Madera was silent.

The Greek looked past Madera, and he noticed a man standing near the directory in the center of the courtyard. He seemed to be watching them. Instinctively, the Greek's gaze drifted up toward the second level. Another man at the railing seemed to have his eye on them as well. The Greek knew in an instant that these men weren't Secret Service agents.

They were part of Madera's other world.

His pulse quickened, and he suddenly realized that putting Sofia at risk and not getting paid for it were the least of his worries. He had to make a break, but even at the peak of his training, he wasn't sure he could have outrun three, four, or maybe more of them. From behind he heard the whine of an electric engine, and with a quick glance over his shoulder he spotted a mall security guard. He was driving a flatbed golf cart that was rigged to transport the handicapped.

Yes!

The Greek threw the rest of his coffee into Madera's face, leaped to his feet, and grabbed the security guard as he rode past their table. A woman screamed as the guard tumbled to the floor and the Greek jumped behind the steering wheel. He put the pedal to the metal and brought it to full speed immediately.

The man on the second floor raced down the escalator. Two other men came running from a bagel shop. The Greek knew they weren't going to shoot him in front of all these people, but if they caught him, they'd soon stuff him in the trunk of a car, never to be heard from again. He was a dead man if he didn't get out—*now.*

He pulled a quick U-turn and sped toward the exit. Shoppers jumped out of the way as he blew past one storefront after another. The security guard and Madera's men gave chase, but the electric cart was fully juiced and fast enough to have been an emergency-response vehicle. The Greek laid on the horn and drove as if he didn't care how many people he mowed down. He rode it all the way to the Pennsylvania Avenue exit, ditched it at the door, and headed for the street at a full sprint on fresh legs. A taxi was at the corner of Twelfth Street. He pushed an old woman aside and stole it from her.

"Hey," said the driver, "that lady was first."

The Greek slammed the door shut and threw his wallet onto the front seat beside the driver.

"Take as much as you want. Get me out of here. Fast!"

The tires squealed, and the cab launched like a rocket. Through the rear window, the Greek saw Madera's men huffing and puffing, cursing one another at the curb.

He was smiling, feeling smug and even a little full of himself over the getaway. But then reality hit, and the smile ran from his lips. The bottom line was that he still owed the Russians five hundred thousand dollars. And if there was one thing worse than having the Russians out to kill you, he had just found it.

Now it was the Russians *and* the Italians.

Chapter 30

The biscotti were selling like hotcakes. That was the noon report from Sofia's nephew, the assistant manager at Angelo's Bakery.

"Hot cakes should be so lucky to sell like my biscotti," said Sofia.

It's wasn't bragging. Angelo's was the go-to bakery in the neighborhood, but people drove miles out of their way for the biscotti, which had always been a point of personal pride for Sofia. The famous cannoli recipe was from her late husband's family, a treat reminiscent of Old World Sicily with traditional thin crust and ricotta filling. The biscotti, however, were her own baby—her way of proving that a Sicilian baker could outdo the Tuscans on their own invention. Sofia came up with something completely new every week, from cranberry-orange-pistachio to vanilla–chocolate chunk. Her latest creation was a softer biscotti with tasty lemon frosting and a texture between a crispy cookie and crunchy biscotti. The secret ingredient was the leavening agent for a controlled release. Customers who hadn't touched biscotti in years for fear of breaking a tooth were addicted.

"Any more of the amaretto cookies?"

It was one of Sofia's regular customers, a tailor who had been making suits in the same shop across the street for thirty years. Sofia smiled from behind the counter.

"All gone, sorry."

"Will you have more tomorrow?"

Sofia's gaze had shifted back to the storefront window—and her attention shifted along with it.

"Sofia, will you make more tomorrow?"

She turned back to her customer, embarrassed. "What? Oh, sorry. Sure. I'll hold you a dozen."

"*Grazie.*"

"*Prego.*"

He left happy, and Sofia went to the window and pretended to watch him cross the street and disappear into his tailor shop. But her gaze wasn't following him. She was focused on the midnight-blue Mercedes-Benz parked a few doors down on the other side of the street.

Sofia's worries had started with Demetri's return. Just the fact that he'd tracked her down and shown up at her bakery, completely out of the blue, had been unsettling enough. Asking her to commit blackmail was unconscionable. She'd refused. He remained determined to convince her, and that was when the confusion had begun. She'd served him cappuccino with hazelnut biscotti, and he'd turned on his charm. She allowed him to talk about the old times, the happy times—that brief period in her life when she had thought everything was possible with Demetri. Back then, it was unheard of for a nineteen-year-old girl to leave Villa Rosa and run off to Cyprus with a foreigner, but Demetri had literally and figuratively swept Sofia off her feet. He was strong, handsome, and filled with the confidence of youth. She'd believed him when he vowed never to make her cry, when he promised on his honor to take her back to Sicily someday and buy the biggest house in Villa Rosa. She had been a willing and passionate partner in his plan to conquer the world. But that was all so long ago. Two old lovers separated by decades and reminiscing about such nonsense had given Demetri an emotional opening, a reason to hope that she would come around to see things his way. It wasn't that he had any real claim to her affection, and she had certainly never regretted her life with Angelo at the bakery. But even after all these years, the good side of Demetri was an undeniable piece of her lonely heart. She only wished that she had never known his bad side.

"You're asking me to be a criminal," she had told him. "Think of another way, and maybe I will try to help you."

He had been sweet to her as long as possible, even shown her a tear—his heart breaking at Sofia's mere insinuation that he would use her. The weird thing was, she had almost stepped into his web, almost believed in his sincerity. For a moment. Then his notorious temper flared, and it had frightened her to the core. He left in a huff, and Sofia had been worried ever since. She'd barely slept last night, but a busy morning at the bakery could cure just about anything. By mid-morning she had just about convinced herself that she was being foolish and paranoid. If Demetri was in as much trouble as he'd claimed to be in, surely he had no time to waste prevailing on his ex-wife for help. It seemed almost inevitable that she had seen the last of him and his way of life.

Then that dark Mercedes had cruised slowly past her bakery and parked across the street. It had been there for over twenty minutes. Something told her that the two men inside hadn't come for the biscotti.

Sofia wiped her hands nervously in her white apron. One of the men on the street was talking on a cell phone. She wondered who he was calling.

Stop it, Sofia.

The telephone on the wall rang, and it gave Sophia a start. Her nephew was about to answer it, but she hurried past the cash register and grabbed it first. He gave her a funny look, but Sofia had a strange intuition about this call.

"Angelo's," she said.

She glanced out the window. The man standing by the Mercedes was no longer on his cell phone.

"Hello?" she said, trying once more.

"Sofia, is that you?"

It was Demetri's voice—not the stranger on the cell phone.

"Sofia is not here," she said.

"*Amore mio*, I know it's you."

"Please don't call her anymore."

She was about to hang up.

"It's life or death, listen to me!"

His desperation gripped her. Her nephew glanced over from behind the counter.

"Hold on," she told Demetri. "Let me go to the other phone."

"No! There's not time. Just listen to me!"

"But—"

"Don't talk, listen. I've done a terrible thing, a terrible, terrible thing. And I am so sorry."

Sofia shifted uncomfortably. Again her nephew seemed to sense her distress, and she turned away, burrowing herself in the corner behind the pastry display cabinet.

"Demetri, please."

"You have to go. Get out!"

"What?"

"I was so desperate when you turned me down, but I knew in my heart that you wanted to help me. I told them that you were the one who tried to sell the secret to Harry Swyteck's son and to that reporter. I told them I could—for money, I said I would . . . eliminate that threat."

The phone shook in her hand.

"I was bluffing," he said. "I was never going to hurt you. I could never do anything to hurt you. Please, please believe me. My plan was to take their money and take you away—back to Villa Rosa, just like I promised you forty-six years ago."

"I have to hang up," she said, her voice quaking.

"No, Sofia! You have to run. Don't you understand? They believed me when I told them you were trying to sell what you know. Now they are going to kill me, and they are going to kill you, too!"

Sofia's heart was pounding. She looked out the plate-glass window, between the lines of the hand-painted name of her late husband. The man on the street who had been speaking on the cell phone was coming down the sidewalk and walking toward the bakery. His partner was at his side. Sofia had seen men like these before, with their felt hats, expensive Italian-made overcoats, black leather gloves, and icy-cold eyes. It frightened her to the core to think that they were coming for her.

"Where can I go?"

"Just go! *Now!*"

Sofia hung up the phone. Her nephew was pretending to be busy rolling out pastry dough on the marble slab, but Sofia knew he had been watching her out of the corner of his eye. She untied her apron and hung it on the hook.

"What's the matter?" her nephew asked.

She grabbed her purse from under the counter, and pulled on her winter coat. Then she punched open the cash register and grabbed a handful of bills.

"*Tia*, where are you going?" he said.

She went to him, held his face in her hands, and kissed him on the lips. Her answer was an old Sicilian saying:

"*Quandu si las 'a vecchia p'a nova, sabe che lasa ma non sabe che trova.*"

When you leave the old for the new, you know what you are leaving but not what you will find.

With a tear in her eye, Sofia turned and ran out the back door.

Chapter 31

J ack went into the office early on Saturday morning
to pack boxes.

Technically his lease wasn't set to expire for another
six months, but the rent was more than he could afford,
and the landlord had agreed to let him out early—if he
could be out before December 31. Under that kind of
deadline, he was willing to take help from anyone. Even
Theo.

"Do you know where you're going yet?" said Theo.
He was wearing a vintage 1970s Allied Van Lines moving shirt that he'd picked up at Miami Twice clothing
store, which made him look all the more authentic loaded
down with a stack of boxes as high as the ceiling.

"There's a little place on Main Highway that I really
like. Hope to sign a lease this week."

Theo went to the lobby and dropped his stack on the floor beside other packed boxes. It sounded like breaking glass.

"Those were my framed diplomas," said Jack.

"Emphasis on *were*," said Theo. "Sorry, dude. But I can make it up to you. In fact, I'm gonna make you rich."

"Spare me. I still have a garage full of Y2K survival kits from the last time you promised to make me rich."

"This is different, dude. I been thinking about it since I called you at Grayson's funeral and we talked about Tara Lee and porn addicts."

"Vivien Leigh."

"Whatever. It's the addicts that's important. I registered the domain name last night: BringBackPorn dot com."

"I didn't know it had left."

"Your father isn't vice president yet. Once he gets confirmed he'll have nothing but time on his hands. All we gotta do is convince him to outlaw Internet porn. And then what do you think the most valuable domain name on the planet will be?"

"Get a Life dot com?"

"BringBackPorn dot com, baby. And we own it. It's like money in the bank, dude."

"Really, what planet are you from, Theo?"

There was a knock at the door. Theo went to the window, pulled the curtain aside, and peered outside.

"Can't really see, but I think it's your *abuela*."

Jack's maternal grandmother had a way of showing up at his office whenever it had been too long since he'd last visited her. Sometimes it was to wonder aloud if she was going to live long enough to teach Spanish to the great-grandchildren who, by the way, Jack needed to hurry up and give to her. Other times, it was to remind her gringo grandson that half the blood in his veins was Latin. Usually, however, it was just to give him a kiss and make sure that he wasn't starving to death.

"Probably bringing us her famous *tres leches*," said Jack. The tasty dessert was a running joke to just about everyone in Miami but *Abuela*, who regularly phoned in to Spanish talk radio and told the world that she'd invented *tres leches*, which the Nicaraguans had stolen from her.

Jack opened the door. It was not his grandmother.

"Mr. Swyteck?" the woman said.

"Yes. Who are you?"

"My name is not important. May I come in, please?"

"The office is not really open today." *Especially to people who won't tell me their name.*

"Please," she said. "It's important. It's about your father becoming president."

"You mean vice president?"

"No," she said. "I mean president."

The woman suddenly had Jack's complete attention. It was odd that she wouldn't share her name, but compared to everything else that had happened to him lately, it wasn't *that* odd. He showed her inside and closed the door.

"Excuse the mess," he said. "I'm moving."

"To Washington?"

"No, I'll be staying in town."

Theo said, "Jack's father fired him."

Jack shot him a deadly look.

"Fired you?" she said.

"This is my friend Judas," Jack said to her. "He was just leaving."

"Nice to meet you, Judas."

Theo nodded. "Later, dude," he said, then left through the front door.

Jack showed his guest into his office and took her coat. It was heavy, he noticed, and even though it was a cool December day by Miami standards, it wasn't winter-coat weather. He moved the boxes out of the way and offered her a seat in the armchair. The clutter made it impossible to get behind his desk, so he leaned on the front edge, facing her.

She sat quietly with her hands folded in her lap as she gazed down at the floor. Jack took a moment to size her up. She was younger than his grandmother, but he could see how Theo had mistaken her for *Abuela*. Both were attractive, elderly women with dark eyes and olive skin that seemed younger than their years. She had the delicate features of a former beauty, but her hands were those of a working woman. At bottom, however, it wasn't her beauty or her subtle resemblance to *Abuela* that gnawed at Jack. There was a deeper familiarity—a distinct sense that he had seen her somewhere before.

"Is something wrong?" she said.

"No, sorry." Jack was staring, but he couldn't help it. She was definitely familiar. "Would you like some coffee?"

"No, thank you."

She was leaning on the arm of the chair with her elbow, as if she were too tired to sit up straight, and her left leg was restless and shaking uncontrollably. She seemed nervous. Maybe even a little scared.

Finally, she looked up into Jack's eyes.

More than a little scared.

"You're in a lot of danger," she said.

Jack had heard some interesting first lines from people in that chair, but this one was up there with the best of them.

"Can you tell me why?"

She shifted uncomfortably. "I had a lawyer once. He did a will for my late husband and me. If I'm your client, you can't tell anyone what I tell you. Not even the police. Is that right?"

"That's the way it normally works."

"Am I your client?"

"You are now. Talk to me."

"I think I know who killed that young reporter in Washington—Chloe Sparks. And," she said, swallowing a lump in her throat, "I think you may be next."

"Whoa," said Jack. That last part had hit a little too close to home. "What's the killer's name?"

"I can't tell you his name."

"That's okay. But what do you say we back up a little and you at least tell me your name?"

She took a breath, and let it out. "Sofia."

"Good. A beautiful name."

"*Grazie.*"

"You're Italian?"

"From Sicily."

"Is that where the killer is from?"

"No."

"Would I be wrong if I guessed he was Greek?"

She showed surprise. "How would you know that?"

"I've been doing a little investigating of my own. Chloe's sister and I tracked that down after we figured out that Chloe and I got the same curious message from an anonymous source."

"I still can't tell you his name."

"How do you know he killed Chloe Sparks?"

"I've known him a long time," she said, then thought better of it. "No, I knew him a long time ago. We talked recently."

"He told you that he killed Chloe Sparks?"

"No. In fact, he denied it."

"You don't believe him?"

The anguish was all over her face. "I wanted to. I've always wanted to. But I've known better for a long time, and I definitely know better now. He told me he was in contact with her about President Keyes. He was trying to sell her newspaper a story. It didn't work out. Now she's dead."

"You assume he killed her."

"He's desperate for money—a lot of money. The only way he can raise it is to sell what he knows about President Keyes. Once the secret is out, he can't sell it. Somehow, Chloe Sparks must have figured out what he was trying to sell her before she had to pay him for it. That was a fatal mistake. Then he tried to sell the same information to you."

Jack processed her words, thinking it through. "So if he thinks I also figured it out without paying for it, then—"

"Then you're next on his list."

Jack took it a step further, wondering if that was what had happened to Paulette Sparks.

"Are *you* on the list?" he asked.

She massaged away the tension between her eyes. "I have even bigger problems."

Jack took another good look at her. It was a safe bet that she hadn't slept much last night. "Are you running from someone?"

She didn't answer. She didn't have to.

Jack said, "Have you thought about going to the police?"

"No!"

"It's just a suggestion," said Jack. "Can we at least talk it out?"

"I can't go to the police."

"Why not?"

"I just can't. That's not possible."

"What if you were to tell me the killer's name and then I went to the police?"

"No."

"I have a friend in the FBI."

"Absolutely *no!*"

Jack paused, confused. "The man killed Chloe Sparks. You think he might kill me. You look scared to death. Why are you protecting him?"

"It's not him I'm protecting," she said.

"Have you done something wrong, too?"

"No," she said, almost laughing in frustration. "This is not about me."

Jack leaned forward and looked her in the eye. "Are you afraid of him?"

Again, she was silent. Then suddenly she rose and said, "I've told you everything I can. You know the danger. Now please take care of yourself."

"Sofia, you are an important witness, and you seem like a good person. I can help you get protection. I've done this many times before."

She closed her eyes, struggling, then opened them. "You have no idea how complicated this is."

"You're right. I don't. But let's agree on this. We won't do anything today. For now, we'll just make you safe. You look like you could use some sleep. Do you have friends or family to stay with in Miami?"

"No one."

"Do you have a hotel?"

She shook her head. "I rode the train all night from New York. I came straight from the station."

He noticed that she had no luggage, but the heavy winter coat suddenly made sense.

Really on the run.

Jack helped with her coat, then grabbed a business card from his desk and wrote an address on the back.

"There's a boutique hotel about three blocks that way," he said, pointing. "The San Pietro. My out-of-town clients stay there and love it. Use my name. Tell the manager to bill it to my account."

"I can't do that."

"Please. It's right on the corner of Alhambra. A pink Mediterranean-style building with a barrel-tile roof and bougainvillea vines climbing up the walls. It will remind you of Sicily."

That brought a smile—just a hint of one, but Jack could see that, trapped deep inside, was a beautiful smile that could have lit up a room.

"Thank you," she said, as she surprised him with a kiss on the cheek.

"You're welcome," he said, and he showed her to the door.

Chapter 32

J ack caught up with Theo for lunch at the Royal
Castle.

Northwest Seventy-nine Street and Unity Boulevard
was Theo's old neighborhood, a hardscrabble part of
town where deadly race riots had made Liberty City
synonymous with violence in the 1980s. Over the years,
crime had shut down or driven away scores of mom-and-
pop businesses, but Royal Castle hamburgers—palm-
sized patties with pickles, onions, and mustard—have
been served at the same location for over half a century.
The orange bubble letters on the windows and vintage
sixties posters on the white tile walls were a nice touch
of nostalgia, though the world's last existing Royal
Castle restaurant did not have a spotless past. It had
taken a civil rights protest march to bring down the sign
on the counter that had once proclaimed WHITES ONLY.

Theo's great-uncle Cy had been one of the first persons of color to sit himself down on one of ten chrome stools at the red-and-white counter, and he'd been coming for lunch every Friday since.

Theo kept eating, but Uncle Cy was so happy to see Jack that he got up and hugged him so hard that the old man accidentally farted.

"Ooops, my bad."

Theo nearly burst with laughter, and Cy slapped him across the back of the head, as if he were ten years old again.

"Ain't funny. Gettin' old sucks."

"You can say that again," said Jack.

Cy introduced Jack to the waitress, a striking young woman who looked like a young Vanessa Williams and whose name was Brandy.

"Brandy?" said Jack.

"Yes. Brandy."

"A fine girl," said Theo.

"And what a good wife she would be," said Jack.

"Huh?" said Brandy.

Jack was feeling all of forty again, referencing a pop song that was almost as old as he was to a woman who wasn't even old enough to know Red Hot Chili Peppers unless they were on her nachos.

"Jack, take my seat," said Cy. "I gotta run. You can have that last burger if you want it."

Theo snatched it from the old man's plate and stuffed his face.

Cy swatted him across the backside of his head again. "The boy's hopeless," said Cy.

"This, from a man who just blew his trumpet at the counter," said Theo.

Cy swatted at him again, but this time Theo ducked.

"Not even my aim's what it used to be," said Cy. "I'll see y'all later."

Jack placed an order with Brandy—two burgers for himself and three more for Theo. Theo slurped down a root beer as Jack told him all about the visit from Sofia. Theo was Jack's unofficial investigator, so, technically speaking, telling him about Sofia wasn't a breach of the attorney-client privilege. More important, Theo knew a thing or two about people on the run, and Jack needed some insight.

"You scared?" said Theo.

"A little. She did say I could be next on the killer's hit list."

"Or he might just wait for you to die, now that you're forty."

"Go to hell."

"So, you're sure that the cause of everybody's problems—yours, Sofia's, Chloe Sparks's—is all the same person?"

"I'd bet my Mustang on it."

"It's this Zorba guy?"

"Yeah. The Greek."

"You know, it's funny," said Theo. "I once impressed the hell out of a chick by humming the theme from *The Munsters* and joining it seamlessly with 'If I Were a Rich Man.'"

Jack pressed between his eyes, staving off a migraine. "First of all, I don't even remember the theme from *The Munsters*. Second, 'If I Were Rich Man' is from *Fiddler on the Roof*, not *Zorba*. You'd know that if you were forty. And, third, why the hell are we talking about this?"

"Sorry. So, after talking to this Sofia, are you going to call the cops?"

"I was thinking about talking to Andie first."

"To get protection for yourself, or to tell her what Sofia told you?"

"I'm still sorting that out."

"Don't you have some attorney-client issues?"

"The privilege starts to break down when your client is talking about a future crime."

"Except that she's not the one who is going to commit the crime. It's someone else."

Every now and then, Theo raised a legal issue that made Jack realize why his prison mates had called him "Chief Brief."

Jack said, "It's a gray area."

Theo checked out Jack's hair at the temples, searching for a pun, and for a brief instant another "forty" joke seemed imminent. He let it go.

"Meanwhile, Sofia is where?" said Theo.

"Hotel San Pietro."

"You want me to talk to her?"

"How could that possibly help?"

"You got me off death row. She might trust you better if she meets someone who trusted you and won the lottery."

The server put the burgers in front of them. Jack poured ketchup on his plate as he considered Theo's remark.

"That's not a terrible idea," said Jack.

Theo grabbed a handful of Jack's fries. It never seemed to matter to Theo that he had his own plate of food. Jack didn't even bitch about it anymore.

"Here's the thing," said Theo. "You could force her to go to the police or to go see Andie. But you know what would happen."

"She wouldn't talk," said Jack.

"And if she won't talk, you can't get her in witness protection."

"That's the worst of all worlds," said Jack. "She's clearly afraid of this guy. If he thinks she's talking to the police but I can't get her protection, she's dead."

"So you have to convince her that she wants to tell the police what she knows," said Theo. "Let me talk to her."

"I want to think more about that."

Theo finished off his root beer, sucking air through the straw.

"Meanwhile, what do you do about protecting yourself?" said Theo.

"I do keep a gun in the office."

"When's the last time you shot it?"

Jack had to think. "Been a while."

"Dude, you need a bodyguard."

"I can't afford that."

Theo put on his dark sunglasses, folded his arms across his chest, and flashed a Secret Service expression.

"No way," said Jack. "I'm not going there."

"Will work for tequila."

"Theo, forget it."

"Suit yourself," he said, then downed his last burger in one bite.

Jack said, "Can you come back to the office this afternoon and help with the packing?"

"Not today, dude. I have a jazz bar to run."

"You're taking this personally, aren't you?"

"Me? Nah. You don't want me to talk to Sofia. Fine. You don't want me to be your bodyguard. That's fine, too. I'm just stepping away from the plate before it's strike three."

"Theo, come on."

"Later, dude. Brandy, see ya, girl. It's back to my life, my love, and my lady, the sea."

"Huh?"

Jack let him go. Theo didn't pout often, but ignoring it was the best strategy.

"Anything else?" said the server.

"Just the bill."

Jack took it. Somehow, he had ended up paying for himself, Theo, and Uncle Cy. Only then did Jack realize that all the pouting had been a ruse.

Theo Knight, you are one smooth operator.

Jack drove his Mustang back to the office, and again he was having second thoughts. Ever since he had decided to buy the fastback, Miami had seen nothing but cloudless blue skies and seventy degrees. It was enough to make him long for his old convertible. Andie would have called it another "Jack Swyteck/grass is always greener moment."

He parked in front of the office and went inside. The only light in the room was a hint of afternoon sun filtering through the closed blinds, but when he switched on the desk lamp, nothing happened.

"It's broken," a man said.

Jack started and turned to see a stranger in the shadows across the room. He held the lamp cord in one
hand and a gun in the other.

"Not another step."

Jack froze. He tried to place the accent, but he could
only guess. *Sicilian?*

"Take whatever you want," said Jack.

"Sit down," the man said. "You and me need to have
a nice long talk. About Sofia."

Chapter 33

The accent, Jack decided, was Greek—the same voice he'd heard on the telephone outside the Smithsonian.

Jack was seated in the chair that was normally for clients, his forearms tied tightly to the armrests with the cord that the Greek had yanked from the lamp. The Greek sat on the desk, his gun aimed at Jack's chest.

"You must be Anthony Quinn," said Jack.

"If that's supposed to be some kind of ethnic joke, Anthony Quinn was Mexican."

"I think I knew that," said Jack. "But when Paulette Sparks and I tried to find out who hired the homeless guy to meet me outside the Smithsonian, we were told that an old Greek man like Zorba was behind it all."

He almost chuckled, as if he'd heard the comparison before, and then he started to fake his way through the lyrics to "If I Were a Rich Man": "ya ha deedle deedle, bubba—"

"That's actually from *Fiddler*—" Jack stopped himself, still unable to recall the theme from *The Munsters*. "Ah, the hell with it. Common mistake. So where's your wheelchair?"

"Do I look like I need a wheelchair?"

He was an imposing figure, standing erect and broad shouldered. "About as much as I do," said Jack.

"That little ploy worked out pretty well, didn't it? I figure maybe one percent of the general population is in wheelchairs. Greater Washington area has—what, nine million people? That's ninety thousand suspects. Threw the cops off the trail looking for a guy who can't walk."

Jack checked out the pistol. It wasn't anything Jack recognized, but he was far from a gun expert. Even though it looked small, he was sure it could do the job at this range.

"You should put the gun away if we're going to talk."

"It's a bad habit. Some people smoke when they do business. I point guns."

"What do you want from Sofia?"

His expression turned complicated—a mixture of anger and nostalgia, Jack guessed, and probably many more conflicting emotions.

"I followed her here to Miami," he said. "And then to your office."

"I figured."

"I saved her life. Those goons in New York would have killed her."

"What goons?"

"Are you gonna pretend she didn't tell you about the wiseguys who came to her bakery?"

"She's scared and on the run," said Jack. "That's all I know."

"She should be scared."

"She is—of you."

Jack's words had truly seemed to pain him. Jack sensed an opening, perhaps a willingness to talk.

"How do you know Sofia?" said Jack.

"We were married a long time ago. In Cyprus. This was way before the Russians took over the island. I had some business problems, Sicilian style."

"You mean organized crime?"

"I don't mean a pizzeria. Crazy Sicilians threw me off a hotel roof."

"You're lucky to be alive."

"Yeah," he said, scoffing. "If you call losing Sofia 'lucky.'"

"Sounds like you're still angry about it."

"You've met her. Imagine what she was like when she was twenty."

Jack did for a moment, and he was starting to understand the man's anger.

"We're getting way off mission here," said the Greek.

"Really, you should put the gun away."

His face reddened, and suddenly he lunged at Jack and pressed the barrel of his gun to Jack's forehead.

"Stop telling me what to do, and listen to me, Swyteck."

Jack was afraid to blink. The Greek had his human and sympathetic side, but with the flip of a figurative switch, it was easy to see him putting a bullet between the eyes of Chloe Sparks, Jack Swyteck, or anyone else who got in his way.

"I could have killed you a long time ago. What does that tell you?"

Jack struggled for the right answer, but he wasn't sure there was one.

The Greek said, "I take you out only when necessary. Don't make it necessary."

"Just tell me what I have to do."

"I need your help with Sofia."

"I won't help you kill her."

He grabbed Jack by the hair and jerked his head back. "You think I would kill my Sofia before I kill you?"

Jack was sure the man was going to hit him, maybe even shoot him. But the Greek took a couple of deep breaths, got himself under control, and returned to his seat atop the desk, facing Jack.

"Why did she come to you?" said the Greek.

"She didn't want to see me end up like Chloe Sparks."

"I didn't kill that woman."

Jack didn't believe him, but now was not the time to argue. "Sofia never said you did. In fact, she wouldn't tell me anything about you. Like I said, she's afraid of you."

"Afraid of *me*? It's your father and his new friends she needs to be afraid of."

"What does my father have to do with this?"

"Grayson comes down to Florida, goes hunting with your father, and dies a sudden death. Next thing you know, Harry Swyteck is the nominee to become vice president. All right after I told Grayson I could make him president."

"Wait a minute," said Jack. "Are you saying that you sent Grayson the same message you sent me?"

"Not directly. I sent it to his wife."

Jack thought back to the FBI telling him that his wasn't the first message. Marilyn Grayson had obviously turned hers over to law enforcement.

"Did you tell her more than you told me?"

"Only after she responded."

Jack bristled. He hadn't heard anything about response.

"You two had a dialogue going?"

"Until her husband died, we did."

"Did you end up telling her as much as you told Chloe Sparks?"

"No more, no less."

"So why was it 'necessary,' as you say, to kill Chloe Sparks, but not Marilyn Grayson?"

"It's one thing to know that President Keyes is controlled by a certain family from Sicily. It's another thing altogether to know *why*."

"You told Chloe why?"

The Greek shook his head. "She figured it out."

"Does Sofia know why?"

"Sofia knows."

"I presume that's why those men came for her yesterday."

"Exactly right. And that's why I need your help."

"What can I do?" '

"You have Sofia's ear. Convince her that she can't go to the FBI or the police with this. No one at any level of government can be trusted."

"What am I supposed to tell her to do?"

"Get out of the country. *Now.* If she hears that advice from me, she will never believe it. But if you tell her, she might."

"I can't promise she'll believe me."

"She'd better."

"What if she just doesn't listen?"

He leaned forward, his nose just a few inches from Jack's, his eyes narrowing. "Then killing you will become *very* necessary," he said, his voice so calm and cold that, for a moment, Jack thought the Greek would actually enjoy it.

Jack returned the glare, but he was looking at a three-eyed monster—the Greek's dark eyes and the muzzle of his handgun.

"I'll do my best," said Jack.

Chapter 34

They waited until dark, and then Jack led the way to the Hotel San Pietro.

"Faster," said the Greek. They were already covering the scenic block along Alhambra Circle at the pace of a much younger man, which told Jack something about the Greek's recovery from his hotel roof fall. The Greek walked a couple of steps behind, his hands buried in his coat pocket. Jack assumed there was a gun aimed at his spine.

The San Pietro was one of the oldest hotels in Coral Gables. The lobby floor was a mosaic of cracked Cuban tile, and crossbeams of pecky cypress supported the high arching ceiling. In daylight, colorful stained-glass windows filtered the strong Florida sunshine, throwing patches of red, yellow, and green against the thickly textured walls. After dark, however, the windows were black against the night sky, and the lobby took on a shadowy, castle-like ambience beneath a broad candlelit chandelier. On the wall behind the front desk were rows of old-fashioned key cubbies with room keys on tassels.

"Good evening, Mr. Swyteck," said the young woman behind the desk.

Jack tried not to look nervous as he returned the smile. "I sent a client over this afternoon. Sofia is her name. Has she checked in yet?"

"Yes, she has. Would you like me to ring her room?"

"Yes, please."

She glanced at the Greek. "And who else should I say is calling?"

"It's a surprise," said the Greek. "I'm an old friend."

She ran her finger across her lips, zipping them. "Your secret is safe with me."

"That's what they all say," said the Greek.

She didn't seem to know how to take his meaning, but she smiled anyway, dialed the room, and announced that Mr. Swyteck was in the lobby.

"Yes, ma'am," she said into the telephone, then hung up.

"Miss Sofia would like you to come to her room," she said.

Jack wasn't surprised. Being on the run, she probably felt safest in the room.

"Then we'll go," said the Greek.

"First floor," said the desk clerk. "Chopin Room."

That was another cool thing about the hotel. All of
the rooms were named after famous composers.

At least she's not in the Salieri Room, thought Jack.

The hallways were narrow, and there were numerous
abrupt turns. Hotel San Pietro was actually several old
mansions linked together into a single hotel, which made
getting to your room a bit like a trip through a maze.
They passed the library and the dining room, and if
Jack hadn't been to the hotel before, he would have had
no way of knowing if he was headed in the right direction. The old floorboards creaked beneath the carpeting
in the hallway as they passed the Bach and Beethoven
rooms. Finally, they reached the Chopin Room.

The Greek stepped aside so that he could not be
seen through the peep hole. Jack knocked three times.
The door didn't open, but he heard Sofia's voice.

"Is that you, Mr. Swyteck?"

"Yes, it's me."

Jack heard the rattle of the chain lock, the deadbolt
turning. The door opened.

"Please, come in," she said.

Jack stayed where he was. "I have someone with me."

Her concern was immediately evident, as if she knew who it was.

The Greek stepped behind Jack. "Hello, Sofia."

"Demetri!" She gasped, and then slammed the door shut.

The Greek leaned into Jack's back, letting him feel the gun in his right kidney. It was still hidden inside the Greek's coat pocket.

"Tell her she shouldn't be afraid," he said in harsh whisper. "Tell her to let us in. Go on. *Tell her!*"

"Sofia, it's okay," said Jack, speaking to the closed door. "I've worked something out with . . . Demetri," he said, repeating the name Sofia had used.

There was no reply. The Greek nudged Jack with the gun.

"It's all a misunderstanding," said Jack. "Please, let us in. This is all going to work out."

The lock clicked. The doorknob turned. Slowly, the door swung open, but Sofia was nowhere to be seen. She appeared to be shielding herself behind the door.

"Come in," she said, still out of sight.

Jack entered first. The Greek was right behind him. The door slammed shut, and in a lightning-quick blur, both Jack and Demetri were hit from behind with the force of a charging bull. Jack went down first, and Demetri fell right beside him, both men facedown on the floor. The man sitting on Jack's kidneys felt like a rhinoceros, and the gun at the base of Jack's skull felt big enough to drop an entire herd.

"Move and I'll blow your head off," the man said.

Jack's right cheek was pressed to the silk rug, and out of the corner of his eye he could see that the Greek was in the same predicament.

"You're early, Vladimir," said the Greek.

The man named Vladimir got off Jack's back and stood over him. The Greek remained pinned beneath the other man.

Vladimir said, "Your deadline was last Tuesday."

"You gave me another week. It's only been five days."

"And what did you do with the extra time?" said Vladimir. "Nothing, except cook up a plan to run from the country with your ex-wife."

"That's not true!" said Sofia.

"Quiet!" said Vladimir.

Sofia cowered in the corner. Jack didn't have a good vantage point from the floor, but he could see that her hands were bound behind her back. He also noticed that behind the long, drawn draperies was a set of French doors that led to a courtyard—presumably the intruders' point of entry.

Vladimir began to pace—not the quick steps of a nervous man, but the slow and confident gait of a man in control.

"We've been watching you, Demetri. We know you went to visit Sofia's bakery. We followed her to Miami. We saw her go to Swyteck's law office. We watched you show up an hour later. Did you really think you could run from us?"

"Of course not. That's why it makes no sense for you to say I would even try."

"Except that now you must believe anything is possible, no? Now that you have the son of the future vice president to help you."

"I'm not helping him," said Jack.

"Shut up!" said Vladimir. He stopped pacing, and silence hung over the room. Finally, he said, "This is how it's going to be. Demetri, you are coming with me."

Vladimir gave a nod, and his partner got up and lifted the Greek to his feet. He patted the old man down, found the gun in his pocket, and threw it on the bed. Then he shoved him face-first against the wall and put the gun to the back of his head.

Vladimir said, "Sofia and the lawyer stay here with Mika. I give Demetri twenty-four hours to pay what he owes. If he comes up with the money, I shoot him. If he doesn't, I kill him any way I choose. And Mika shoots Sofia and the lawyer."

"Can't we talk about this?" said Jack.

"We're done talking," said Vladimir.

He pushed the Greek toward the door, then stopped before opening it.

"Twenty-four hours," he said. "Mika, if you don't hear from me before then, you know what to do."

Jack listened as the door opened, the men filed out, and the door closed.

Mika locked it and took a seat in the reading chair. "Let's decide," he said.

There was smugness in his tone, and Jack didn't bite. Sofia did.

"Let's decide what?" she said.

He released the ammunition clip from his pistol, then shoved it back into place for effect.

"Who will I shoot first?"

Chapter 35

Ortanique on the Mile was bustling, and Andie sat alone at an outdoor table for two. A brightly painted, seven-foot statue of a flamingo stood guard on the sidewalk beside her. She was halfway through her second mojito—Ortanique's were *numero uno* in Miami—and she already knew what to order. It was creative cuisine with a Jamaican flair, and everything was exceptional, but the special West Indian bouillabaisse with lobster and Key West shrimp in a curry broth was a lock.

Andie had spent all day preparing for an undercover role. She'd been looking for ways to stay busy ever since Thursday's phone conference with the Washington ASAC. He'd told her things about Harry that she probably would have been better off not knowing, and ever since she'd been cool to the idea of spending too much time around Jack. She worried about a slip of the tongue. Saturday was their standing date night, however, and she'd decided to keep it. She'd called that morning to tell him that it was going to be a crazy day and that she would just meet him at the restaurant at seven.

It was now after eight o'clock. Andie dialed him once more on her cell, and for the seventh time, her call went straight to voice mail. Desperate, she dialed Theo. He picked up from behind the bar at Cy's Place, the jazz club he'd named after his sax-playing uncle.

"Theo, do you have any idea where Jack is?"

"Last I looked, he was right here on the shelf next to Mr. Bacardi."

It took her a moment to realize he was talking about Jack Daniel's.

"I meant *my* Jack, wise guy."

He shouted something to a customer. It was getting hard to hear him, between the traffic noise on the Mile and the weekend roar over the line from Cy's Place.

"Sorry," said Theo. "Haven't seen him since lunch."

"Do you know if he had something going on? He's over an hour late. He hasn't even called, and I can't get him to pick up on his cell."

"You might want to call Hotel San Pietro. He had . . . er—uh."

Andie definitely sensed backpedaling. "What?"

"He has a client staying there. I gotta go. See ya."

Andie looked at her phone, confused. Theo had clearly just committed a slip of the tongue of some sort. Calling a hotel probably wasn't a lead she would have followed if Theo hadn't acted so weird. She pulled up the number for Hotel San Pietro, dialed it, and connected to the front desk.

"Hello, this may sound like a strange request, but I'm trying to reach Mr. Jack Swyteck. I understand that he has a client staying at your hotel."

"Yes, actually he paid for the room."

"He did? Is he there now?"

"I believe so. He went back to her room a couple of hours ago. I haven't seen him come out."

Her? Andie suddenly felt numb. "Does . . . she have a name?"

"I'm sorry, but I can't give out that information. Would you like me to put your call through to the room?"

"No!" she said, her tone way too sharp. It was suddenly difficult to breathe, and she struggled to get the words out. "I mean, that won't be necessary. Thank you."

Andie closed her flip phone and laid it on the table. Her hand started to shake, and she suddenly had the same sick feeling that she thought she had left behind with her ex-fiancé in Seattle. The pit in her stomach was widening, and part of her wished that she could just fall into it and disappear forever.

"Will it be just you this evening, miss?" the waiter asked.

She looked off toward the traffic on Miracle Mile. "Yes," she said. "I guess it is just me."

For the second time in one day, Jack's hands were tied with electrical cord. Sofia's were bound in the same way, which left no working lamps in the hotel room. Mika was reclining comfortably on the bed, shoes off, basked in the colorful glow of the flat-screen television on the wall. His gun rested within his reach on the nightstand. Jack and Sofia were sitting side by side on the floor near the closet, their backs against the silk wallpaper.

It had been at least two hours since Vladimir had left with the Greek. Jack had no idea what kind of debt Demetri owed the Russian mob, but he had no hope that Demetri would somehow pull a rabbit out of a hat and come up with the money. Bottom line: Jack had about twenty-two hours to figure out how to stop Mika from putting a bullet in his head.

"*Goooooooooooooooooal!*" said Mika.

A soccer game was playing on Spanish-language television, and Mika was joining the sportscaster in the universal language of celebration.

Mika rolled off the bed and grabbed his gun. Then he picked up the complimentary copy of *City Beautiful* magazine and started toward the bathroom.

"I make shit now," said Mika.

"Knock yourself out," said Jack.

Mika pointed at Jack with his gun. "You move, you shit. Understand?"

Jack could have explained that "shit" could be either a noun or a verb, but he assumed he meant the noun. "Understood," said Jack.

"Good."

Mika thumbed through his magazine, went into the bathroom, and closed the door almost all the way, leaving it open just a crack.

The televised soccer game played on, and the world suddenly felt surreal to Jack. A half Cuban man and a Sicilian woman held captive in a Coral Gables hotel room. A Mexican sportscaster calling Brazil versus Argentina on the television. A Russian mobster "making shit" in the bathroom. All they needed to complete the quintessential Miami moment was a disgraced politician and a dead body—and in a matter of hours, the Greek would probably be that body.

"He doesn't learn," Sofia said, speaking softly so that Mika would not overhear.

"Who doesn't learn?"

"Demetri. Whether it's the casino, the track, or whatever business they asked him to run, he always thinks he can take a little extra for himself."

"Is that what happened with the Russians?"

"Of course. And before that it was the Sicilians." She shook her head. "He never learns."

"He told me it was the Mafia looking for you."

"Yes," she said. "But it all goes back to Demetri."

"How do you mean?"

She breathed a sigh, as if not sure where to begin.

"You can tell me," said Jack. "I can't get us out of this mess if I don't know the players."

She hesitated, but only for a moment longer. "I know of three times for sure. This is the latest. The last time was with the Sicilians."

"When?"

"Right before the election."

"President Keyes' election?"

Sofia nodded. "They were going to kill Demetri. But he talked himself out of it."

"How?"

"Demetri gave them the power to control him."

"To control the president?"

"Yes. He told them the truth about Daniel Keyes."

"Which is what?"

She looked Jack in the eye but said nothing. It was clear that she had no intention of telling him.

Jack said, "How do you know about this?"

"Demetri told me when he came to see me last week."

"Demetri also says that he told you the secret about Keyes."

Sofia didn't answer.

A shout came from the bathroom: "Quiet out there!"

Sofia waited a moment, then lowered her voice. "There is more history," she whispered. "It was in Cyprus. We were young, married less than a year."

She stopped, as if reluctant to continue.

"It's all right," said Jack. "You can tell me."

Jack listened as she described that night in their apartment. The noise outside that woke them. Demetri naked and leaping from the bed. The pounding on the door, and their panicked good-bye before the door burst open, the armed men rushed in, and Demetri escaped out the window.

"One of the men stayed with me," she said. "When the others finally came back, they told me they had thrown Demetri off the roof. I thought he was dead."

"So did they, I'm sure."

Sofia nodded.

"Then what happened?" said Jack.

"When?"

"After the men came back to your room and told you about Demetri. What happened?"

She shifted uncomfortably, and Jack could read her body language. He'd seen it in many clients before. It was something Sofia clearly didn't want to talk about.

"There were five of them," she said. "Do you really want to know?"

"Only if you want to talk about it."

"I've never actually told this to anyone."

"You don't have to. Really, it's okay."

"No. I want you to know the truth."

Chapter 36

The Greek stared at the telephone on the table.

"Go on, use it," said Vladimir. "Make your big money phone call."

They were in a conference room at a ground-floor office suite somewhere in North Miami Beach. The Venetian blinds on the picture window were shut, but a few slats were twisted and out of place, offering Demetri a glimpse of the courtyard and the parking lot beyond. It was impossible to tell what kind of business had once been conducted in this place. The cubicles outside the conference room were vacant. Employees were nowhere to be found, and there were no computer terminals, telephones, office supplies, or other signs of an active workplace. Some desks didn't even have chairs. The Greek figured that it was the ghostly remains of a

Mafya-controlled boiler-room operation. "Gemstones" was his guess. In a month's time from a place like this, they could have phone-blitzed the over-seventy population in North Miami and sold five thousand dollars' worth of colored glass for over a million bucks. The Greek had run similar operations over the years. Only about one time out of a hundred did the bosses catch him stealing from them.

"You think that's all it takes?" said Demetri. "I make a phone call, and I can pay you back?"

"I don't care what it takes. One call is all you get. So make it count."

"You need to work with me. I'm close, really close to making a deal. This is money in your pocket. What good am I dead?"

Vladimir pushed the phone toward him.

"One call," he said. "If you're that close, then pick up the phone and seal the deal."

Demetri lifted the receiver and then put it down. "Why should I do this for you? You said you were going to kill me even if I get the money."

"You get the money, you save Sofia."

"I don't care about her," he said. It hurt to say it, but a bluff was his only way out.

Vladimir smiled. "Nice to see you haven't changed."

"Come on," said Demetri. "I'll make the call, but if the money comes in, we're square. No need to kill me."

Vladimir's smile drained away. Some men were capable of showing no reaction, putting themselves in the emotional equivalent of "neutral." Vladimir, however, was always in gear. When he was happy, he was the life of the party. His every other waking moment, however, seemed to be driven by contempt or anger, albeit in varying degrees. It all depended on how much the poor slob on his hit list reminded him of the bastards who had cut open his nine-year-old son and left him on the doorstep to bleed to death.

"I've had it up to here with your disrespect," he said. "We give you a job, you steal from us. We give you another chance, you steal more from us. This is the end of it. You pay your debt, and you go out with no pain. You don't get the money, I take you to the Kamikaze Club."

"Moscow?"

"Idiot," he said, shaking his head. "You're not worth the plane fare. We got one in Brighton Beach now. Just like the original."

Those words—*just like the original*—sent his heart racing. Demetri had never visited the Kamikaze Club, but stories of it were Russian *Mafya* legend. It was for men only, except for the high-priced prostitutes brought in to service them. The night's entertainment climaxed with the arrival of two unlucky souls who had been yanked off the street. It was not just a fight, but a barehanded fight to the death—the human equivalent of cockfighting. Guys like Vladimir would place their bets, wagering on everything from which of the two warriors would win to which of the whores sitting ringside would end up with the most blood splattered on her tits.

"Who wants to watch an old man like me fight?" said Demetri.

"Don't give me that 'old man' crap," said Vladimir. "Plenty of young men have fallen for that line and ended up in the dirt. We'll have to give your opponent a hatchet just to keep it interesting."

Before Vladimir could laugh at his own joke, the window suddenly exploded and the Venetian blinds danced with the rattle of machine-gun fire. Demetri dove to the floor. Vladimir slammed against the bullet-riddled wall, smearing the white wainscoting with a bright crimson streak as he slid to the floor. His body collapsed in a heap right beside Demetri, bits and pieces of his shattered skull sticking to the wall.

Another spray of machine-gun fire popped the fluorescent ceiling lights. Groping in the darkness, Demetri yanked Vladimir's gun from its holster.

The machine-gunning stopped as suddenly as it had begun.

Demetri lay perfectly still, his body covered with thousands of glass pellets. He listened. With the window blown out, he could hear footsteps outside. The click of leather heels on asphalt sounded like two men. The clicking turned to crunching on grass made stiff by the winter drought. The men were crossing the courtyard and coming closer.

Demetri got a comfortable grip on the pistol. At first touch, fumbling in a blackened room, he couldn't tell what it was. He was certain now that it was the Russian MR-444 Baghira, a 9-millimeter pistol that incorporated thermoplastics and many other of the Glock's best design features. It was no machine gun, but with a seventeen-round magazine of Parabellum ammunition, he had more than enough stopping power for any gunfight.

The approaching footsteps slowed with caution and then stopped altogether. The men were standing right outside the window. Demetri waited, his pistol at the ready. A flashlight switched on and shined into the conference room. Busted Venetian blinds cast zebra-like shadows on the walls, and the sweeping beam of light came to rest on Vladimir's bloody streak on the wall.

"*Bel colpo!*" said one of the men. *Good shot.*

They were Sicilian, Demetri realized, and instinctively his forty-year-old thirst for revenge took over. He rolled to his right and squeezed off a half dozen rounds—rolling and firing, rolling and firing. The fall of the flashlight and painful cry in the night told him that at least one round had found its mark. The return of machine-gun fire told him that one wasn't nearly enough. Bullets whizzed overhead as Demetri scrambled through the noise and darkness to the door.

The machine gun fell silent.

Demetri quieted his breathing and listened. For a moment—it seemed much longer—he heard nothing. Then, faintly at first, he heard something in the distance. He started counting the number of rounds he'd fired, trying to see how much ammo was left, but then his focus returned to that growing noise.

Sirens blared in the distance, and for a brief instant Demetri almost let himself believe in God.

Someone called the cops!

Suddenly, the sound of footsteps returned—crunching of dry grass, then heels clicking on the asphalt— but this time it was the sound of one man running. A car door opened and slammed shut, the engine turned over, and tires squealed in the night. The gunman was making a run for it, leaving his dead partner behind.

Demetri hurried back to Vladimir's body and rummaged for his car keys. They were bloody, but they would still work. He jumped to his feet, pushed the busted blinds aside, and hopped out the window. He was at full speed when he stepped on the dead man's chest, his pulse pounding with adrenaline.

Hang on, Sofia.

Chapter 37

From across the room, Jack counted the small liquor bottles on the nightstand. There were at least a dozen. Mika had gone through the entire minibar stock—brandy, scotch, bourbon, rum, gin, vodka—and stacked the empties into a pyramid.

Jack wondered how much longer Mika would stay awake.

Mika had the look of Miami's first-generation *Mafiya*, an insanely arrogant breed that Jack had prosecuted during his brief stint at the U.S. attorney's office. The undercover agents used to joke about how easy it was to walk into a bar in North Miami Beach or Hollywood and pick out the Russian mobsters who consciously played to the stereotype—loud, muscle-bound, tons of gold jewelry—so that people would know not to mess with them. Most feared was a guy called Tarzan, famous for his drug and sex orgies on his yacht off South Beach, until he landed in jail for trying to buy a nuclear submarine from a former Soviet naval officer. His plan was to smuggle Colombian cocaine to Miami—underwater. For every criminal visionary like Tarzan there were scores of foot soldiers like Mika, street thugs who would shoot you just to see if their gun was still working.

"I'm starving," said Sofia. She was seated on the floor beside Jack, their backs against the wall.

"I'm hungry, too," said Jack.

Mika propped himself up on one elbow. He was still shoeless but fully dressed, relaxing atop the bedspread.

"What do you want me to do about it?"

"Order us some food," said Jack.

"How about champagne and caviar?" said Mika, clearly being facetious.

Jack said, "The room is on my account. It all gets billed to my credit card."

Mika smiled. It was as if Jack had said the magic word: *free*.

Mika climbed off the bed and grabbed the room service menu from the desk. He started flipping through the pages, but the confusion on his face said it all. He looked as if he were trying to calculate the square root of 367,000 divided by nineteen.

"You want me to read that to you?" said Jack.

"Fuck off," said Mika, and then he threw the menu across the room. Jack ducked, and it hit the wall behind him.

Mika raided the minibar one more time, grabbed a can of beer, and went back to the bed. The soccer game was over, and he started channel surfing.

"There's news at ten o'clock on channel seven," said Jack. He was hoping to find out if the police were looking for him or Sofia.

Mika ignored him. He switched to paid programming and started scrolling through the adult movie menu. The screen lit up with the provocative images of a dozen soap opera rejects turned porn star. Mika chose the sexy blonde in a flick called *April Showers*. It took about thirty seconds for her to land in the shower with a pizza delivery boy who could only be described as a freak of nature from the waist down.

"Can you at least kill the sound?" said Sofia.

Mika laughed and hit MUTE. "You no like the movie?"

Sofia didn't answer.

The shower scene was getting steamier. Jack wasn't really watching, but it did trigger a brief recollection of the one and only time he and Andie had showered together. She washed her hair, conditioned it twice, shaved her legs, applied the exfoliant to her entire body—all while Jack stood off to the side shivering and waiting for someone to throw him a coat or a blanket.

Mika stood up and grabbed his crotch.

"Hey, old lady. Come jerk me off."

"Leave her alone," said Jack.

"Come on," said Mika. "All I need is thirty seconds. I just got out of prison three days ago."

"I said leave her alone," said Jack.

A sinister smile creased his lips. "I got a better idea."

Mika went to the closet and pulled a gun from the coat pocket. It was much smaller than the 9-millimeter pistol on the nightstand. A .22-caliber, Jack guessed. Then Mika found another piece of equipment—a suppressor. He fastened it to the barrel of the .22, unzipped his fly, and stuffed the whole thing down his pants. It was nearly a foot long, still short of pizza boy. He walked toward Jack with the business end of the equipment sticking out of his trousers.

"Here, big mouth. Suck on this."

"Get away, you pig."

Mika kicked him in the stomach so hard that it knocked Jack over. It was a well-placed boot in the

BORN TO RUN · 283

solar plexus that left Jack gasping for breath. Then Mika went to Sofia.

"Here you go," he said, as he brought the weapon to her lips. "A little Russian roulette, Mika style."

"Don't!" said Jack.

She jerked her head back so quickly that it bumped against the wall behind her.

"Come on," said Mika. "Last time I did this, a little whore in Moscow sucked her brains right out the back of her head."

"Sofia, don't," said Jack.

"You listen to him," said Mika, "and I'll put a bullet right in your face."

A tear ran down her cheek.

"Open your mouth!" said Mika.

Jack was about to lash out, but he stopped himself. Across the room, through a crack between the closed drapery panels, Jack saw movement on the patio. Someone was standing right outside the room, behind the locked French doors.

"*Do it,*" said Mika.

Jack drew his knees to his chest and coiled up like a catapult, then shouted at the top of his lungs as he sprang into action. His right shoulder hit Mika squarely in the belly, and Jack kept pushing against him with every bit of strength and momentum he could muster.

A glass panel shattered in the French door on the other side of the room, but the noise couldn't drown out the discharge of Mika's gun and the unmistakable sound of his suppressor doing its work.

Sofia collapsed as Jack and Mika tumbled to the floor.

The French doors burst open. Demetri raced into the room and squeezed off a quick shot that sounded like a bazooka. Mika went still, a dead heap, the left side of his head a bloody mess. Jack pushed himself away from the body, and Demetri charged across the room.

"Sofia!"

Chapter 38

"Stay away!" said Sofia.

She had withdrawn to the corner, well away from the bullet that had whizzed past her ear and lodged in the wall behind her. Demetri started toward her.

"Sofia, please."

"Stop!" she said, her tone bordering on hysterical.

"Put the gun away," said Jack.

Demetri seemed to have forgotten that he was holding a weapon. He shoved it into his coat pocket and approached slowly. Sofia cowered, clearly overwhelmed. Demetri tried to switch on the lamp, but it didn't work. The muted porn on the flat screen was still the only light in the room. Demetri knelt beside Sofia and untied the frayed lamp cord that bound her wrists.

"We have to go," he told her gently.

She sniffled, on the verge of tears. Demetri embraced her, but she did not hug back.

"Sofia, listen to me," he said in the same soft but urgent voice. "We need to get out of here. They found us. Madera's men know we're in Miami."

"*Agent* Madera?" said Jack. "That's the new head of my father's Secret Service detail."

"Gee, what a coincidence."

Jack sank even lower. His father's role in all of this was getting cloudier at every turn.

"Sofia, we don't have much time," said Demetri. "Come with me."

She shook her head, and for a moment in the dimly lit room, Jack felt as if he were watching a twenty-year-old Sicilian beauty struggling in the middle of the night as she came to terms with her fears about a new life in Cyprus and her new husband's line of work.

"I can't do this," said Sofia.

"You must," said Demetri.

"Where's the Russian guy?" said Jack.

"Dead," said Demetri. "They killed him."

"Who are *they*?" said Jack.

"The same people who are going to kill us if we don't get out of here right now. Sofia, I'm begging you. Don't stay here to die."

Jack heard panicked voices and footsteps in the hallway outside their door. Guests were running from their rooms.

"They're evacuating the hotel," said Jack. "Obviously they heard your gun go off."

"We're running out of time," said Demetri.

"You go," said Sofia.

"I don't make the same mistake twice. Tonight you come with me."

"That time has passed," she said, "a long, long time ago."

"Don't let yourself believe that. We're older, but it's still me, and it's still you. That will never change."

His words seemed to play on her very conflicted feelings, but before Sofia could speak, police sirens sounded on the next block. Demetri pulled his pistol and checked his ammunition clip.

"Don't be a fool," said Jack.

Demetri held Sofia's hand tightly and looked her straight in the eye. "You know what will happen if you go with the police, don't you?"

She didn't answer.

Jack said, "It's the only choice."

Demetri ignored him, continuing in his soft, persuasive voice. "Sofia, that's not what you want."

The approaching sirens grew louder. Sofia shot a nervous glance at Jack, and he shook his head, as if to tell her *Don't even think about it*. Then her gaze swept back to Demetri, her voice filled with more resignation than resolve.

"I'll go," she said.

Demetri threw his arms around her and helped her up. Then, like a guy turning the doorknob in a gas station bathroom, he reluctantly reached inside Mika's pants and grabbed the gun. He pitched the silencer aside and tucked the little .22-caliber pistol into his pocket.

Suddenly, sirens were blaring right outside the hotel.

"It may be too late," said Sofia.

Demetri aimed his pistol at Jack's face. "You're coming, too."

"Leave him," said Sofia.

"He's our ticket out."

"I won't be a kidnapper," she said.

Demetri's face flushed with anger. It was as if the pressure of the past two weeks, the stress of the past two days, and the events of the past two hours had finally come to a crescendo. All patience—even for Sofia—had run out.

"Then be a hostage," he said as he pointed his gun at her.

"What?"

"Let's go."

Sofia was dumbstruck.

"Go on!" he said. "Move!"

Sofia obeyed, and the way his command sent her moving toward the busted French door reminded Jack of the battered wives he'd defended.

Demetri spotted Mika's 9-millimeter pistol on the nightstand, did a quick check of the ammunition clip, and smiled like a man who'd just hit the daily double. He tucked the extra weapon into his other coat pocket, and then he grabbed Jack and took him out at gunpoint.

The narrow alley outside the hotel had been converted into a pedestrian walkway with vine-clad walls and colorful flower boxes adorning the windows. The streetlights resembled old-fashioned gas lamps, and the cobblestone path had just enough twists, turns, and depressions to remind Jack of old Sienna at midnight. Right around the corner, at the main entrance to the hotel, blue beacons from police cars swirled in the night. Demetri stopped.

"Where's your car?" he asked Jack.

"My car?"

Demetri shoved the gun up under his chin. "Where is it?"

"In the parking lot behind my office."

"Can we get to it the back way?"

Jack struggled. "You really want to take my new car?"

Demetri cocked his pistol.

"Follow me," said Jack, and he led them down the narrow walkway.

"Faster," said Demetri, even though Sofia was already struggling to keep up.

Jack picked up the pace to a near trot. They reached a T-intersection in the walkway, and Jack took them to the left. A paved parking lot opened up before them, and they stopped for Demetri to make sure there were no police.

"It's the green Mustang," said Jack.

Demetri almost smiled. Jack cringed.

"Keys," said Demetri.

Reluctantly, Jack handed them over. Jack crammed himself into the tiny backseat, and Sofia rode shotgun. It was a bad time for Jack to discover that the rear seat belts were broken. Demetri fired the engine and raced toward the exit, gaining speed until another car pulled out and blocked his way. Demetri stood on the brake, and Jack slammed into the backside of the front seats as the Mustang screeched to a halt.

"Shit!" said Demetri.

Jack looked up in time to catch a glimpse of the other driver's face, but it was Demetri who told the story.

"It's him!" said Demetri.

He slammed the five-speed into reverse and steered backward with the intensity of an Indy racer.

"Slow down!" said Sofia.

"Hang on!" said Demetri.

Still in reverse, Demetri steered the speeding Mustang toward the walkway. Jack was still in the back, which meant that he was effectively in the front, as Demetri gunned it straight toward the narrow opening between buildings.

"It won't fit!" said Jack.

"Will too," said Demetri.

"My car!"

A quick glance at the speedometer nearly stopped Jack's heart. Tail end first, the Mustang shot into the narrow walkway, its side mirrors brushing the leafy vines on either wall as they burrowed deeper and deeper into the darkness.

"Stop!" said Sofia.

Demetri pressed on. Jack spotted a pair of window boxes ahead. Behind. Whatever.

"Look out for—"

Too late. The rear fender took out the window boxes like a wrecking ball.

"Ouch," said Jack, cringing. It was like a bad dream—his beautifully restored *Bullitt* Mustang in a "bass-ackward" chase scene, all with Jack at the mercy of a crazy son of a bitch who was no more Steve McQueen than the flat streets of Florida were the hills of San Francisco.

"Hold tight," said Demetri.

They flew past the T-intersection in the walkway, the brick walls on either side a blackened blur in the night. Finally, the Mustang came out on the other side of the Hotel San Pietro and spun to a stop in the middle of a four-lane street. An SUV was about to T-bone them when Sofia screamed and a horn blasted. Demetri found a gear and hit the gas to speed out of the way.

Sofia reached over and slugged him. "You're going to kill us!"

Demetri didn't seem to care. In seconds he had the fastback in fifth gear, weaving in and out of urban traffic at double the speed limit.

"Red light!" said Jack.

Demetri blew through it, sending a crossing car into a screeching tailspin.

"You're scaring me!" said Sofia.

He didn't respond.

"Demetri, I'm too afraid."

"This will work."

"I don't like this," she said.

He kept driving.

"I don't *deserve* this!"

Demetri hit the brakes, and the car skidded to a stop at the curb. Jack expected to see another temper flare, but Demetri didn't look angry. Sofia's last remark—*I don't deserve this*—had simply resonated on a level that even Sofia could not have expected.

Demetri reached across her lap and opened the passenger-side door.

"Run!" he said.

"What?"

"It's just like the first time. It's me they really want. Run fast and disappear."

Sofia looked at him for several long moments, her eyes welling. It seemed to Jack that she didn't know how to say good-bye. Finally, she just turned away and got out of the car without a word. The door closed, and Demetri spun the tires.

"What now?" said Jack.

Demetri didn't answer. The speedometer was quickly up to seventy.

"This is pointless," said Jack. "You've got the Russian *Mafiya* after you. By your own admission, Madera's men are out to kill you. And in about two minutes the police will be chasing you down. It's over."

"Ain't over yet," he said.

"What are you going to do?"

The tires squealed as Demetri made a sharp turn toward the expressway ramp.

"You and me are gonna talk to the president," he said.

Chapter 39

They were flying past cars as if traffic were standing still.

The speed limit on this stretch of interstate was seventy miles per hour, and Demetri was pushing well beyond that. Jack was about to tell him to slow down when a pair of motorcycles shot past them like silver bullets. The bikers weren't wearing helmets, of course, and their girlfriends clung to them like frightened koalas as they maneuvered around cars with the precision of slalom skiers. For a second, Jack wondered if one of them was Theo. No such luck.

"You think we can catch those guys?" said Demetri.

"Before or after they kill themselves?" said Jack.

Demetri snorted. "You're a funny guy, you know that?"

Jack's hands were feeling numb. The cord around his wrists was too tight, and sitting in the cramped rear seat with his knees up to his chest and his hands behind his back didn't help the circulation.

"You don't actually plan to drive my car all the way to Washington, do you?" said Jack.

"What are you worried about, the mileage on your precious Mustang?"

"No," said Jack. *Well . . . yeah.*

"Just sit tight and don't make trouble."

"You said we were going to talk to the president."

"And that's what we're gonna do."

"That's just crazy. Do you know how many crackpots have demanded to speak to the president? It never works."

"Your father is about to be vice president. I bet he'll have something to say about that."

"I'll tell you exactly what he'll say: *N-O.* It just won't work. Don't you get it? It's time to give it up."

Demetri raised his pistol. "Did you ever see *Pulp Fiction?*"

"Yeah."

"Remember that scene with Travolta and Samuel Jackson in the front seat and the guy that gets blown away in the backseat?"

Jack got the point.

Demetri suddenly fell silent, his eyes darting back and forth from the road to the rearview mirror. Jack checked over his shoulder and saw the reason for concern. A Florida state trooper was several hundred yards behind them but closing in, its beacon flashing.

"Hold on," said Demetri.

The Mustang lunged forward, and Jack sank even deeper into the rear seat. Jack knew his Mustang had the horses, but Demetri was pushing it harder than Jack had even thought Theo would push it. At this speed, Jack felt as if they were passing mile markers like hash marks on the highway, and in just a few minutes they caught up to the motorcycles. The leader extended his tattoo-covered arm to flash them a thumbs-up. Jack glanced back through the rear window. The Florida state trooper had actually gained ground—and there were three of them now.

Demetri slammed his fist against the dashboard. "What does it take to lose these assholes?"

"It's not going to happen," said Jack.

"Shut up!"

"Check it out," said Jack. "Choppers are already here."

Demetri leaned forward and looked up through the windshield. The whir of the helicopters was audible even over the roar of the Mustang. It was a dark night, but the lights from the helicopter were bright enough for Jack to read the painted logo on the side.

"It's the media," he said.

"How the hell did they get here so fast?"

"What did you expect?" said Jack. "You're driving straight toward the studio for the biggest news station in Miami."

Jack could almost see Demetri's despair transform to hope.

"That must be the station over there, right?"

Jack peered out the passenger-side window. The sign and network logo were lit up against the night sky, easily visible from the interstate: ACTION NEWS—SOUTH FLORIDA'S NEWS LEADER.

"Yeah, that's it."

"What time do they do their late news?"

"Right now," said Jack. "All the networks but Fox do it at eleven. But you're not thinking of—"

Before Jack could finish his sentence, Demetri drove off the interstate and headed straight for the station. It didn't seem to faze him that they'd missed the exit ramp a half mile back. The whine of rubber tires on pavement gave way to the pop and crunch of flying mud and gravel as they blazed a virgin trail off the shoulder, across the swale, down into the ditch, and into a field. Jack tumbled around in the backseat like tennis shoes in a dryer. The ride was so rough that the headlamps were pointing up one moment and down the next, making it impossible to see the chain-link fence ahead in the darkness. The speeding Mustang ripped right through it, but it sounded as if they'd hit a train. The windshield cracked into a starburst pattern, both headlights were gone, and the Mustang suddenly sputtered like most cars its age.

"Flat tire," said Jack.

Demetri gave it more gas, mowing down bushes and other landscaping that surrounded the studio. Jack braced for one more bounce as they jumped the curb and sped into the parking lot. The sound of shredded rubber flapping against the pavement told of at least two flat tires, maybe three.

"You think the doors are locked?"

"It's nighttime in Miami," said Jack.

Demetri pressed the accelerator to the floor, steered the Mustang up onto the walkway, and drove straight for the main entrance. It was a three-story wall of plate-glass windows.

"Down!" said Demetri.

Jack dived to the floor, and it sounded like a hurricane as the car crashed through the door and took down the entire wall of glass with it. Windows shattered, metal twisted, and furniture and debris flew everywhere. The wheels screeched across the tile floor as the car slammed into the reception desk and came to a sudden stop in the main lobby. Through it all, Jack's hands remained tied behind his back, the knotted lamp cord holding like handcuffs.

Demetri drew his pistol, flung open the door, and yanked Jack from the backseat. Fortunately, no one had been in the waiting room or at the reception desk at this hour, but the alarm sounded, and a security guard came running down the open flight of stairs from the upper level.

"This man has a gun!" Jack shouted.

The guard drew his weapon, but not fast enough. Demetri dropped him with a single shot. As the guard tumbled down the stairs, Jack lunged toward the Greek, but he wasn't much of a threat with his hands bound behind his back. Demetri wheeled and clubbed Jack across the side of the head with the butt of his pistol. The blow knocked Jack to his knees. He was even stronger than Jack had thought.

"I'll kill you, too!" he said. "Is that what you want?"

Jack's head was throbbing, and it took a moment to process what he was hearing. The Greek didn't wait for a response. He lifted Jack to his feet and put the gun to his head.

"Now let's do this right, Swyteck. And if you're a good boy, maybe one of us will get out of here alive."

He took Jack past the open stairway first, grabbed the security guard's gun, and tucked it under his belt. Then he pushed Jack through the long hallway, past the darkened set for the *Food, Glorious Food* show, past the managerial offices and dressing rooms, and through the final set of doors that led to the evening news set.

"Nobody move!" shouted Demetri.

Chaos had already broken loose. Dozens of cubicles with computer terminals occupied a large open work area in front of the set, and the reduced staff that worked the eleven o'clock news were either racing for emergency exits or already outside the building. All but one cameraman had fled the set, along with the weekend producer, the director, the co-anchor, the former Miami Dolphin football player who did the sports wrap up, and the former Miss Florida who guessed at the weather. A single cameraman and an ambitious young anchorwoman were bringing up the rear, dutifully keeping *Action News* on the air as they raced toward the door.

"We have breaking news literally breaking into the *Action News* studio!" she said into the wireless microphone clipped to her lapel. She was a weekend substitute, not the regular nightly anchor, and Jack recognized her as the rising *Action News* star who had chained herself to a palm tree to keep from getting blown away during her report on Hurricane Wilma making landfall.

She was just steps away from the door when Demetri fired a warning shot. It tore through the carpet three feet in front of her, stopping her and the cameraman in their tracks.

"I said, *Nobody move!*"

Chapter 40

At 11:10 P.M. Andie's home telephone rang. She was awake but in bed, wearing her most comfortable and unsexy pair of pajamas, all geared up for a night alone watching *Saturday Night Live*. Her gut told her it was Jack calling, and she was afraid to answer. She'd probably overreacted to the news that Jack was in a hotel room with his "client," and she feared that if she picked up the phone she might still saddle Jack with the sins of her ex-fiancé. No way would Jack do what that creep had done to her.

Then again, where the hell has he been for the past four hours?

She let it ring through to her answering machine.

"Andie, pick up."

The voice wasn't Jack's. It was the assistant special agent in charge of the Miami field office, Guy Schwartz.

Andie launched herself across the bed and grabbed the phone from the nightstand.

"I'm here," she said.

"Turn on *Action News*," he said.

It probably would have been fair to ask *why*, but Schwartz's tone was too urgent to invite questions. Andie fished around beneath the covers and found the remote control beneath an empty bag of mini-marshmallows—consolation food that had nearly made her sick, which was one more reason to be angry at Jack. With a punch of the button she switched channels.

"That's Jack," she said.

It was stating the obvious, but the words had come like a reflex. Andie moved to the foot of the bed, closer to the TV.

Schwartz gave her a two-minute summary of everything the FBI understood about the standoff so far. Andie listened as she watched it unfold in real time on television. *Action News* was broadcasting in a split-screen format, the live hostage standoff on the left and, on the right, their lead anchor broadcasting from the parking lot outside the station. Andie heard her mention something about one dead security guard inside the building, which jibed with what Schwartz had just told her.

Andie said, "The media need to assume that the gunman is listening to everything they're saying. We need to muzzle that reporter."

"We're on it," said Schwartz.

On the split screen, Andie could see that police were indeed trying to move the entire *Action News* team to a safer distance.

"Once again," said the reporter, "*Action News* has not yet confirmed the gunman's identity. However, we do know that he has taken at least three hostages, including *Action News* weekend anchor Shannon Sertane, cameraman Pedro Valdez, and Miami attorney Jack Swyteck, whom you may know as the son of former governor and vice presidential nominee Harry Swyteck. The gunman has not—wait a minute. It looks as though he may be about to say something."

Andie increased the volume. *Action News* changed the on-screen format from split screen to a picture-in-picture mode, relegating the reporter to a small box in the upper right-hand corner. But she kept talking.

"Up until now, we have seen the gunman securing the set inside the *Action News* newsroom, checking things out, tying up his hostages with electrical cord. Basically getting situated. So far we have only been able to speculate as to his demands and . . ."

Andie spoke into the phone. "Somebody needs to tell her to shut up and let him talk."

The reporter's microphone suddenly went silent, someone presumably having pulled the plug.

The gunman looked into the camera and said, "Good evening."

Andie noted the accent and waited.

"My name is Demetri, and I want everyone to know right up front that I don't want to hurt any of these fine people who are here with me tonight."

Tell that to the dead security guard, thought Andie.

"But I will do whatever is necessary if my demands are not met. Or if anyone is foolish enough to storm the building." He was speaking very slowly, as if determined to hide his accent from the television viewers. "Let me assure everyone right now that there is no way for the FBI or anyone else to get inside this building without turning this into a bloodbath. I've checked it out, and the newsroom has no windows. Sorry, snipers. I've locked all the doors and rigged them up nicely so that I'll hear it if anyone tries to sneak in. I'm sure some genius at the FBI is probably coming up with a plan right now to climb in through the air-conditioning ducts. Well, I've thought of that, too. I'm not going to get into specifics, but let me just say that it would be a very bad idea."

"He's into this," Andie said into the telephone.

"A very desperate man making his last stand," Schwartz replied.

The Greek continued, "I will have several demands to make, so let's start off with a simple one: we stay on the air. This is a live broadcast, and everything is in real time. There are television screens all over the place in here, so I'll know if this demand is being met. If it's not, one of these hostages will die. It's as simple as that."

He walked across the set toward the news desk. Jack and the anchorwoman were seated on the floor in front of the desk, their hands tied behind their backs. He stepped closer to Jack, and the camera followed him.

"You don't want that to happen, do you, Swyteck?"

He didn't answer.

"Do you?" said Demetri.

Andie gripped the phone tighter. "Answer him, Jack," she said to the television. Even if Jack couldn't hear her, maybe she could will him to do the right thing.

"No," said Jack.

"No *what?*"

Jack glared at him, and Andie was getting nervous again. *Don't antagonize him.*

"No, sir," said Jack.

"That's better," said Demetri. "So, all you folks at home, sit back, relax, pop yourselves some popcorn, and enjoy the show. I promise you this: it's going to get good. Really good."

Demetri walked over to the morning-show couch, made himself comfortable, and put his feet up on the cocktail table. The cameraman kept the show rolling.

On-screen, *Action News* resumed the picture-in-picture mode, and the reporter returned with a new microphone.

"There you have it, ladies and gentlemen. The man's name is Demetri, and he has demanded that *Action News* remain on the air. I'm told that we will honor that request, but sources inform me that, even as we speak, *Action News* officials are coordinating with law enforcement to determine how best to handle this extremely dangerous and unprecedented situation."

"Can somebody *shut her up*?" said Andie.

"I'm about to shoot her myself," said Schwartz.

"Where do things stand logistically?" said Andie.

"We're setting up a mobile command center right now. Should have a dedicated line into the newsroom in a few minutes. I don't want to wait much longer to make contact. How soon can you be here?"

Andie hesitated. "Are you sure you want me to be your negotiator?"

"You're the best one I've got."

"But I date one of the hostages."

Schwartz grumbled. "We'll sort that out when you get here. I at least need you here on the premises as part of the team. How long till you can get here?"

Andie got off the bed and walked to the closet. "It'll take a good thirty minutes," she said.

"Make it sooner," said Schwartz, and the line disconnected.

Chapter 41

S ecret Service Agent Frank Madera stepped out of a warm taxi and into a pile of cold New York slush. Black skies over the boroughs had been trying to snow since sundown, succeeding at times, but the rain was stubborn. By 11:15 P.M., an ankle-deep mess of wet slop covered the sidewalks of Queens.

Madera cinched up his overcoat, popped open his umbrella, and waited at the corner. He was one of just a handful of pedestrians braving the weather. Across the street, outside a restaurant called Café Luna, was a black limousine. The dark tinted windows made it impossible to see inside, but the motor was running and the headlights shone. The car pulled away from the curb and started to swing around before Madera could even signal the driver. It stopped in front of him, and the rear door opened.

"Get in," the man said.

It had been two years since Madera had last seen Joseph Dinitalia. He looked the same—handsome, slightly overweight, and still showing the jet-black hair and dark Sicilian eyes that had labeled him a lady killer since high school. That was where the two men had first met. Every day after baseball practice they'd head over to Corona Heights, hit the Lemon Ice King, and talk about their plans to take over the world while watching the old Italian men play bocce ball in the park. After graduation, Dinitalia stayed in New York to join the family business, so to speak. Madera chose the straight path, went to college on an ROTC scholarship, served two tours of duty in the Middle East, and finally came home to a coveted job with the Secret Service. Then he hit a wall: not once, not twice, but six separate times the service turned down his request to work directly for the president. At their twentieth high-school reunion, Dinitalia took him for a limo ride. It was then that he laid out his plan to have the president work for them.

Sometimes Madera cursed his old friend for getting him involved, but it was all too perfect—the two smartest kids from the old neighborhood in Queens, one with the goods on the president of the United States, the other a Secret Service agent who was suddenly—but not coincidentally—handpicked by the president to be his right-hand man. All Madera had to do was whisper into his new boss's ear, and the most powerful man in the world had two choices: grant Dinitalia his wish, or pack his bags and leave the White House.

"LaGuardia," Dinitalia told the driver. "Go the long way around Jackson Heights and come back past St. Michael's."

"Yes, sir."

The privacy partition rose automatically, and the men were alone, facing each other in the split rear seating.

Madera had just come from the airport, but he didn't complain about returning. No one ever complained to Dinitalia. The last guy to do it had been mad enough and stupid enough to twist his surname into "Genitalia"— and he promptly lost his with a flick of the knife in a scene right out of *The Valachi Papers*. Stories like that became legend. So if Dinitalia wanted you to hop on an airplane, fly into LaGuardia, and cab it over to his restaurant just so that he could have a backseat talk while taking you straight back to the airport, then you hopped on an airplane, no questions asked.

"My father is unhappy," said Dinitalia.

Madera's throat tightened. There were ways to smooth things over between friends, but Dinitalia's old man still ran the show. If he was unhappy, friendship didn't matter.

"How do we fix that?" said Madera.

Dinitalia looked out the window as he spoke. It had the desired effect, making Madera feel as if he were of no more substance than his reflection in the dark tinted glass.

"We get the job done right," said Dinitalia. "That's how we fix it."

"That was not my fuckup in Miami tonight."

"Of all the stupid plans," said Dinitalia, scoffing. "Spray the office with machine-gun fire? What do your boys think this is, an old rerun of *Miami Vice*? They should have walked up and put a bullet in the Greek's head. Bang. Game over."

"It was impossible to just walk up to him," said Madera. "He was with some Russian *Mafiya*. We don't mess with them."

"So thanks to you cowards, not only is the old man still alive, but he's got complete control of a newsroom and is ready to talk to the camera."

"What?" said Madera.

"You haven't seen the news?"

"I've been on an airplane."

Dinitalia filled him in on everything that he'd missed since boarding the shuttle from Washington. It was the proverbial bad-to-worse scenario, and by the time Dinitalia had finished, Madera was literally feeling sick to his stomach.

"I don't think anybody saw that coming," said Madera.

Dinitalia's gaze drifted back in Madera's direction. "My father paid the Greek good money for valuable information. It changed everything. Two years ago we were still paying off city managers to grant us recycling contracts so that we could haul bottles and newspapers straight to the dumps for pure profit. A nice piece of change, if you like small potatoes. This year, when the new contract comes in from the Pentagon, we'll be over a hundred million dollars in private security contracts alone. Pretty good work for a company that doesn't even have a private security force, but who the hell is gonna fly over to Iraq and check? And all this is possible because we know something about President Keyes that nobody else knows."

"That's still the case," said Madera.

"For now. But it's all over if the Greek starts blabbering on television. And once that unravels, do you have any idea what kind of problems we'll have on our hands?"

Madera lowered his head. "I'd say no one has a better understanding of that than I do. Except for the president himself."

The two men rode in silence for several minutes. It was a dark night, but Madera recognized much of the old neighborhood passing by outside the car windows. Finally, they'd completed the big loop, and the limo was back on Grand Central Parkway and headed toward the airport. St. Michael's cemetery was coming up, and right next to it was the former Bulova watch headquarters. A famous watch manufacturer beside a cemetery. Madera had always thought it was the world's greatest metaphor for time marching on.

"I have friends there," said Dinitalia.

Madera knew he wasn't talking about the Bulova Corporate Center.

"My father has friends there, too," said Dinitalia.

Madera glanced out the window. He couldn't really see anything, but he'd traveled past St. Michael's so many times that he knew what was there.

"We've *put* friends there," said Dinitalia, crossing himself.

Madera said nothing.

Dinitalia said, "You and I have been friends for a very long time, Frank."

"A long, long time."

Dinitalia nodded. "But this is business. Very important business."

"I understand."

"I'm not sure you do. So let me spell it out. The Greek dies tonight—before he starts shooting his mouth off.

Period, end of story. Tell me you can get it done, and I'll tell my father to let you live."

Madera felt numb. Never before had the disparity in power between the two old friends been more apparent.

"I can do it," said Madera.

Dinitalia leaned forward, deadly serious.

"Listen to me. At this point, I don't care if you, personally, have to run into that television studio with a machine gun and shoot the place up. This problem has to be taken care of."

"It'll happen," Madera said.

Dinitalia grabbed Madera by the earlobe and forced his old friend to look him straight in the eye.

"I want your word on it."

Madera met his stare and said, "You've absolutely got my word on it."

"Good man," said Dinitalia, as the limo steered onto the airport exit ramp. "There's a twelve-fifteen red-eye to Miami. Be on it."

Chapter 42

Andie almost had to shoot her way through the media.

The two-lane access road to the *Action News* studio was completely choked off. Police had established a perimeter around the property with teams of uniformed officers stationed about every twenty feet. Outside the police tape, hungry reporters poked and probed at the yellow membrane like free radicals on a skin cell. The largest concentration was at the main entrance to the parking lot. Media vans with satellite dishes and microwave antennae were parked two and three deep. The story of a newsroom held hostage was to the media as mirrors were to supermodels, and everyone from CNN to *Noticias 23* was on the scene.

Andie tried dialing Jack's father on his cell. It was her second attempt in the past twenty minutes.

This one went to voice mail, too, so she left another message.

"Harry, it's Andie. I'm just arriving at the scene. I know you must be worried. Technically, I can't tell you much, but I just want you to know that I'm . . . involved."

She frowned at her choice of words, but she'd never had such a personal stake in a standoff, and she didn't really know what to say.

"Call me if you can," she said.

She hung up and inched her car forward toward the perimeter, where television reporters with roving camera crews were staking out positions for live updates. They all seemed to want the same backdrop in the distance: the gaping hole that Jack's car had punched through the main entrance to the *Action News* studio. A motorcycle cop finally had to part the media in order to get Andie to the entrance gate, where a highway patrol officer stopped her car.

"FBI," she said, flashing her credentials.

He looked at her skeptically, as if he'd seen reporters pull much cleverer stunts to get past him.

"She's legit," said the motorcycle cop. "I checked."

The trooper let her pass. Andie parked her car in the nearest open space and started walking across the parking lot to the FBI's mobile command center. The

lot wasn't quite the state of confusion that raged outside the gate, but things were buzzing. In addition to
the FBI, the sheriff's department was out in full force,
as was Florida Highway Patrol. Three dozen squad
cars surrounded the building in a first line of containment, forming a tight and fortified circle within the
wider circle of crowd control. This close to the building, patrol officers wore flak jackets, just in case the
gunman came out shooting. Andie also noted the obvious duplication of effort between local and federal law
enforcement. There were actually two mobile command centers on site, one from the FBI, and the other
a large motor van bearing the blue, green, and black
logo of Miami-Dade Police Department (MDPD).
The antennae protruding from the roof indicated
that it was equipped with all the necessary technical
gadgets to survey the situation and make contact with
the hostage taker. Andie could smell the turf war
already.

Just then, another MDPD vehicle rolled past her
and came to a stop beside the sheriff's command center. It was a SWAT transport vehicle, and before the
engine cut off, the rear doors flew open and the tactical team filed out. They were armed with M-16 rifles
and dressed in black SWAT regalia, including Kevlar
helmets, night-vision goggles, and flak jackets. They

were on hold for the moment, but they appeared ready—eager, in fact—to go on a moment's notice.

The turf war had just gone from cold to hot.

Andie's cell rang, and she answered. It was the Miami ASAC, Guy Schwartz.

"Where the heck are you?" he said.

"Headed straight toward you."

"Walk faster. We have some . . . logistics to work out."

She knew that "logistics" meant "politics." It was the part of her job that she hated most, and the last thing she needed was to waste time arguing with the local sheriff over who was in charge. Unfortunately, resolution of these matters was never as simple as pointing out that the gunman inside had three hostages at his mercy, that the coroner's van was already on the scene for a dead security guard, that three ambulances were waiting in the wings for the next victims, and that there was no time to waste.

"Why should today be different from any other?" she said, and hung up.

A helicopter whirred overhead, its bright white spotlight illuminating the demolished entrance to the building. She'd seen the damage on television, and she'd even recognized Jack's new Mustang in the rubble. But seeing it in person impacted her anew and with much greater force. She was doing her best to sustain her unemotional work mode, but it was impossible to keep a certain hostage out of the equation. Her gaze again drifted toward the ambulances, and she said a little prayer that it wouldn't be Jack who needed it.

She found Schwartz on the other side of the FBI mobile command center. He was standing in the parking lot, just him and someone from the sheriff's office. The conversation didn't look friendly, and she approached with trepidation, landing in the middle of a heated argument.

"Nobody called for FBI support," he said to Schwartz.

They would, if they could, thought Andie, meaning the hostages.

"Andie Henning," she said, introducing herself.

"Manny Figueroa," he said, "MDPD crisis team leader."

He and Schwartz looked as if they'd been cut from the same mold—or, more accurately, chiseled from the same block of granite. Some men shrank in a crisis. Andie wondered if there was enough room in Miami for these two angry warriors who were standing eyeball to eyeball at about six-foot-three.

"Any contact with the subject yet?" asked Andie.

"Just what you've seen on the air," said Schwartz.

Andie said, "Are we sure the phones are even working? The crash may have taken out the landlines."

"Our techies say they are," said Schwartz.

"That's good, but we don't need him talking to some overactive journalist. We'll want to block out all calls except those coming from our communications vehicle."

"You mean *my* communications vehicle," said Figueroa.

Andie ignored it. That was Schwartz's battle. "Has anyone contacted Building and Zoning yet?"

Figueroa said, "Before we get into this—"

"We'll want blueprints of the building," said Andie, stemming the jurisdictional argument. "The more detailed, the better. Bearing walls versus nonbearing, crawl space, duct work, attic clearance. Have we located the water main?"

"These are all good questions," said Figueroa, "but the first thing we need to talk about is who is in—"

"We may want to turn that off at some point," said Andie. "The same goes for electrical, though that will take some real thought. The gunman's one and only demand so far is to stay on the air, and it may actually play to our advantage to have an eye on the inside. Have we been able to confirm that no one else is in the building—just the gunman and his three hostages?"

"I can answer that," said Figueroa.

Andie almost smiled. She had him talking about the important stuff, and that was always step one toward cooperation.

"Great," she said. "Fill me in."

"MDPD officers swept all areas of the building, other than the newsroom, when we went in to retrieve the body of the security guard. We found one other guard hiding in a closet on the first floor. That's all we know."

"Was there a sign-in register at the front desk—anything to show if there were visitors in the studio?"

"The lobby is completely demolished. My guess is that the sign-in log is buried somewhere under that Mustang."

Andie looked at Schwartz and said, "We should establish contact ASAP."

Figueroa said, "Excuse me, Agent Henning. But exactly what is your role here?"

Schwartz said, "She's the lead negotiator."

Figueroa chuckled. "I don't mean no disrespect, but I saw the gunman on television. He looks like a sixtysomething-year-old mobster. Do you really think a guy like that is going to negotiate with a woman half his age?"

More helicopters buzzed overhead. The fleet of television helicopters had grown from one to three, and

Andie could see that they were media choppers. One of them cruised by so low that it stirred the cool night air around them. Andie shot a look at her boss, as if to say that it was time to end this squabble or take it inside.

"Here's the deal," said Schwartz. "The FBI makes the first contact with the gunman. If he won't speak to Andie, you're in charge."

Figueroa gave Andie an assessing look. He seemed reluctant to take Schwartz's challenge at first, sensing that Andie might be a ringer of some sort. Soon enough, however, the testosterone came bubbling back up to the top.

"All right," said Figueroa. "You make that first call, Henning. And a hundred bucks says I'll be taking it from there."

Chapter 43

J ack was counting bullets.

The warning shot and the security guard made two. Mika was three. That was the sum total, as best Jack could recall. Could Demetri really have come this far on just three spent rounds? On the other side of the balance sheet, he'd picked up the security guard's gun, Mika's pistol on the nightstand, and the .22-caliber, pizza-boy special from Mika's pants. At this rate, the chances of this guy running out of ammunition before killing a hostage were not good.

"Are you packing?" Shannon whispered.

Jack and the *Action News* anchor were sitting on the floor in front of the news desk.

"Packing what?" said Jack.

"Do you have a gun?"

"If I did, do you think my hands would be tied behind my back?"

"Good point," she whispered. "Pedro's our only hope."

Pedro was the cameraman. Demetri needed him to operate the equipment, so he was the only hostage with free hands. Demetri had also used him to move furniture and barricade the entrance to the newsroom, turning the place into a windowless fortress.

Jack looked up at the ceiling. It was about twenty feet high. Scores of stage lights hung down in rows over the set, leaving about six feet of inky black crawl space between the suspended lights and the ceiling. The entire newsroom was built that way, though the suspended fixtures over the work cubicles were far fewer in number and not nearly as bright as the set lighting. Jack liked the idea of SWAT moving in like Spider-Man above the lights a whole lot better than Pedro the cameraman playing hero.

"It's getting miserably hot here under these lights," said Jack, speaking loud enough for Demetri to hear.

"Must be male menopause," he said. "Deal with it."

Does the whole freakin' world know I'm forty?

"Smart ass," said Shannon.

She'd muttered it beneath her breath, but the acoustics on the set were state of the art. Demetri threw her a deadly glare.

"Did you say something?" he said. He was seated on the couch that was part of the morning talk show set, just away from the news desk.

"Me?" she said. "No."

Demetri rose, then pointed his pistol at Pedro and said, "Keep the camera right on me."

The camera followed his slow walk across the set. Jack had noticed Demetri stretching his legs and massaging his hip as the night wore on, the way back-pain sufferers did, and the flare-up seemed to make him more ornery. Demetri stopped right in front of Shannon, showing the television audience his profile. A wireless microphone was clipped to his shirt, and he reached for the control pack on his belt and switched it off. Then he lowered himself onto one knee and pressed his gun between Shannon's breasts.

"I don't like a woman with a mouth," he said.

She seemed on the verge of telling him where to go, which impressed Jack, but she held her tongue.

"We have two choices," said Demetri. "You can behave yourself. Or," he said, glancing toward the camera, "we can have ourselves a public execution. What's it going to be, sweety?"

Switty. His accent seemed to creep in with fatigue.

A phone rang in the newsroom. It was in one of the cubicles nearest to the news set.

"Gee, who could that be?" said Demetri.

"You pressed your gun to her chest on live television," said Jack. "You're lucky the cops didn't come busting through the door. That's the way it works, pal."

It rang for the second time, and then a third.

"Aren't you going to answer it?" said Jack.

Demetri switched on his wireless microphone. The speakers whined with a bit of feedback, but a quick adjustment cleared it.

The phone continued to ring.

"You should talk to them," said Jack. "What can it hurt?"

Demetri stepped down from the set and walked to the phone. For a moment, Jack thought he might answer it. Then he yanked the wire out of the wall and threw the phone across the newsroom.

The ringing stopped.

Demetri faced the camera and said, "As the saying goes, folks: 'Don't call us, we'll call you.' "

Then he walked back toward the news desk, pacing back and forth in front of his hostages as he spoke to his television audience. His movements were fluid now, as if his anger had a way of cutting through any amount of pain.

"Let me make something real clear," he said. "This is not a negotiation. There will be no private conversations, no side deals here. Everything I have to say will be said on the air. There is only one reason for anyone to call this newsroom—and that's to tell me when my demands have been met. So let's get the ball rolling. Demand number one. Money." He stopped pacing and looked at Jack. "How much do you think I want, big mouth?"

Jack didn't like playing his games, but he'd seen Demetri's temper. The guy had even lost it with his beloved Sofia.

"I have no idea," said Jack.

"Come on, you can do better than that. You met one of my Russian friends tonight. He must have told you how much I owed them."

"He wasn't much of a talker," said Jack.

"Even less now," said Demetri.

"Like Chloe and Paulette Sparks."

Demetri stopped pacing, his expression sour. "Now why'd you have to go and mention them already? That's like killing off Jack Bauer in the second episode of the season. You gotta build up to these things. Where the fuck is—oops, sorry. Network television. Where the hell is your sense of drama, Swyteck?"

"The whole world knows what you did," said Jack. "You're just kidding yourself here. I have it figured out, the FBI has it figured out. I bet if you turn on CNN, they've even got the scoop. It's all on the table. You don't have any secrets left."

Demetri fell silent, but that ember of anger that seemed to burn continuously inside him was about to burst into flames. He took a deep breath and swallowed his rage.

"That's where you're wrong. I got one left. The big one."

Demetri turned away from Jack and spoke to the camera.

"I'm talking to you, big man. That's right. *You.* I know you're watching, so here's the deal. I want five hundred thousand dollars in cash. Hundred-dollar bills will be fine. Old bills, not new ones. For you novices out there who've never worked as a bagman, that's five thousand bills, which comes out to about ten pounds of money. And I want it delivered here to the newsroom by . . . let's see."

He checked the clock on the wall.

"It's going on one o'clock. I'll give you till seven A.M. That's more than enough time. Don't you think, Swyteck?"

Jack didn't answer.

"You're right," said Demetri, again making that extra effort to speak clearly for his American audience. "We're dealing with a very powerful man here. He can make things happen fast. Five hundred thousand in cash delivered right here to the studio by six A.M., not a minute later. Stay glued to those television sets, folks. I'm going to count it live and on the air. And if it's not here by six," he said, taking a step closer to his hostages, "then one of our lucky guests here will take a bullet to the head. I might even let you call in and vote on which one should get it. The pretty blond anchor woman, or the greedy lawyer whose father is a slick politician? Hmmm. Tough choice. But if I'm a betting man, Swyteck, I'd say you're toast."

He stepped even closer to the camera, his face filling the screen.

"I told you it was gonna get good."

Chapter 44

*A*ction *News* was playing in real time on the Air Force One television.

Harry Swyteck had been sound asleep in his Washington hotel room when the president called. He'd switched on the television to see the Miami broadcast of the hostage standoff, which had been picked up nationally. A split second was all it had taken for Harry to realize that he needed to be back in Miami. It took even less time for him to accept the president's offer to take him there ASAP. By 1:00 A.M. they were in the executive suite of Air Force One, just forty minutes away from Miami. The president sat behind his desk, and Harry was in a leather chair facing the flat-screen TV.

"More coffee, sir?" the flight attendant asked.

"None for me, thank you," said Harry.

"You have to try this one," said the president. "I have these beans shipped to me every day from a little coffee shop called the Flying Goat in Healdsburg, north of San Francisco. I drank it every day I campaigned in California, and it definitely brought me luck."

"We could all use some luck," said Harry.

The flight attendant filled his mug, and then she put down the pot and cupped her hands. It confused Harry at first, but then he noticed the remnants of a napkin that he'd nervously and methodically torn to shreds. He gathered up the mess and gave it to her.

"Sorry," said Harry, as he glanced toward the television screen. "This is a really stressful time for me."

"I understand, sir."

Harry had missed not a single frame of the live broadcast since boarding the plane, but absolutely nothing had happened since Demetri's on-the-air demand for $500,000. The camera was locked onto Jack and the anchor woman seated side by side on the floor in front of the news desk, their hands tied behind their backs. Stress had a way of playing with the mind, and staring at an image that virtually never changed had Harry thinking all the way back to Jack's college graduation, when Harry had rested the old VHS recorder on the floor and forgot to switch off the

RECORD button. Ninety minutes of Agnes's shoes on videotape.

"You all right?" said the president.

"I'm not sure."

"I feel for you. It's every politician's worst nightmare. Just the thought of something like this happening to one of your children is terrifying. It doesn't seem to make much difference that they're not kids anymore."

Harry looked at him. On some level, he appreciated the words. But he didn't have time for this.

"I need to ask you a question, Mr. President."

Sensing the gravity in Harry's tone, Keyes stepped out from behind his desk and sat in the chair facing Harry.

"Sure," said the president, "what is it that you want to know?"

"Who was he talking to?"

"What?"

"This Demetri character. When he demanded the half million dollars, he was obviously speaking directly to someone he chose not to name on television—someone he couldn't just pick up the telephone and call, so he chose to speak to him over the television airwaves. Who is it?"

"What makes you think I would know?"

Harry drilled him with his stare. "Is it you?"

Keyes stared right back.

Harry said, "Am I to take silence as a 'yes'?"

The president rose and walked to the window. He was staring into a vast blackness above the clouds, millions of stars in the distance. Worry was staring right back at him in his reflection in the glass. The president seemed oddly fixated on his receding hairline, checking it with his fingers.

"I'm getting old, Harry."

"We all are, sir."

The president turned away from the oval window and placed his hand atop his head, slicking his hair back to show Harry just how far it had receded. The large and distinctive birthmark on his scalp, normally hidden in part by his comb-over, was fully exposed.

"I look more and more like Mikhail Gorbachev every day, don't I?"

Harry wasn't sure how to answer.

The president lowered his hand and let his hair fall back into place. He returned to the chair facing Harry.

"My question," said Harry. "I'd like an answer."

The president drew a deep breath and let it out slowly. "I suppose you have a right to know."

"My son is being held hostage in a newsroom with a gun to his head. I have *every* right to know."

The president nodded, then took another deep breath, as if not sure where to begin. "The answer to your question is yes," said the president. "Demetri was indeed talking to me when he demanded that half million dollars."

"Why would he look to you for the ransom?"

"It's not a ransom," said the president. "It's blackmail, pure and simple."

"So the things I've been hearing are not just talk? There truly is some secret out there that could have made Phil Grayson the next president of the United States. And just as Jack was told in that e-mail message, the same bit of information could make me president, too, if I'm approved."

"All I can tell you is that it's bullshit. Trust me on this. I've done nothing wrong. I swear on my mother's soul, this is not about anything I did, anything I could have prevented."

"If it is bullshit, as you say, then how could it be that bad—to bring down the president of the United States, just like that?"

"I'm sorry, Harry. I'm simply not going to dignify any of it by repeating it to you tonight, tomorrow, or any time coming."

"I want to know what this is all about."

The president's gaze drifted back toward the television. "Then watch the show like everyone else. And see if Demetri tells you."

Chapter 45

"If he doesn't answer this time," said Figueroa, "it's time to start thinking about a breach."

A breach meant a forced entry. Andie wasn't ready to go there yet, even if this was her fifth attempt to bring Demetri to the telephone.

"He'll answer."

She waited in the tense silence, watching the television screen. Demetri had just one operational boom microphone on the news set, which wasn't enough to pick up the sound of the ringing telephone in the business pods adjacent to the set. The on-screen reaction of the hostages, however, told Andie that they could hear it. Precious seconds ticked away with each hollow, unanswered ring on Andie's line. On the fifth one, the call went to the *Action News* voice mail. Andie disconnected.

Figueroa said, "How much longer do you intend to keep this up?"

"These things take time."

"He's watching the television," said Figueroa. "I say we tell *Action News* to go to a split screen. I'll go on the air and tell him to answer the phone or we're coming in."

"Let's hold off on the threats," said Andie.

"Look at this," said Schwartz, pointing at the television screen.

Andie watched as Demetri slowly crossed the set toward the desk phone at the nearest cubicle. The camera followed him, keeping him on-screen.

"He's picking up," said Schwartz.

Demetri appeared to punch two or three buttons, not enough to place a call. Andie hoped it was star-69—returning her call. Her hope materialized, and the phone rang. She answered in a cordial tone, speaking into her headset.

"Is that you, Demetri?"

He hesitated. Even though his image on the television screen was far from a close-up, Andie could see the confusion in his body language.

"Who is this?" he said. His voice played over a speaker, allowing everyone inside the mobile command center to hear.

"FBI Agent Andie Henning," she said.

Andie watched on-screen as he lowered the phone and shouted across the set.

"Hey, Swyteck. You're not gonna believe this. I got your girlfriend on the line."

Back in the command center, Figueroa made a face. *"Girlfriend?"*

Andie shushed him, then spoke into the phone. "Demetri, I want to talk to you."

"Go right ahead," he said.

"I think it would be best not to share our conversations with the television viewers. This should be between us."

"Sorry, nothing's off the air. You got something to say, just say it."

"All right. We can do this your way. But you know how this works, right? If I give you something, you give me a little something, too."

"I don't have time for your games."

"Don't hang up," she said, catching him just before he did. She watched him carefully on the screen, and he was awfully close to ending the call. It was time to change the subject.

"Are you guys getting hungry in there?" she said.

He laughed. It was totally forced, like a bad actor all too aware that the camera was rolling. Then he lowered the phone, looked into the camera, and spoke to the television audience.

"The FBI wants to know if I'm hungry. If I say yes, she'll probably offer to send us a sack of Big Macs or Whoppers. We call that product placement. All the reality shows do it."

Andie and her boss exchanged glances. A sense of humor could be a good sign. A man about to pull the trigger didn't usually crack jokes. But you never knew for sure.

"Demetri, talk to me," said Andie.

"No, we don't want any food," he said into the phone. "I just want my five hundred thousand dollars."

Andie had to handle this one carefully. She never promised anything she couldn't deliver. "I'm working on that," she said.

"You better work hard."

"You have to understand that I'm getting resistance on that. It would help if you showed us some goodwill by letting one of the hostages go."

"Get me my money and they all can go."

"Taking the hard line isn't going to do any of us any good, Demetri. I can't help you if you won't show us that you're willing to work this out."

"I'm not letting anyone go a minute before I get my money."

"I hear what you're saying, but let me be straight with you. This is not a threat. All I'm trying to do is give you an accurate picture of what you're up against. The police have surrounded the entire building. The FBI is here. Miami-Dade Police Department is here, too. They have shut down the entire area. It's going to be really difficult for you to escape with or without your money. So let's make a deal here and now, all right? You let one of the hostages go, and I'll tell the boys in the SWAT van to back off. We cool with that?"

Demetri didn't answer. Andie saw that as a good sign. Immediate rejection punctuated with profanity would have been a bad sign.

Andie said, "You just take a deep breath and think about letting one of those hostages go. It would count for a lot if you did, Demetri. A little goodwill goes a long way."

"Who the hell are you to be talking about goodwill?"

The sudden change of tone took Andie aback. "Take it easy, Demetri."

"No, you just shut up and listen to me. I know it was you who tried to set me up when your boyfriend went to the Smithsonian. I watched the whole thing go down. I saw you come running out to get Swyteck on the museum steps. I know who you are, and I know you're a liar."

"Things are going to be handled different this time."

"No they aren't. You are no different from any cop I've ever met. You will lie to get whatever you want."

The mood swing was startling. Despite that brief display of humor at the top of the phone call, Demetri was obviously starting to feel the pressure.

Andie said, "I won't lie to you."

"Like hell you won't. Liars always lie. And you are a fucking liar!"

"Demetri, calm down."

"Don't tell me to calm down! I'm in control here, not you. Just get me my money, and stop stalling."

"I'll call you in an hour."

"Don't. Just *don't*—unless you're calling to tell me you got my money."

"Let's work this out together. You've got two hostages. Why not let one go?"

"I ain't letting nobody go."

"Demetri, listen to me. Let one of the hostages go. You don't need three. You only need one."

"That's exactly right. All I need is one. So get me my money, or somebody's gonna die—live on television."

Demetri hung up.

Andie breathed deep and let it out.

"You okay?" said Schwartz.

Andie felt her hand shaking just a bit as she put the phone down. "Yeah, I'm good."

Figueroa said, "It's time to consider a breach."

"No," said Andie.

"He's this close to snapping. Can't you hear it in his voice?"

"It's his accent. Greek uses a narrower pitch range than English, and to our ear, he can sound angrier than he really is."

"How do you know that?" said Schwartz.

She'd learned it while watching the 2004 Summer Olympics from Athens on TV, but that wouldn't have impressed anyone. "I just know these things," she said. "Just like it's time to work something out with the money."

Figueroa said, "The director has made MDPD's position on this crystal clear: We don't give money to hostage takers. Period."

"Why not, if it gets the hostages released? We have two SWAT teams here. He isn't going to leave the building with it."

Figueroa said, "We can't let the entire television world see us hand over a half million dollars in exchange for three hostages."

Andie looked at her boss. Schwartz said, "He has a point there, Andie. We don't want copycats across the country."

"Use marked bills. That won't encourage copycats."

"It just won't work," said Figueroa.

"We have to *try*," said Andie. "He's already killed a security guard, at least one and maybe two Russian mobsters, and two sisters in Washington. He has absolutely nothing to lose by killing again. If we can get the hostages out of there in exchange for a suitcase full of marked bills, I say that's a good deal."

Figueroa looked as if he were going to explode. "You think maybe your judgment is clouded because your boyfriend is one of the hostages inside? The FBI conveniently failed to mention that little detail to me."

"Nothing is clouding my judgment," said Andie.

"If you think that, I say you're out of your mind."

"I say it isn't your call," said Andie.

His eyes were like lasers.

"We'll see about that," he said.

Figueroa turned on his heel and slammed the door on his way out.

Chapter 46

"Swyteck, get over here," said Demetri.

Jack was sitting alone on the floor in front of the news desk. Shannon had talked Demetri into letting her use the nearest bathroom, which was just off the back of the set. Two untied hostages—the anchor woman and the cameraman—were clearly making Demetri edgy, not to mention the constant threat of SWAT bursting into the newsroom at any moment. He stood by the weather-forecast green screen, where he could keep one eye on the barricaded entrance to the newsroom and the other on the bathroom door behind the set.

"What do you want?" said Jack.

"I said come here."

Jack climbed to his feet and walked to the back of the set. Demetri had been extremely quiet since his last performance in front of the camera, and as 2:00 A.M. approached, he was looking tired. He'd been mumbling about his back hurting until he found a first-aid kit with some pain reliever inside. The red box was sitting on the news desk. Jack wondered if there was a pair of scissors or maybe a knife inside.

"What now?" said Jack.

Demetri turned off his wireless microphone. Whatever he was going to say, it wouldn't be for the television audience.

"I need your help," he said.

"My help?" said Jack, almost smiling at the absurdity of the situation. "Look, you've got three guns by my count, which clearly puts you in the driver's seat. But I'm not interested in helping you do anything that could get someone killed. Especially me."

"This isn't going to hurt anyone. I just need you to help me draft something."

"You mean like a demand letter?"

"No," he said, pausing for a moment. "It's something legal."

"A confession?"

"No—*hell* no. I need a will."

"You're kidding, right?"

"Do I look like I'm kidding?"

Jack studied those dark, piercing eyes. Being held hostage was bad enough. Getting stuck with a hostage taker who was so prepared to die that he seriously wanted a will was enough to ruin your whole damn day.

"I'd have to say you look pretty serious to me."

"You're a lawyer. I assume you do wills, right?"

"Well, not really. I'm a trial lawyer."

"Are you trying to tell that me you've never helped anyone with a will?"

Jack could have told him about the time he'd represented Theo's older brother Tatum—a reformed hit man who had stood to inherit millions in a six-way battle of survival of the greediest—but that probably wouldn't have helped matters.

"I could do a will if I had to," said Jack.

"You have to," he said, pointing the gun at Jack's forehead. Demetri called down the hall to the bathroom. "Hey, hurry it up in there, princess."

The toilet flushed. A minute later, the door opened, and Shannon emerged.

Demetri said, "Hands up over your head where I can see them."

She complied, walked straight to Demetri, and stopped.

"Facedown on the floor," he said.

She did as he told her. Demetri quickly retied her hands behind her back, and then he directed both her and Jack back toward the news desk.

"You," he told Shannon, "get on the floor."

Jack remained behind the news desk. Demetri found a pad and paper in the drawer.

"Here's the deal," said Demetri. "When I get this five hundred thousand dollars in cash, I want it all to go to Sofia. I have some other personal things I want to leave to her, too."

"It's a nice sentiment," said Jack. "But that's not going to work."

"Why not?"

"You can't steal money and leave it to your heirs."

"I have friends who do it all the time. Hell, how else do you expect an entire generation of baby boomers to leave something to their kids?"

Jack glanced toward the camera. "The problem is, you're trying to do it on television."

"Just tell me what to write. I promise I won't sue you for malpractice."

Jack suddenly had visions of *Body Heat* and Kathleen Turner saying that she liked him because he was "not too smart."

"It would be a lot easier if you just untied me and let me write it for you."

Demetri gave it some thought, and to Jack's surprise he called the cameraman over, whose hands were free.

"Untie Swyteck," said Demetri.

He did so at gunpoint, and then Demetri ordered him back behind the camera. Jack took the chair at the news desk, pen and paper before him. Demetri stood off to the side, where he could keep the gun trained on Jack and still read what he was writing. Jack took a deep breath. He'd become a trial lawyer for many reasons, and disdain for drafting legal documents of any kind was one of them.

"I need your last name," said Jack.

"Pappas."

Jack inked out some language he recalled from law school. It was probably archaic, but clients expected that kind of stuff.

I, Demetri Pappas, being of sound mind and body . . .

"What's Sofia's last name?" said Jack.

He started to answer, then checked his words. "Pappas," he said.

"You understand that Sofia remarried, right?"

Demetri's eyes narrowed. "Her name is Sofia Pappas."

Jack sensed another opening, an emotional point of leverage that could shift the balance of power. It was a skill he had honed on death row, where careful navigation through his clients' personal demons could spark connections with men who were beyond reach.

Jack put down the pen and said, "Why are you doing this?"

"Keep writing."

"You're doing this for Sofia? Is that it?"

He looked angry for a second, but if Jack was reading his expression correctly, it seemed to be morphing into something more complicated.

"I'm not mocking you," said Jack. "I'd just really like to know."

On the desk was a cup of water left over from the evening news, and Demetri drank it, as if his throat suddenly needed oiling.

"Right before I let Sofia out of your car tonight, do you remember what she said to me?"

"Not really," said Jack.

"She said 'I don't deserve this.'"

"That meant something to you," said Jack. It was an observation, not a question.

Demetri nodded. "I know she wasn't trying to hurt me or blame me, but it opened up old wounds. Things that I had hoped were healed. She was talking about a night a long time ago in Cyprus, when we were young. It began as pure pleasure."

Plezoor. A nostalgic moment seemed to trigger the accent.

"Until you got thrown off the building," said Jack.

"She told you about that?"

"Yes."

He seemed surprised, then tentative. "Did she tell you what those bastards did after they thought I was dead?"

"She told me what happened."

"Everything?" said Demetri. "She told you *everything*?"

"Yes."

Demetri breathed in and out. "I suppose it's healthy that she can talk to people about it now. That wasn't always the case. She wouldn't even report it to the police. We tried to work through it, but it was too much. We lasted less than a year. Nine months."

"Do you mean exactly nine months?"

"Yeah. Exactly."

"Nine months from that night, or nine months after you got out of the hospital?"

"From that night."

"Are you saying that Sofia was—"

"Just write the damn will, Swyteck."

Jack took a moment to read the man's eyes, his body language, his voice—trying to gauge whether the opening was still there. On death row, if you pushed the wrong emotional button, you called for the guard. The gun in Demetri's hand made the risk of error prohibitive.

Jack picked up the pen, explaining aloud as he wrote.

"I'm drafting this so that everything you have when you die—whether it's five hundred thousand dollars or five cents—goes to Sofia."

"That's the way I want it," said Demetri.

Jack finished the paragraph in short order, then drew several signature lines at the bottom of the page.

"We'll need three people to witness your signature," said Jack.

"Aren't we in luck? I have three hostages."

"Yeah, but here's an important point. In order for this will to be valid under the law, all three witnesses have to be alive to confirm that this is really your signature. So if any one of us gets killed here—well, there goes your will. Sofia gets nothing."

Demetri gave him an assessing look. He seemed to sense that Jack was bluffing—and in fact, Jack had been bluffing all the way, starting with his claim that three witnesses were required.

"I got a better idea," said Demetri.

He took the handwritten will and the pen from Jack and walked across the news set to the camera. Holding the paper right in front of the lens, he put his signature at the X. Then he folded up the will and tucked it into his pocket.

"Now I have a million witnesses," he said. "All of us can die."

Chapter 47

S ecret Service Agent Frank Madera went straight from the Miami International Airport to the *Action News* standoff.

He hadn't told the FBI that he was coming, and he assiduously avoided contact with the feds after his arrival. Instead, he tracked down Manny Figueroa in a coffee shop adjacent to the studio. The MDPD SWAT unit had made it their official staging area. Its location was strategic—in a building separate from the studio but within the traffic control perimeter, so that they could mobilize without the entire world knowing about it. Figueroa was standing beside a table of doughnuts and coffee when Madera introduced himself as a member of the president's elite personal security detail. It was enough to impress anyone, and Madera had his full attention as he explained—falsely—that the Secret

Service had arrived to help protect the son of the vice presidential nominee.

"I hope you didn't bring your own mobile command center," said Figueroa.

"No," said Madera. "That's not what we do. Can you and I talk in private?"

A half dozen members of the SWAT unit were seated nearby in the dining area, waiting for the green light from Figueroa. They seemed incredibly calm, as they were trained to be. In a matter of minutes, one of these guys might storm a building and pump hollow-point ammunition into a man's skull. Or not. It all depended on how things went. Madera was determined to have a say in that.

"Sure," said Figueroa. "Step into my office."

Madera followed him into the men's room. Figueroa locked the door. Madera stood near the sink with his back to a cracked mirror. Figueroa leaned against the wall beside the electric hand dryer. Madera had never met the man, but he was trained to make quick judgments about people, and he'd already concluded that Figueroa was capable of blowing more hot air than the hand dryer.

"Let me just say this up front," said Figueroa. "I've already backed down to the FBI on leading the negotiations, and I can see that it was a mistake. I'm not backing down to the Secret Service on top of it."

"Take it easy, all right?" said Madera. "I told you that's not what this is about, and I'm shooting straight here."

Figueroa looked skeptical, but he didn't argue.

"Here's the bottom line," said Madera. "This gunman has to go."

"Excuse me?" said Figueroa.

Madera gave him his most serious look. "The man is a threat to national security. It's time to take him out."

Figueroa paused, taking in Madera's words. "What kind of threat to national security?"

"I can't divulge the details, but I can tell you this much. It's no coincidence that one of his hostages is the son of the next vice president of the United States. Nor is it a coincidence that he's taken control of a television news station. The secrets he intends to reveal on the air are a direct threat to our national security."

"That's all fine and good," said Figueroa. "But you've got the FBI here, and they have their own SWAT. Why are you talking to me?"

"It's not like I'm enlisting a bunch of yahoos. MDPD is the one of the largest local law enforcement outfits in the United States. Its SWAT unit is top notch, and unlike most tactical units, your men have experience, not just training."

"Well, thanks for the blow job, but I'm not sure I really heard an answer to my question."

"I can't use the FBI."

"Why not?"

"Again, I will be totally honest with you, but if you ever repeat it to anyone, I will deny it vehemently. But only after cutting your balls off. Is that clear?"

"Crystal."

"Have you ever dealt with the Federal Bureau of Investigation?"

"Of course."

"And has it ever occurred to you that it's impossible to spell bureaucracy without the bureau?"

Figueroa smiled. "You've got a point there."

"We need to neutralize this threat immediately, and it'll be dawn before I can get kill-shot authority from the 'bureau-cracy.'"

"Longer," said Figueroa.

"To be honest, I'm not sure they'd ever approve it. It's been over a decade since the FBI botched things up at Waco and got seventy-four hostages killed along with David Koresh, and even longer since the shootings at Ruby Ridge. Those events live on, and the FBI worries about its image. I'm sure there are plenty of people here in Miami who will never forget the midnight raid that sent Elián Gonzalez back to Cuba. With this hostage crisis unfolding live on television, an exit plan with this kind of finality is bound to die from an acute case of paralysis through analysis as it works its way up the chain of command."

Figueroa considered it, but not for long. "There has to be precise coordination. The instant my men make the breach, the power has to be cut off. Or at least the broadcast has to be killed. The MDPD may not be as image conscious as the FBI, but I don't want a take-down on television either."

"So you're up to the task?"

Figueroa was deadpan. "I need to clear it with my director."

Madera shook his head. "If you go up in your department, I might as well call in the FBI. You're the MDPD crisis team leader. This is a crisis of national significance. Find some balls."

Figueroa drew a breath, his chest rising. "All right," he said. "We're in."

Chapter 48

Things were quiet in the mobile command center. Too quiet.

Andie had been staring at the television screen too long. If Demetri was striving for must-see TV, he was failing miserably. The single camera was aimed at Jack and the anchorwoman, who could do nothing but wait quietly and try not to freak out. Demetri was somewhere off to the side, out of view. Long periods of silence gave the *Action News* commentators and guest analysts way too much time to fill. She tried not to listen to them. Her focus was on the hostages, and it suddenly struck her how unusual this situation was. Hostage negotiation rarely depended so much on sight. In fact, one of the City of Miami's finest, Vincent Paulo, was blind. For the first time in her entire career, Andie was able to see the people she was trying to save. In some ways it was an advantage. At least she knew they were alive. But being able to see into their eyes, to watch the ever-growing worries on their faces from one moment to the next, more than canceled out any advantage. That constant reminder on the television screen only seemed to emphasize the fact that their fate depended entirely on her next choice of words.

The fact that one of the lives hanging in the balance was Jack's upped the stakes beyond measure.

Andie stepped outside for some air.

A circle of squad cars was still stationed around the *Action News* studio, but the uniformed officers had downgraded from a state of readiness to a hunker-down-and-wait mode. It was a subtle difference in posture and demeanor, but it came like clockwork about two hours into every hostage standoff Andie had ever handled. Andie looked up at the stars and breathed in the cool night air. A helicopter whirred above the edge of the crowd-control perimeter, and she was relieved to see that police air coverage had replaced the media choppers. A spotlight swept the strip mall at the western edge of containment, and Andie noticed snipers on the rooftops. They were well within range of the studio. She knew the position of all the FBI snipers. These were not FBI.

Andie checked her cell phone. Still no return call from Jack's father. She wondered if he'd gotten her messages. Andie was big on vibes, and she didn't like the one she was getting at the moment. It had been almost an hour since Figueroa had last stopped by the FBI mobile command center to tell her "I told you so, I knew you'd get nowhere in negotiations." She sensed that something was afoot, and that she wasn't part of it.

She was about to dial Harry's cell again when a car door slammed and Guy Schwartz stepped out.

"Good news and bad news," he said as he approached.

An ASAC spending this much time on-site wasn't the norm, but this was a standoff with some very long tentacles, ones that reached all the way back to Washington. Schwartz was showing every intention of remaining hands-on from start to finish.

"Okay, I'll bite," said Andie. "What's the good news?"

"We have approval to deliver five hundred thousand dollars in marked bills to Demetri."

"Can it be here before the six A.M. deadline he gave us?"

"That's the bad news. He specified old bills, not new bills. That makes it impractical to track by serial numbers. Only reliable way to mark it is with fluorescent ink, and we don't keep half a million dollars sitting around, premarked."

"What am I supposed to tell him? Headquarters is concerned that there's a one-in-a-million chance that he might actually escape with the money after we deliver it to him, so we need more time to mark the bills?"

"It's Sunday morning. You need to make him understand that we need additional time to pull that much cash together."

"How much additional time?"

"Keep it open-ended."

Andie shook her head and said, "I worry about this."

Schwartz took a half step closer, showing his concern. "Are you okay?" he said.

"Yes. Why?"

"I shouldn't have to tell a Quantico-trained negotiator that you don't let the hostage taker set the timetable, that you never agree to deadlines. I'm beginning to think that your initial reluctance to get involved has some validity. Maybe you are too personally invested to exercise proper judgment."

"Jack is not the issue," she said.

"Are you sure?"

"Yes. My concerns are based solely on maintaining credibility as a negotiator. Demetri is holding the future vice president's son hostage, he's broadcasting the whole thing live on television, and he must be thinking that he's dealing directly with the president. He isn't going to accept an excuse as lame as 'Sorry, the bank is closed.'"

"Then lower his expectations. You have to convince him that the president isn't watching and doesn't care. Television or not, you can't let him believe for a minute that he has a direct line to the White House."

Tires screeched as a Florida highway patrol car flew around the perimeter-control barricade and cut toward the mobile command center. The brakes grabbed, and the front bumper nearly kissed the pavement as the car came to an abrupt halt just a few feet away from Andie. The trooper jumped out of the car, and the single gold bar on his uniform told Andie that he was a lieutenant.

"I just got word that Air Force One touched down at Miami International."

Schwartz said, "That's not possible. There's no way Air Force One would fly into Miami without the FBI knowing about it."

"Well, maybe the rest of the FBI just didn't bother to tell you folks. All I know is that I have to take about half my troopers and my entire tactical response unit off this site to assist with the motorcade."

"Is the president on board?" said Andie.

"That's what I'm told," said the lieutenant. "Harry Swyteck is with him."

"How do you know that?" said Schwartz.

"That part was on the news."

"The news?" said Schwartz.

Andie raced inside the command center and checked the television monitor. Jack and the anchorwoman were still on the left side of the *Action News* split screen. But sure enough, Air Force One was on the other side. The banner below it read, PRESIDENT AND V.P. NOMINEE LAND IN MIAMI.

Schwartz came up behind her, and Andie's heart sank.

"So much for convincing Demetri that the president isn't watching."

"The hell with that," said Schwartz. "I wasn't just puffing my rank when I said Air Force One couldn't land in Miami without me knowing about it."

"So what do you make of that?"

"I want to know who's keeping you and me out of the loop," he said. "And why."

Andie paused. Thursday's telephone conversation with Stan White, the ASAC from the Washington field office, was replaying in her mind—when he told her "there is something you need to understand about

Harry Swyteck." It suddenly made perfect sense to her that Miami was "out of the loop," so to speak.

"Were you about to say something?" said Schwartz.

Again she paused. If Schwartz didn't know what Washington knew about Harry, it wasn't her place to tell him.

"No," said Andie. "I wasn't going to say anything."

Chapter 49

"*Yesssss!*" said Demetri, clenching his fist like a tennis star who'd served an ace.

Jack glanced across the news set to see him standing in front of the flat-screen television mounted on the wall.

Shannon leaned closer to Jack and whispered, "Is that Air Force One?"

The television was a good forty feet away, too far for Jack to read the news banner at the bottom. But the red, white, and blue Boeing 747 was unmistakable.

"It sure is," said Jack.

"Do you see that?" said Demetri, as he stepped toward his hostages. "You see how seriously they are taking this?"

Shannon whispered, "He's delusional."

Jack knew that he wasn't, but he didn't argue with her.

Every half hour or so, Demetri had been doing fifty push-ups at a time to keep alert as the night wore one, and he definitely had renewed energy in his step as he crossed the set and looked into the camera.

"All you doubters out there who have been watching on your televisions at home, do you understand how important this is? How important *I* am? The president of the United States has just landed. Do you think he flies into Miami at"—he checked his watch—"two thirty on a Sunday morning for just any old reason?"

Shannon said, "If he thinks the president flew down here to negotiate with him, we're in bigger trouble than I thought."

"Just don't panic," said Jack.

Demetri's television address was gaining momentum, his excitement growing. "*Now* we are seeing some action!"

Shannon leaned closer and whispered, "I have a nail file."

"What?" said Jack. He was trying to hear Demetri talk.

"It's the metal kind with the pointy tip, like a knife. I found it in the bathroom and hid it in my hair."

Jack checked her hairdo. It was full enough to hide a machete.

Shannon said, "All we have to do is get Pedro to step out from behind the camera and come over here. He can take it from me and then he can—" She paused, as if it were difficult for her to speak of such things. "Pedro can slit his throat."

"That's a suicide mission."

"You got a better idea?"

Jack's gaze swept toward Demetri, who was still speaking to his television audience.

"A word of warning," said Demetri, almost shouting with renewed energy. "If sending down Air Force One is part of a strategy to stall, I got no sense of humor for it. That money—all five hundred thousand dollars—still needs to be here at six A.M., period. No extensions."

Jack whispered, "Okay, let's assume we can get Pedro over here and that he can get it out of your hair without Demetri noticing. Do you have any idea how hard it is to overtake an armed man and slit his throat with a nail file?"

"No, do you?"

"It's hard," said Jack.

"But not impossible?"

Jack's thoughts suddenly flashed back to Eddie Goss, a former client on death row who had decapitated one of his victims with nothing more than brute strength and a nylon stocking.

"No," said Jack. "Not impossible."

"Then we have a plan. You got a problem with that?"

Jack glanced again at the Greek. He was down doing push-ups again, this time for the television audience.

"Is Pedro a former navy SEAL?"

"No," she said.

"Green Beret?"

"Pedro? Heck no."

"Then yeah," said Jack. "I got a big problem with that."

As the ground crew tended to Air Force One, Harry ducked into the bathroom and placed another call to his FBI contact.

Supervisory agent Glenn Perkins had told Harry to call whenever he wanted an update, and Harry was more than taking him at his word. Perkins was head of the FBI's Critical Incident Response Group in Quantico, and for this standoff, the Miami negotiators—including Andie—reported to him. No decision to pull the negotiators and send in the SWAT could be made without Perkins's approval.

"What's the latest?" said Harry.

"You saw the same thing I saw on the TV," said Perkins. "It's what I cautioned about before you boarded the plane: bringing you and the president down to Miami would only embolden him."

"Andie should call him again."

"With all due respect, sir, you're micromanaging."

"That's my son in that newsroom."

"All the more reason not to micromanage."

"I should give Andie a call."

"Governor, I'm urging you not to do that. Agent Henning was not my first choice, not because she isn't qualified, but for the same personal reasons I worry about you getting too close to this. I agreed to put her in as lead negotiator, but you promised to stand clear."

"I have four voice mails from her on my cell. I should at least return the call and tell her I'm behind her."

"I'm expecting an update from her in five minutes. I'd be happy to tell her for you. I hope I'm not being too blunt, but the last thing she needs is the pressure of you breathing directly down her neck."

Harry grumbled into the phone, nervously picking at the Air Force One bar of bathroom soap with his fingernail. "I feel so useless."

Perkins said, "There is one thing you can do to help."

"Name it."

"Ask the president to power up Air Force One and fly you right back to Washington."

"That's ridiculous."

"Sir, we went over this before, but now that you've seen the gunman's reaction on television, maybe you'll understand my position. The next time Demetri makes a demand, Agent Henning needs to be able to buy time and tell him that she has to check with her superiors. If he knows that you're in town with the president, he's going to expect and demand immediate answers."

Harry considered it, picking even more furiously at the bar of Air Force One soap.

"It's basic negotiation 101," Perkins continued. "In fact, I use Jimmy Carter as a case study for training here at Quantico. Back in the seventies, he offered to intervene in a hostage standoff and accede to a gunman's demand to speak to the president. The bureau couldn't have been any quicker or clearer in its response: 'Thanks, but no thanks, Mr. President.'"

"I understand your point," said Harry.

"Good. Then you'll do it?"

"Maybe I can disembark in secret, and I'll get the president to fly back without me."

"Not a good plan," said Perkins. "It's best that you stay with the president."

"I need to stay near my son."

"Sir, that is a totally understandable feeling, but there is nothing you can do to resolve this standoff. In fact, there is nothing President Keyes can do, either. My advice is to stay with the president and help him understand that. Most important of all, make sure he doesn't pull a Jimmy Carter, try to intervene, and get somebody hurt."

The bar of bathroom soap was almost entirely a pile of white flakes, and Harry was still a bundle of nerves.

"All right," he said. "I'll stay with the president. But I'm not leaving my son."

Chapter 50

It was officially "last call" at Sparky's Tavern, and Theo was wiping down the cracked linoleum bar top.

The band had packed up at 2:00 A.M., but the tavern was emptying out slowly. Theo had started the night at Cy's Place, his jazz club where music was the priority. The typical crowd at Sparky's would rather line-dance to "The Electric Slide" than listen to Duke Ellington reincarnated. It had been a good night, nonetheless, and it was winding down to the usual suspects: a handful of regulars and some Keys-bound college kids who'd challenged a couple of bikers to a game of eight ball. Not smart. They'd lost their shirts. Literally, they were stripped down to their waists. If it didn't end soon, they'd be walking out stark naked.

"You're cute," said the leggy blonde on the bar stool.

Theo hadn't arrived till 1:00 A.M., and by his count she was on her third martini. He had no intention of serving her a fourth.

"Cute?" said Theo as he rinsed another beer glass in the sink. "I don't think so."

"I'm Mia," she said. "Mia from Miami."

Theo smiled and shook her hand. "Now that's cute."

"My ex-husband's name is Phil. He was from Phila-delphia. Mia from Miami, and Phil from Philadelphia. Isn't that too funny?"

"Funny, yeah," said Theo.

"Where you from, hon?"

"Never-bed-the-last-chick-in-the-bar . . . berg."

"What?" she said, smiling as if she wasn't quite sure she should be.

"It's a little town in Sweden near—ah, never mind."

She tried to rest her elbow on the bar and missed. "Hey," she said, regaining her balance. "Do you ever watch anything but ESPN here?"

Theo glanced up at the TV behind him. "Nope."

"How many times do we have to see the same high-lights?"

They were showing the Ohio State Buckeyes' game-winning goal-line stand—for the fifth time of the night. Theo grabbed the remote and scrolled down quickly through the cable news channels. He soon realized that they all had the same coverage, and when he finally stopped surfing to check out the "breaking story," his mouth fell open.

"Jack?" he said.

"You know that guy?"

Theo ignored her and turned up the volume to hear the live update from outside the studio.

"We are now well into our third hour of a tense hostage crisis here at *Action News* studio," the reporter said.

Theo stepped closer to the television, not quite believing, as the report continued. Jack and another hostage, whom Theo recognized as the *Action News* anchor, were on the left side of the split screen, their hands tied behind their backs. On the right side, a camera outside the studio was zooming in on what appeared to be Jack's demolished Mustang in the rubble.

"Not the 'stang," said Theo.

"More on this story," said the newscaster, "after this commercial break."

Theo checked his cell. There was a call from Andie just before midnight that he'd missed. He speed-dialed a return call, but it went to her voice mail. He left a quick message, and the time flashed on his phone:

2:52 A.M. Not quite closing time, but close enough. He rounded people up, starting with Mia from Miami, and herded them toward the door.

"That's it folks, we're locking up."

A few grumbled, but even first-timers at Sparky's seemed to grasp that when Theo Knight said it was time to go, you went.

"Call me," said Mia on her way out the door.

"Sure thing," said Theo.

He pushed the last customer out, locked the door, and ran to the back office. His uncle was sound asleep on the couch, snoring like a grizzly bear. Theo shook him till he woke.

"Cy, I need your help."

His eyes blinked open, but he was still half asleep.

"Jack's in trouble," said Theo.

Cy yawned into his fist. "What else is new?"

"I'm serious. I need you to close up for me."

"Tonight?"

"Yes! Can you do it?"

Another yawn. "Yeah. I guess so."

Theo grabbed his car keys and ran from the room before Cy could change his mind. He went out the front, locked it with his extra key, and started toward the parking lot. A voice in the darkness stopped him in his tracks.

"Mr. Knight?"

It was a woman's voice, definitely not Mia from Miami. He turned, but it was too dark to see anything but a silhouette.

"Who are you?"

She stepped out from the shadows, and the face fit the voice—that of an older woman.

"My name is Sofia," she said, "and I want to help your friend."

Chapter 51

The television screen closest to Jack suddenly went gray.

The news set remained lit, and the ceiling lights and computer monitors still glowed in the newsroom. But each of the half dozen flat-screen televisions mounted on the walls throughout the newsroom was without a picture, and the audio was silent, as if someone had literally pulled the plug on the broadcast.

"What's happening?" shouted Demetri.

It wasn't clear whether he was talking to someone or thinking aloud. His gaze quickly swept the newsroom—up into the open catwalks above the lights, then across the newsroom to the barricaded doors. He walked completely around the news desk, then over to the weather set, then back to the sports desk. It was purely adrenaline-driven motion—short spurts of energy and panic that put the hostages even more on edge.

"I said what's going on!"

"I have no idea," said Pedro.

Jack cringed at the sound of Pedro's voice, knowing that all of the hostages would have been better off to remain silent and let Demetri vent.

Demetri hurried toward the cameraman, almost frantic in his approach, and pressed the muzzle of his pistol up under Pedro's chin.

"What did you do?"

Pedro went white, fumbling for a response. As far as Jack could tell, the camera appeared to have electrical power, and Pedro looked as befuddled as anyone as to the cause of the interrupted broadcast.

"I didn't do anything," said Pedro.

"Fix it!"

"I—I don't know what happened."

Demetri whacked him in the head with the butt of his gun, knocking Pedro to his knees.

"I said *fix it!*"

Blood ran from the gash above Pedro's eye, and the left side of his face was quickly streaked with crimson rivulets that ran to his chin and dripped onto the floor. Pedro didn't answer, either too stunned or too scared to speak.

Jack leaned closer to Shannon and said, "Did you two somehow cook up a plan with the camera?"

"No," she whispered. "I don't know what's going on either."

"Fix the damn camera!" said Demetri. Another swift kick to Pedro's ribs left him flat on the floor.

"Stop!" Jack shouted.

Demetri ignored him, or perhaps he was too enraged to hear Jack's voice. He was suddenly caught up in destroying Pedro, as if each and every setback of the night mandated its own blow to the defenseless man's torso.

"Stop, or you're going to kill him!" said Jack.

A telephone rang in the newsroom, and Demetri froze. It was the same phone that Andie had called on earlier. Slowly, Demetri seemed to pull himself together long enough to process things. A final kick to the kidney elicited a deep groan from Pedro. Then Demetri went to the phone and snatched it up, his voice filled with contempt.

"What the hell are you trying to pull?" he said, his voice booming throughout the newsroom.

Andie bristled, not sure what to make of Demetri's accusation. She adjusted her headset and spoke into the microphone from her command center.

"We have a little situation here," she said. "I need you to take a deep breath and calm down, all right?"

"Get me back on the air—*now!*"

"I was about to tell you the same thing," said Andie.

"Don't mess with me. Get this show back on television, or the blood of one of these hostages is on your hands."

Andie glanced at Guy Schwartz, who was seated beside her and listening to every word. The initial word from their technical unit was that the cause of the broadcast interruption was internal, not of the FBI's doing. Schwartz scribbled a quick note on a scrap of paper and slid it toward her.

SWAT, it read.

"Demetri, listen to me," said Andie.

She exchanged another glance with Schwartz, making sure that he wanted to go this route. He took back the note and double-underlined the word *SWAT.* The message was clear.

Andie said, "I am being totally straight here, Demetri. I told you before that there is a tactical team on-site. SWAT is ready to bust down the door if you don't turn the cameras back on."

"Aren't you listening, damn it? It wasn't me who turned them off!"

"It wasn't me, either," said Andie. "Obviously we have some kind of technical difficulty beyond our control."

"Oh, what bullshit! I knew you were a liar, I absolutely knew it."

"I'm being totally honest with you, Demetri."

"I'm not going to listen to your excuses."

"Wait, *wait*," said Andie.

"Wait for what? More lies?"

"I'm telling you the truth. Come on, you're a very smart man, Demetri. Think about it this way: Why would I *not* want a camera inside the newsroom with you? My biggest concern is the safety of you and those hostages. If those cameras aren't rolling, I have no way of knowing if anyone is hurt or not."

There was silence on the line, and instinct told Andie that her point was registering.

"Doesn't that make sense, Demetri?"

He didn't answer, but he didn't hang up, either. She was definitely getting through to him.

"Okay, I'll tell you what," said Andie. "We are going to do our best to fix this problem. But you have to stay on the line with me until you're back on the air. If you hang up before that happens, SWAT will move in. That is not a threat. I don't want that to happen, but if you break off contact now, I won't be able to stop them. That's just the way it is."

He still didn't speak, but Andie heard a cross between a grunt and a shriek, and she envisioned him pulling his hair out in frustration.

"You think you can take control away from me?" he said. "Is that it? Because if that is what's going through your head, you need to give it up right now."

"You have to trust me on this," said Andie. "It's not about control. I'm just trying to keep everyone on an even keel here. I can't do that if you hang up on me. Just stay on the line till we figure out what happened."

"I need to be on the air."

"Like I said, we are going to do our best to make that happen."

"You got ten minutes," he said, and she could hear the anger in his voice. "Or Swyteck is the first to die."

Chapter 52

President Keyes gripped the telephone tightly, biting back his anger. Harry Swyteck was still in the bathroom, leaving the president alone in the executive suite of Air Force One. But if Agent Madera had been there with him, the president probably would have slugged him.

"Who do you think you're talking to, Frank?"

"The better question is who am I talking *for.*"

Like so many times before, the president held his tongue. Even though he was speaking on his encrypted personal phone line, he feared the mere mention of the name Joseph Dinitalia.

"I'm fed up with this," said the president.

"It will be over before dawn."

"I don't mean the standoff. I mean this whole . . . arrangement."

"It's not going to change."

"I'm sick and tired of you telling me what to do."

"That's not going to change either."

"Did you hear what I said? I'm tired of it."

Madera scoffed. "Do you think you're the first politician in history to feel this way?"

"I think—"

"We don't care what you think," said Madera. "Listen to me. You need to assert yourself with the Critical Incident Response Group. Go straight to the director if you have to. No FBI SWAT. Get Swyteck's father to sing the same chant."

"I thought we wanted SWAT to go in."

"Not ours. If the FBI unleashes its own SWAT, there is no guarantee that they'll make the kill. I have the local SWAT on board. You need to rein in the FBI and make way for the Miami-Dade police."

Keyes considered it, then answered in a firm voice. "No."

"Excuse me?"

"I'm not going to do it."

Madera said, "I can't let FBI SWAT go in. I need a guaranteed kill shot."

"That's not my problem."

"Yes, it is. I convinced MDPD to shut down the broadcast. Now, the FBI thinks he's going to hurt the hostages. If you don't rein them in, the only way to keep FBI SWAT from busting down the doors is for MDPD to put the Greek back on the air. And if that happens, there's no telling what he might say."

"I'm not going to strong-arm the FBI or do anything else that might put Harry's son at risk. That's where I draw the line."

"That's funny, because you sure seemed willing to draw the line differently when it came to Phil Grayson."

"I'm going to ignore that," said the president. "You're on your own this time."

"I'm losing my patience."

"Join the club."

"You've picked the wrong time to find a backbone."

The president walked around to the other side of his desk, where there was a framed photograph of his mother and father looking back at him.

"Like I told you, Frank," he said as he stepped toward the door, "I'm tired of you and everyone else telling me what to do. That's the last I have to say about it."

The door to the executive suite opened, giving Harry a start. The president hung up his phone.

"How long have you been standing there?" said the president.

"Not long."

The president seemed unconvinced, but he stepped aside, allowed Harry to enter, and closed the door. He directed Harry to sit, which he did.

"Let me ask you again," said the president. "How long were you standing out there?"

Harry shrugged. "Maybe a minute."

The president walked behind his desk and took a seat. He looked directly at Harry but said nothing for about sixty seconds, as if to make his point. Finally, he said, "A minute can be a very long time."

"Long enough, I suppose," said Harry.

The president leaned forward, his hands folded on top of the desk. "Long enough for what?"

Harry also leaned forward in his chair—just enough to convey that he was not intimidated. Harry said, "Long enough to know that you were on the telephone with Frank Madera."

The president tightened his glare, but Harry didn't flinch.

"You said something about being tired," said Harry. "And it had nothing to do with being sleepy."

"Look, I don't know what you think you heard, but things are not always as they seem."

"You can say that again."

The president was silent.

Harry said, "There's something I want you to know, Mr. President."

"Tell me."

"I know so much more than you realize. Everyone from Marilyn Grayson to this Demetri character has pumped me full of suspicions."

"Well, you're wrong if you think for one minute that—"

"Please," said Harry, halting him, "let me finish. There's something else you need to know."

Harry leaned closer still, resting his forearms on the edge of the president's desk.

"I don't give a rat's ass about any of it. All I want is to get my son out of that newsroom alive. So I need you to tell me the truth. The whole ugly, stinking truth."

Chapter 53

Jack felt Shannon's body press against his. They were still seated on the floor in front of the news desk, and the cameraman was there, too. Pedro lay on his side next to Jack, coiled in the fetal position, recovering from the beating. He was so out of it that Demetri hadn't even bothered to bind his wrists.

"Do you see it?" Shannon whispered.

She nuzzled against his chest, pretending to be asleep. Jack lowered his eyes. Tucked into her hair, the pointed metal nail file glistened beneath the studio lights.

"Yes," he whispered back.

"Get it to Pedro," she said.

Jack glanced to his right. Pedro was conscious but grimacing in pain. "He's no help," said Jack.

"Then cut yourself loose with it," she whispered.

It was a huge long shot, but fighting back seemed like their only option now, with Demetri at T-minus-ten-minutes to either going back on the air or killing his first hostage. Shannon leaned closer, and slowly Jack worked his jaw deep into Shannon's big hair. It was sticky with a television dosage of extra-hold hair spray, and it smelled of tangerines or some other citrus-scented shampoo. Jack kept one eye on Demetri, who was across the set and sitting by the phone with Andie on speaker. The volume was high enough for Jack to hear her voice.

"Keep talking to me, Demetri," said Andie.

Jack felt the metal file against his chin. He tightened his jaw and tried to slide it out, but it didn't budge.

"Can't get it," he whispered, and in that same instant, he wondered what he would do with it even if he got it. Cut himself loose—and then what? Strangle Demetri with his bare hands? Sneak up and slice open the jugular? Jab it into his eye orbit? Shove it into his ear? Those were bizarre thoughts for a lawyer to have, especially when up against a seasoned killer who had barely lost a step despite his age and injuries.

"Use your teeth," Shannon whispered.

Jack tucked his jaw and tried to clench it, but Shannon had buried it so securely that not even a badger could have chewed it loose. Jack went for the lion-sized bite.

"Ow!" said Shannon, as the nail file fell to the floor behind her.

"Swyteck!" shouted Demetri.

Jack started, his heart pounding, and Shannon jerked away from him.

"How much time is left?" Demetri said.

Jack could breathe again. For a moment, he'd thought Demetri had noticed that they were plotting something. Jack checked the clock on the wall.

"Eight minutes," said Jack.

"Liar," said Demetri, and then he addressed Andie on the speakerphone. "By my count, you're down to six minutes to get me back on the air, Henning."

"We might need more time," said Andie.

"You're not gonna get it."

"Saying things like that only makes it harder for me to keep the SWAT out of this."

"That's why you get paid the big bucks," said Demetri.

Jack felt the nail file sticking him in the thumb. Shannon had it in her hands behind her back and passed it to him. Jack grasped it and worked it around in his fingers until the tip pointed to the knotted cord that bound his wrists.

Andie was still talking on the speakerphone. "You have to keep working with me, Demetri. It would help matters on this end if I could hear the hostages' voices."

"You just heard your boyfriend. We're on speaker."

"You must be too far away from him. I couldn't pick up his voice. That makes everyone on this end of the line nervous. They wonder if the hostages are okay. Come on, Demetri. Work with me. I'm busting my butt over here trying to get you back on the air. The least you can do is let me hear their voices."

Jack worked faster, jabbing the nail file at the knot.

Demetri said nothing, thinking. Then he rose and walked toward the hostages, the phone wire trailing behind him. Fully extended, it was plenty long to reach across the set.

Jack's heart sank. He knew what Andie was doing, but her timing wasn't good. *So much for cutting myself loose.*

Demetri put the phone on the news desk and said, "I'll give you one hostage a minute for the next three minutes. Ladies first. Say something, news lady."

Shannon looked up, as if caught off guard.

"Come on," said Demetri. "I know you bubbleheads like a script, but we don't have one. Say whatever you want."

"I love you, Jeff," she said.

"Aww, isn't that sweet?" said Demetri. "Will Jack Swyteck say the same to his girlfriend? Will Agent Henning think he's just being a copycat if he does? Will she think he's a schmuck if he doesn't? We'll find out in exactly sixty seconds. Damn, this is good televi-sion. Turn the fucking cameras on!"

Andie read the handwritten message from Guy Schwartz in front of her: *He's losing it.*

Andie worried that her supervisor might be right.

"Demetri, I know it's late, and you must be getting tired. Maybe even a little punchy. But this is no time to lose focus. This isn't a game. Don't act as if it is."

"Are you lecturing me?"

"I just want us to keep working together, Demetri."

"You keep saying that. Is that the only line they teach you at hostage negotiation school? And stop saying my name over and over again, like we're a couple of old drinking buddies. Do they teach you to do that, too?"

Andie checked the text message on the computer screen in front of her. It was from the SWAT unit leader.

Team in position, it read.

Andie spoke into her headset. "Isn't it about time to hear from another hostage, Demetri?"

"I told you to stop saying my name!"

"I need to hear from another hostage," she said as she typed out a response to SWAT: *Hold your position.*

Demetri said, "I'm not giving you another hostage."

"That's not smart," said Andie. "We had a deal."

"No," he said. "A deal is where I give you something, and you give me something in return. I already let you hear from the anchorwoman. Now get me back on the air."

She checked another computer message, this time from the technical unit, which was working to restore the *Action News* transmission.

Need ten minutes, it read.

"Demetri, I need more time to get you back on the air," said Andie.

"You've got four minutes, by my clock."

"Give me ten, and I'll send in food."

"Not hungry."

"You must be."

"I said *not hungry*."

"Demetri, be reasonable."

"Three minutes and counting down," he said.

Another message from SWAT: *Condition yellow.* Green would be next, which was the breach.

Hold, she typed back to SWAT.

"False deadlines are a bad idea, Demetri."

"This one isn't false. I'm putting the gun to your boyfriend's pretty head right now."

That made her throat tighten. A SWAT breach now would be a disaster, but she put that out of her head and forced herself to negotiate.

"Deal with me, Demetri."

"Make me another offer," he said.

"I won't bid against myself. Take the food, give me ten minutes."

"You need to do better than food."

"How much better?"

"I want to talk to the president."

"What?"

SWAT messaged her again: *Thirty seconds to green.*

Demetri said, "I saw Air Force One on TV. I know he's at the airport. I want to talk to him."

"That's not going to happen," she said.

Fifteen seconds, SWAT wrote.

"Tic-toc," said Demetri.

"Give me ten more minutes, Demetri. Just say yes."

Green in ten.

The television screen flickered in the command center, and Andie typed a quick message to SWAT: *HOLD!*

"What's happening?" said Demetri.

Green in five—

The television screen brightened, and the *Action News* broadcast from the news set was back on the air.

Abort breach, Andie typed to SWAT.

"Are we back?" said Demetri.

Roger, was the response from SWAT.

"Yes," Andie told him, breathing out. "Thank God."

"Nice work," said Demetri. "Two minutes to spare."

More like two seconds, thought Andie. "We aim to please," she said.

"Then get me President Keyes on the line."

"I can't promise you that will happen," said Andie.

"You don't have to," said Demetri. "I have every confidence that he heard what I said. And this time, he knows I mean it."

The line clicked in her earpiece.

Chapter 54

Jack could see himself on the television screen. The *Action News* camera hadn't moved since the transmission outage, and it was still aimed at him and Shannon. Same image, with one major difference: Jack looked scared to death.

"You're a lucky boy," said Demetri as he pulled the gun away from Jack's scalp.

Jack breathed out. He'd heard of mock executions, terrorists putting a gun to the back of a prisoner's head and pulling the trigger with the chamber empty. Jack hadn't been pushed to that point, but he'd been close enough to understand how it made people crack.

Demetri turned his back to the hostages and stepped toward the camera. Jack's gaze followed him, and then he glanced over to the TV screen. The cameraman was still on the floor beside Jack, but he wasn't in the television shot. Lucky for Demetri. If Andie saw that bloody face on television, SWAT would be busting down the door.

"I want to welcome our television viewers back to the show," said Demetri, "but I don't think we'll be having these technical difficulties again. The bad news is that our most compelling episode so far happened while we were off the air. But there's some good news. We will be offering the entire block of missing footage as a bonus feature on the DVD edition of *Action News Standoff*, the first and only season, to be released this spring."

"He's snapped," Shannon whispered. "You have *got* to get us out of here."

Jack clenched the nail file and picked furiously at the knot behind his back. It was hard to tell, but he felt as though he might be making progress. He worked the file around to another angle, then accidentally jabbed himself in the wrist, and he had to bite his lip to keep from crying out in pain.

Demetri turned his back to the camera and faced the hostages.

"What was that face for, Swyteck?"

Jack felt hot blood trickling down from his puncture wound to his fingertips. It hurt like hell.

"I didn't make a face."

"Don't lie to me. I saw you on the television screen, right behind me. You better not be trying to throw signals at someone."

Jack was about to deny it, then reconsidered. He didn't know what the punishment would be for throwing signals, but it had to be a lesser offense than trying to pick himself free with a nail file.

"Sorry. It won't happen again."

"Make sure of it," said Demetri.

The television screen flickered, and Jack thought for a moment that they might be going off the air again. *Action News* was simply resuming its split screen broadcast. This time, however, it was a different reporter with a live update from just outside the traffic-control perimeter.

"This is Haley Vacaro, *Action News*. I'm standing about a mile from the *Action News* studio, which is now as close as police will allow traffic to approach on Frontage Road. Police have actually set up a second perimeter of traffic control here to prevent the crowd around the studio from swelling to an unmanageable level. With me is a close friend of Jack Swyteck, one of the three hostages. Sir, if you could step right over here, please, and give us your name one more time."

"Theo Knight."

Jack's jaw dropped, but that was definitely the one and only Theo Knight on television, wearing a T-shirt that read BRINGBACKPORN.COM.

"Mr. Knight, how is it that you know Jack Swyteck?"

"Jack's a dude, man. He was my lawyer when I was on death row, and we been hangin' ever since. No pun intended."

The reporter stepped away. "Well, obviously this is someone's idea of a joke, and I apologize to our viewers for—"

"It's true," said Theo as he stepped back into the picture. "Look at this," he said, holding up a key.

"What is that?"

"A key to a 1968 Mustang GT-390 Fastback. That's the green car that crashed through the front door to your studio. I was with Jack when he bought it, and I kept the extra key."

You kept my damn key? thought Jack. He'd been looking for the spare.

The reporter put a finger to her earpiece to receive a message. Whatever her producer was telling her, it seemed to satisfy her.

"All right, Mr. Knight. What can you tell us about this hostage standoff? Any idea what it might be all about?"

"I really couldn't tell you, but I have someone with me who definitely knows the story. Her name is Sofia, and she used to be married to that dude with the gun inside the studio."

The reporter's eyes lit up, as she'd just hit the jackpot.

Demetri screamed at the top of his lungs, *"Nooooo!"*

Jack understood the Greek's reaction immediately, but he also realized that Theo had no idea how much danger he was putting Sofia in.

Demetri moved faster than Jack had ever seen him move as he cut across the set, grabbed the phone, and punched star-69 to get the FBI command center. He shouted his demand in a voice that was more than loud enough for Jack to hear.

"Henning, get Sofia protection, or all bets are off! Do you hear what I'm saying? The same thugs that want me dead also want her dead. You get her some protection right now!"

Agent Frank Madera was in a conference room inside the *Action News* complex. The business-office wing was a new two-story building that ran perpendicular to the studio, and at Madera's suggestion, Sergeant Figueroa had moved the Miami-Dade SWAT unit there from the coffee shop. It would serve as their staging platform into the newsroom—partly for logistical reasons, but mostly because it was on the opposite side of the building from the FBI SWAT staging area.

The tactical team was suited up in black gear and ready to deploy, eight contemplative men leaning against the wall in silence. A ceiling-mounted television in the corner was tuned to *Action News*, keeping them apprised in real time. Madera stood at the head of the conference table, an architect's blueprint of the newsroom spread out before him. At his side was Officer Sam Reed, MDPD's top-rated sniper.

"You'll move in through the main air-conditioning duct," said Madera, pointing to the blueprint. "There's a large intake vent here, which provides access to the catwalk over the newsroom."

"I wouldn't be surprised if the perp has already sealed off the A-C vents," said Reed.

"You'll need to be careful," said Figueroa. "He did say in his first communication that he had a surprise for anyone who tried to come in through the A-C ducts."

"If it's impassable, radio us," said Madera. "Sergeant Figueroa will have to waive off the sniper shot and breach with his tactical team."

"Got it," said Reed.

Figueroa said, "What's the likelihood of success on a shot from up there?"

Reed processed it aloud, his mind a human calculator of angles, percentages, and timing. "Subject on an open news set. Distance about a hundred feet.

Possible obstructions—lighting fixtures, hanging cameras, other equipment. Elevated shooting platform should have only minimal adverse impact on bullet trajectory. No wind or other elements to worry about. If that vent isn't blocked, I'd say we're looking above the ninety-ninth percentile."

"For a kill shot?" said Madera.

"T-zone," said Reed.

A shot to the T-zone—the imaginary area that covered a person's eyes and nose—was exactly what Madera wanted. It shut a man down like the flip of a light switch, no reaction.

Madera said, "SWAT will breach at the crack of sniper fire. If for some unknown reason the head shot doesn't take him out, the team does."

"Roger," said Figueroa.

Madera turned to address the tactical team as a group.

"Gentlemen, I want to thank each of you for your willingness to serve in this crucial matter of national security. You heard the gunman's latest demand to speak to the president of the United States. While I cannot go into details, I can assure you that this latest demand is not just another delusional request from a crazy man. This subject has already shot and killed a security guard. He has nothing to lose by killing again, and he has no intention of releasing these hostages alive.

Most important, he has put himself on television for the sole purpose of compromising this country's vital national security interests. We've done everything we can to avoid loss of life, even literally pulling the plug on his television broadcast. The gunman's response was to guarantee the execution of a hostage if he did not get back on the air. Our only option was to resume broadcasting, but that concession cannot stand. Again, on behalf of the president, I thank you. I don't have to tell you what needs to be done. Each of you is a trained professional. You know the assignment."

"We do," said Figueroa.

"Good," said Madera. "Then let's get it done."

Madera checked the television for a quick update. It was a split screen, and an *Action News* reporter was interviewing a big, muscular black guy dressed in civilian clothes. Madera wasn't really focused on the interview, but even with divided attention he was able to pick up the important part.

"*. . . but I have someone with me who definitely knows the story. Her name is Sofia, and she used to be married to that dude with the gun inside the studio.*"

Madera nearly choked, and the scream he heard from Demetri over the television—"*Noooooo*"—was his sentiment exactly. His cell rang almost immediately, and he checked the number. It was not a call he could ignore.

"Team, hold your position," said Madera. He stepped out of the conference room and closed the door, making sure he was alone in the hallway. Joseph Dinitalia was on the line.

"You heard?"

"I'm on it," said Madera.

"We need them both out."

"I said I'm on it."

"You need help?"

"No. The Greek is all lined up."

"What about Sofia? Do I have to send someone?"

"You mean like the idiots last night with the machine gun who shot up everything but the Greek? Thanks, but no thanks."

"Then who's got the old lady?"

Madera drew a breath. "You know what they say: If you want something done right . . ."

"You got this one?"

"Send a couple men to help me look for her. But when we find her, then yeah," he said, "I got it."

Chapter 55

"Where the hell did she go?" said Theo.

A crowd of onlookers, some of them press, had gathered around the camera and lighting crew. The *Action News* reporter appeared on the verge of losing her patience.

"Mr. Knight, we are still on the air."

Theo looked out beyond the crowd, up and down the dimly lit parkway. A couple of stray dogs ran loose, and a homeless guy was pushing a shopping cart toward the overpass. Theo was in a neighborhood of two-bedroom ranch-style houses, each with five or six beat-up cars parked in the front yard—a family of four, as far as the U.S. Census Bureau was concerned; more like twelve or fifteen, if everyone had been accounted for. At four o'clock on a Sunday morning, many of them were either coming from or heading to a second or third job, which explained the crowd's steadily growing numbers.

Sofia was nowhere to be seen.

"She was standing right here a minute ago," Theo said into the microphone.

"I'm sure she was," said the reporter.

A squad car passed on the street.

"The cops must have spooked her," said Theo.

"This *is* live television, so perhaps you could tell us what she would say, if she were still here."

Theo ignored her. He was getting concerned.

"Mr. Knight, can you please—"

"Sofia!" he shouted, as he sprinted away. A woman was standing at the street corner a block away. She turned, saw him, and ran.

Definitely her.

Theo gave chase for about fifty yards, then thought better of it. He'd already seen one MDPD car cruise the area, and a former death row inmate chasing an elderly white woman down the street definitely wasn't cool. He walked briskly and kept an eye on her, confident that she would soon tire.

His cell rang. It was Andie.

"Finally, you return my call," he said.

"I've been a little busy. How was I to know you have the gunman's ex-wife with you?"

"You mean 'had,'" said Theo.

"Don't tell me she's gone."

He rose up on his toes and looked ahead. He spotted Sofia cutting across the parking lot in front of a convenience store. Her gait was short, as if the run had already given her a side stitch.

"Not gone," he said into his phone. "I got a bead on her right now."

"Where? I'll send a squad car to pick her up."

"Don't. She doesn't want to talk to the cops. I think that's why she snuck away from me in the first place."

"I need to get her under police protection. That's what Demetri wants."

"I'll call you when I catch up with her, all right? We'll go from there."

"I don't have time to waste."

"Let me handle this," said Theo. "Five minutes ago she was willing to go on television and ask Demetri to let the hostages go free. I'm not exactly sure why she doesn't want to go to the cops, but she doesn't. If you send a bunch of squad cars into the area, you can kiss her help good-bye."

"You don't understand," she said. "There are mob connections here. She wasn't running from the police. She's running for her life."

"I understand plenty," said Theo. "I'll call you in two minutes. Tops."

He closed his flip phone and started after Sofia, gaining ground quickly. Sofia was tiring. As Theo cut across the street, she checked over her shoulder, and their eyes met from a distance. He expected her to run, but she'd already blown through her second wind. She sat on the curb outside the entrance to the convenience store, and Theo caught up with her there.

"My friend Jack needs you," he said. "Why did you take off?"

She was still trying to catch her breath, and her response came out in bursts. "I—saw them."

"You mean the cop car?"

She shook her head, pausing to take another breath. "The black car."

"What black car?"

Her eyes widened with fear, as if she'd just seen death itself. "That one," she said as she jumped to her feet. "They want to kill me!"

Theo looked toward the street. A black sedan rolled past the entrance to the parking lot and then hit the brakes. The driver threw it into reverse, and the car backed up so fast that the tires squealed. Obviously, Sofia wasn't blowing smoke.

"It's them!"

Theo picked her up in his arms—he was at least double her weight—and ran inside the store. They ran past the cookies and knocked over a tray of snack cakes.

The sight of Theo moving that fast was enough to push the skinny white kid mopping the aisle to the brink of cardiac arrest.

"Don't hurt me!" he said as he dove behind the malt-liquor floor display.

Theo stopped, glanced back through the storefront window, and saw two men jumping out of the black car. Hiding was futile. He turned, Sofia still in his arms, and ran past the beer coolers into the stockroom.

"Hey, you can't go in there!" the cashier shouted.

Theo headed straight for the store's emergency exit in the back. The alarm sounded when he pushed the door open, and Sofia shrieked at the shrill noise. Theo carried her into the alley, not sure which way to go. It was a narrow block of barred doors and windows, the back entrances to restaurants, bars, and Laundromats that had closed hours earlier. The glow of high-voltage crime lights gave the night a yellowish tint. The alley was actually bright enough for Theo to read the graffiti on the walls—not a good thing, when you were trying to disappear. He sprinted to the left, past a mound of green garbage bags, past a pickup truck that had probably been there since the Clinton presidency. Thin as Sofia was, she was feeling heavy in his arms, and outrunning these goons was not a winning strategy.

Hide. Gotta hide.

He nearly blew past a narrow walkway between buildings, but he spotted it out of the corner of his eye and made a quick right turn into total darkness. The lone streetlamp in the side alley was burned out, and the passageway was so narrow that Theo had to be careful not to bump Sofia's head and feet against the walls of painted cinder block on either side. He went deeper and deeper into the darkness until he could walk no farther. A blind alley. He turned around, but backtracking was not an option. He could hear the echoes of footsteps— the men in pursuit—in the main alley.

"What now?" Sofia whispered.

Theo was breathing heavy and weighing his options. The business establishment at the very end of the alley was a mom-and-pop grocery story, and a nine-foot tower of crushed corrugated boxes was stacked up behind it. A fine hiding place—for pussies. The ten-foot mound of green garbage bags, filled with stinky rotten produce, was a much better choice.

"There," Theo whispered.

He made a beeline for the bags, Sofia in his arms, and they buried themselves beneath Mount Trashmore.

"What are—" Sofia started to say, but Theo shushed her.

Theo peered out from beneath the bags of trash and saw two silhouettes standing at the end of the

narrow alley, their black bodies backlit by the yellowish streetlights of the main alley. Sofia reached over
and held Theo's hand—Theo could feel hers shaking—
and they waited.

Then slowly, the silhouettes came walking toward
them, the click of leather heels echoing in the darkness.

Theo watched as they approached. It had taken all
this time for his eyes to adjust to the total darkness,
and the men's tentative steps told him that he would
have the advantage of night vision for a few minutes
more. He looked around quickly and found a box of re-
jected apples. The first two he handled were so rotten
that they turned to mush in his hands. He found one
that was still firm, and he grasped it like a baseball.

The sight of Theo armed with nothing but fruit
triggered a look of utter terror from Sofia.

"They have *guns*," she whispered.

He shushed her again, then slowly maneuvered
himself into throwing position, down on one knee, still
hidden behind the mound of garbage bags. He reared
back and let the apple fly with all his strength. It soared
into the night sky, invisible in the darkness. It seemed
to take forever to return to earth. Then, finally—
splat—it landed somewhere in the lighted alley behind
the men.

The two men turned quickly, weapons drawn.

For a moment, Theo thought they'd been fooled. He was only half right. The larger man signaled his partner to check it out. The good soldier turned and retreated, but the leader stayed on mission. He was headed straight toward the mound of garbage bags behind the grocery store.

Theo glanced at Sofia, and the look of terror in her eyes had just popped off the charts. Theo gave her hand a reassuring squeeze, and then he squatted even lower, ready to pounce like a cat.

The gunman was just fifteen feet away and closing.

Keep coming, thought Theo. *I can use a new pistol.*

At five feet away, Theo grabbed a big green bag of garbage with both hands.

One more step.

The man stopped and aimed his pistol. Before he could shoot, Theo leapt from hiding, hitting him first with the bag of garbage, and then laying into him with his entire body. The gun flew across the alley as Theo took the man down, hard, to the pavement.

"Get the gun!" Theo shouted, but Sofia was frozen.

The man was a tough fighter, but Theo had top position, and his fists battered him like a jackhammer.

"Sofia, get the gun!"

Out of nowhere a knife appeared and slashed Theo across the forearm. His cry of pain jolted Sofia into action. The men rolled toward the center of the alley, and when they stopped their tumble, Theo was on the bottom. His arm and fingers were cut from fending off the blade, and the blood from his wounds had splattered into his left eye, turning half his world into a dark blur. He saw his attacker's arm jerk back, and he saw the tip of the blade coming toward him.

Then he heard the gunshot, and the man fell, his body draped over Theo like a lead blanket.

Theo pushed him off and ran to Sofia. She was trembling, tears running down her face, the gun still in her hand.

Theo grabbed the gun and pushed her behind the mound of garbage. Another gunshot rang out in the alley just as Theo dove into the mound behind her. He whirled and fired at the shooter, who fired right back. Theo squeezed off another half dozen rounds, unleashing enough firepower to send the message that he meant business. Then there was silence.

Once again, he heard the click of heels on pavement, but they were unsteady and fading this time—the sound of a wounded man in retreat.

Chapter 56

Frank Madera knew it was bad.

He staggered through the alley, stepping in a pile of juicy mush as he crossed from one side to the other. It smelled like apples. Stinky, rotten apples. It was amazing how the sense of smell could remain robust even as the rest of the body was shutting down from trauma.

His feet were heavy and could carry him no farther. His knees buckled, and he fell against a Dumpster. He managed to grab the rusty lid and hold himself up, but not for long. Slowly, he slid down the side of the green Dumpster, his back swiping it with a long crimson streak. Too much blood. The exit wound from the bullet was even worse than he'd feared.

He reached inside his jacket to assess the damage. The entry wound was just to the right of the sternum.

The clean hole on his shattered rib could have been full-metal-jacket ammunition, but Madera sensed that something even more deadly was at work. Though his body was slipping into shock, the pain not fully expressed, he could tell that this bullet had yawed violently on impact and blown through his body like a snowplow, compressing soft tissue, shredding his lung, and pushing bone fragments out what had to be a devastating hole in his back. Perhaps it was just his mind running wild, confusing rifle with pistol ammo, but the wound had modified .45-caliber FMJ written all over it, probably a tail-heavy cartridge with an interior tip of aluminum, or possibly wood pulp. What did it matter?

I'm a dead man.

He pulled his cell phone from his inside pocket. It felt incredibly heavy in his hand, and he had to wipe the blood off the keypad with his sleeve. He was about to dial 911 when he noticed that the eerie black flow at his sternum was starting to foam. Pneumothorax—a sucking chest wound. He'd watched a fellow soldier die from one on the battlefield. Two weeks later, he'd shoveled the remains of his best friend from a street in Baghdad after a car bombing. He himself had been wounded in combat in a second tour of duty, this one in Afghanistan. None of the suffering or sacrifice, however, had diminished his sense of duty. He'd come home and joined the Secret Service, the only member of his class to have seen combat and hold a Purple Heart. But as time wore on, others were promoted, and Madera was not. Two of his classmates made it to the presidential protection team, and he was denied. That was when he'd cut his deal with Joe Dinitalia. The way he saw it, Madera was good enough to fight for his country, good enough to kill for it, and good enough to die for it. He was good enough to lose a tiny bit of hearing in his right ear in service to his country, only to have the Secret Service hold it against him. He was damaged goods, not good enough to guard the president. So, he figured, he might as well own him.

His breath was short. The foam around his wound was thickening. Madera had even less time left than he'd thought. Calling for an ambulance would have been pointless. He could have called Dinitalia to tell him that he'd failed, but that, too, seemed pointless. Nothing seemed to matter, except for one thing.

Maybe the loss of blood was making him delusional. Perhaps the shame of a good soldier turned bad finally came to a head. Or it simply could have been a dying man's bitter sense of irony. Whatever was driving him in those final moments, Agent Madera chose to make things the way they should have been.

He did his Secret Service duty and called the commander in chief.

The call came on an encrypted cell line that only one man ever used. The message, however, was unlike any that President Keyes had ever received.

"Agent down," said Madera, "and it's me. Sergeant Chavez, MDPD, is your go-to on the Greek. Texting you his number now. You're on your own with Sofia."

"What?" said the president, but in the time it had taken to put the question, he grasped Frank's meaning. That hollow, fragile voice reminded the president of his father's final breath.

"Frank, are you still there?"

The line was silent, but the president didn't hang up right away. No matter how he felt about Frank Madera, hearing him utter his last words—a warning—was unsettling.

The president tucked away the phone and peered out the dark tinted window of the armored black Cadillac DTS.

Traffic was stopped at every intersection as the presidential motorcade, thirty-five vehicles in length, headed away from the airport. The president and Harry Swyteck were alone in the rear compartment, the president facing forward and Harry seated directly across with his back to the driver. The television was tuned to *Action News*, and Harry's eyes had been glued to the standoff—until Madera's phone call.

"You look upset," said Harry.

They passed a Japanese car dealership that was flying a lighted American flag as big as Montana. The president looked at Harry and said, "You really want the truth?"

"I told you I did."

President Keyes nodded, turning very serious. "The truth is that my worst fears have been realized."

"How so?"

"Frank Madera killed Phil Grayson."

Harry's mouth fell open. "How do you know?"

"He just confessed to me. He said he's going to turn himself in to the FBI immediately."

"I can't believe this."

"Think about it. Frank was in Florida when Phil died. He was head of his security detail. He had access to and control over everything Phil did, everyone he saw, everything he ate, everything he drank. It's entirely plausible that he overmedicated Phil, so to speak, which caused the heart attack."

Harry took a moment. "That's a lot of information you just gathered from a half-minute phone conversation."

"Much of it is deduction on my part."

"I don't understand the motive. Why would Frank Madera kill the vice president?"

"Like I mentioned to you before, Phil had his thing with Chloe Sparks when she worked for him. Things were heating up between the two of them again. Don't quote me on this, but it's beginning to sound to me like some kind of deadly vice president, Secret Service agent, girl-gone-wild triangle." The president glanced at the television, then back at Harry. "And this Demetri character seems to have figured it all out."

"Incredible," said Harry.

"Incredible, yes," said the president, wondering how much of the story Harry was really buying. "And yet entirely plausible."

The telephone rang in the FBI command center. It was another star-69 return call from Demetri. Andie answered on the second ring.

"Do you have protection for Sofia yet?"

Andie hesitated. The worst thing for any negotiator was to be caught in a lie, but she could tell from Demetri's tone that there was only one acceptable answer.

"Yes," she said.

"Good girl. Let me speak to her."

"She's not with me."

"You said you had her, liar!"

"No, you asked if I had protection for her, and we do."

"Don't play word games with me! Where is she?"

"Everything's cool, all right? I'm going to follow up right now and prove it to you. I can call you back in ten minutes with an update."

"You've got five minutes, and counting, to put Sofia on the line. Or I start shooting."

He hung up on her.

Andie's hand trembled, but not for long. As quickly as she could, she dialed Theo's number.

Chapter 57

Theo couldn't hear his cell phone ring over the sounding alarm, but he felt the vibration in his pocket. He kept running, leading Sofia by the hand.

Theo had backtracked halfway out of the dark alley when he thought he'd heard reinforcements coming. His only choice was to push onward, and in a blind alley, that meant breaking *through* the mom-and-pop grocery store. A single gunshot to the door lock had done the trick—and triggered the alarm.

"Keep moving!" said Theo.

An orange beacon swirled overhead, and a shrill pulsating alarm assaulted their ears as they raced up the aisle and past the bread and cereal. Sofia was keeping pace, just barely, as Theo pulled, more than led, her past the checkout lanes and to the entrance doors.

"Stand back!"

Sofia ducked as Theo fired a shot at the sliding glass door, shattering it into thousands of pellets of safety glass that scattered across the floor. Theo grabbed Sofia, and together they ran through the busted door and out into the parking lot.

A police siren sounded a few blocks away. Theo stopped and faced Sofia, a hand on each of her shoulders, as he tried to talk sense into her. "We should stay right here and let the police find us."

"No!"

"That's the safest thing."

"If Demetri thinks I turned myself in to the police, he will never listen to me. And then I'm no help to your friend or those other hostages."

The siren was getting closer, and the old woman had a point. Some folks were raised to trust cops, but Theo hadn't grown up in that neighborhood.

"This way," he said.

He led her across the parking lot to the street. A pizza delivery car was rounding the corner. Theo threw himself down in the middle of the lane, flat on his back, as if he were dead.

"Flag him down! I'm hurt and I need to go to the hospital."

"You're hurt?"

"Just do it!"

Sofia waved her arms at the approaching set of headlights. Theo watched with eyes wide open and his ear to the pavement. The delivery car didn't seem to be slowing down. Sofia waved more frantically. The car only sped up, and when it was close enough for Theo to read the spoof license plate—DRIVE IT LIKE YOU STOLE IT—Theo rolled into the gutter. The car zipped past him, a split second away from turning him into roadkill.

"Asshole!" said Theo—though he knew that in Miami he was lucky if the guy didn't back up and try to kill him on the second pass.

Theo jumped to his feet, grabbed Sofia by the hand, and led her across the street. The siren blared even louder, and Theo could see flashing police beacons in the intersection up the street. No way would the cops arrive at the scene of a break-in and ignore the black guy standing on the sidewalk. They needed to get out of sight and fast. Just then, Theo noticed a second pizza delivery car parked outside the strip mall.

"The pizza joint!" said Theo.

They hurried across the parking lot to the little storefront pizza parlor. The sign in the window said OPEN TILL 4 A.M., and they'd just made it. A bell chimed as Theo yanked the door open, and they ducked inside.

Behind the counter, an old man was tossing a giant Frisbee of dough high into the air, singing along to "Saturday in the Park" by Chicago.

Theo walked up as if nothing had happened. "Medium pepperoni, two Cokes, one with extra ice, and the key to your bathroom."

"Takeout only," he said. "Dining area's closed."

"No problem, dude."

Theo glanced out the parlor window and saw police cars pulling up to the grocery store across the street. "We really need to use the bathroom."

"They're in the back."

"Perfect," said Theo.

"You'll need a key."

"Even better," said Sofia.

"Men's or women's?"

They answered simultaneously, Sofia saying "Men's" and Theo saying "Women's."

The pizza chef looked at the two of them as if they were the strangest couple he'd ever seen, and he handed over both keys. Theo led Sofia into the men's room and locked the door. It was a small room with a pedestal sink and a single toilet. Sofia put the lid down on the toilet and took a seat. Theo checked his cell and found a missed call from Andie. He dialed her back.

Andie said, "I have three minutes to get Sofia on the line with her ex-husband."

"You're in luck," said Theo. "She's right here with me."

"Thank God. Stay on the line, I'm going to do a three-way. Oh, one other thing, I'm going to identify you as Agent Knight. You're Sofia's assigned body-guard."

"Sofia says he won't trust her if he thinks she's with the cops."

"Just trust me on this. No time to explain. Can you put your cell phone on speaker?"

Theo laid the phone on the sink and hit the speaker feature.

"How's that?" he said.

"Good," she said. "Sofia, this is Agent Henning. Can you hear me?"

"Yes," she said weakly.

"You'll need to speak up. I'm going to do a three-way conversation with you, me, and Demetri. I have about fifteen seconds to coach you, so listen to what I'm saying. You cannot promise him anything. You should ask him to surrender, and that's it. If things start to go badly, I will drop you from the call. Under-stood?"

"Yes," she said, her voice even weaker.

"I can hardly hear you," said Andie. "Theo, take the phone off speaker and get back on the line."

He switched off the speaker and spoke, just the two of them. "It's me."

"You think she understands?"

"I do," said Theo. "She really wants to help these hostages."

"Okay. Hold on."

Theo listened as she dialed up the three-way call. The next thing he heard was Demetri's voice on the line.

"You better not be stalling, Henning."

"I have good news. We have Sofia. Would you like to speak to her now?"

Theo could almost feel the release of tension on the line. The change in Demetri's tone was a complete emotional turnaround.

"Yes," he said. "Put *amore mio* on the line."

"Agent Knight," said Andie. "Give her the phone."

Chapter 58

"Sofia?" said Demetri.

He had her on speakerphone, leaving him free to hold his pistol in one hand and the dead security guard's gun in the other. Jack could hear both ends of the conversation, and he was close enough to Demetri to get a sense of what he was feeling as well. The hot spotlights above the set were taking their toll. Jack was sweating, and Demetri was having an even harder time with the heat, the back of his shirt stuck to his body with perspiration. Demetri looked upward to the catwalk. Jack subtly followed his gaze. The Greek was clearly on alert to a possible SWAT maneuver, but he was determined to talk to Sofia even as he kept watch.

"Demetri," she said, her voice quaking over the speaker on the news desk. "I want you to put down your guns and give up."

"I can't do that, love."

"Please."

"No. And don't ask me to do that again. There's work to be done here."

"I don't understand why you're doing this."

He paused, and even though it probably didn't come across on television, Jack was close enough to see him swallow the lump in his throat. Whether she was trying to push his emotional buttons or not, Sofia clearly had a hold on him.

"It's all I got left," he said.

"That's not true."

"It is," he said. "From the day you left, I had nothing. Now I got something. And I'm going to use it."

"I have it, too, Demetri. The same power. But you don't see me using it. It's wrong. You're destroying a man's life."

"They destroyed our life!"

"This isn't going to fix that."

"Those bastards—"

He stopped himself and looked up. Something had drawn Demetri's attention up to the darkest shadows in the catwalk, and it wasn't just the paranoia of a stressed-out gunman. Jack had heard the noise, too.

Demetri climbed up on the news desk and redirected one of the suspended spotlights toward the newsroom.

The beam of light swept over the maze of office cubicles and up into the catwalk.

"Are you sending someone in, Henning?"

"No, Demetri. There's nothing going on."

"I heard something. You heard it, too, Swyteck. Don't lie. You heard that noise, didn't you?"

Jack could have lied, but he didn't want to antagonize him. "Buildings can make all kinds of sounds," said Jack.

"Not like that one. They're up to something." He climbed down from the news desk and stepped closer to the speakerphone.

"Tell them to back off, Henning. Back off right now."

Sofia said, "Please, Demetri. Just give up."

"Stay on the line, love. We'll talk. Just as soon as I deal with this pest."

Andie muted the landline to the newsroom and dialed up Sergeant Figueroa on her other phone.

"Please don't tell me that MDPD has a sniper in the catwalk."

"All right, I won't tell you," said Figueroa.

"Damn it, Manny. Stop working against me."

"Cool your jets. He couldn't get a shot. Too many obstructions. We pulled him."

"Are you redeploying him?"

"Are you telling me not to?"

"I'm asking for a little interagency cooperation," said Andie. "One more rattle from anywhere up in that catwalk and we are going to have one ticked-off gunman on our hands."

"One more reason to have a sniper in position."

"We've got it covered."

"Your tactical team has a shoot-to-kill order?"

"I said we've got it covered."

Demetri was still studying the catwalk, even as he spoke. "Sofia, this might not play out the way I want it to tonight. But it will all turn out for the best."

He looked at Jack and said, "Tell her, Swyteck."

Jack withdrew. "Tell her what?"

"Tell her what we did about the money that's coming."

Jack took a moment. Demetri was giving him the opportunity to speak, maybe his last chance to take control of the situation. Jack had to make it count.

Demetri walked over and put the gun to Jack's head. "Tell her!"

"Okay, no problem," said Jack. He was waiting for Demetri to lower the gun, but it remained fixed against the back of Jack's head.

"Sofia," he said, "this is Jack Swyteck."

"I know. I can see you on the TV."

Demetri nudged Jack's head forward with the gun. "Stop stalling."

"Right," said Jack. "I'm a lawyer, so Demetri asked me to help him make a will."

"What for?"

"Just like everyone else, he wants to make sure that he has control over where his possessions go after he dies."

"Demetri, stop this," said Sofia. "It's scaring me."

"Love, just listen to this. Go ahead, Swyteck."

The gun at the back of his head made it tough for Jack to think clearly, but a second chance to talk his way out of this mess would probably never come. He had to go for it.

"Demetri and I got to talking about what's important to him," said Jack, laying on a little schmaltz. "He wanted everything to go to you."

The Greek seemed pleased with the way Jack had characterized it.

"Did you hear that, love?"

"You see," said Jack, keeping himself involved, "a married man doesn't even need a will for everything to go to his wife. But you two were divorced, so it's different. If Demetri didn't have a will, it might go to nobody. Or it might go to another heir. Maybe even an heir he didn't know about. Do you understand what I'm saying, Sofia?"

She didn't answer, and her silence told Jack that he was on to something—something that had been percolating in the back of his mind ever since Sofia had confided in him about the terrible night in Cyprus that had changed everything for her and Demetri.

"Love, did you hear what he said?" said Demetri.

Jack said, "Of course, none of this surprised me—"

"Enough, Swyteck."

"—after what you told me about Demetri."

Jack's words hung in the air. He'd planted the seed, and he waited. Demetri bit.

"What did she say about me?"

Success. Jack almost smiled to himself, but that simply wasn't possible with a loaded gun pointed at his brain.

"Sofia, do you remember what you told me?" said Jack.

She didn't answer immediately, which again told Jack that he was on the right track.

"Yes," she said finally, her voice laden with reluctance.

"We talked about that night in Cyprus," said Jack. "We talked about what happened after those men threw Demetri off the building and came back into the apartment."

"Don't go into that," said Demetri.

"Do you know what happened?" Jack asked him.

"Of course I know," said Demetri. "I told you."

"Sofia," said Jack. "Demetri thinks he knows what happened after he was thrown off the building. Does he?"

Demetri pushed the gun even harder against Jack's head, so hard that Jack feared it might go off.

"I told you not to go into that!"

"No," said Sofia. "He doesn't know."

Jack breathed. Demetri froze.

"What?" said Demetri.

Jack said, "He's got the wrong idea, doesn't he, Sofia?"

Jack could see himself and Demetri on the television screen. Demetri looked ready to hit someone, and if Sofia bailed out on Jack now, it could be deadly.

"Sofia?" said Jack. "He's wrong, isn't he?"

The line was silent, and Jack worried that his gamble was about to backfire. Finally, Sofia answered.

"He was misled," she said.

Demetri was speechless for a moment, as a wave of anger slowly washed over him.

"How do *you* know what happened?" he said, jabbing the other gun into Jack's spine.

Jack measured his words, careful not to make Demetri look or feel stupid on television. That, too, could have been deadly.

"I'm a criminal defense lawyer," said Jack. "People have told me terrible stories—things they did or things that were done to them. Each of you told me in our own words what happened that night in Cyprus. Demetri, you told it like someone who believed it. Sofia, you told it like someone who wanted others to believe it."

"That's a crock," said Demetri. "How did you *know*?"

"It was a process," said Jack. "But the moment it came clear to me was when Sofia came to my office. Do you remember that, Sofia?"

"I remember being there. But I'm not sure what moment you're talking about."

Jack said, "Somebody was tracking you down to kill you because you knew something about the president— something so powerful that it could end his presidency. You wouldn't tell me how you got that information. At first I thought you were protecting yourself. Then I thought you were protecting Demetri. Then I realized I was completely off base."

Demetri said, "What are you saying?"

Jack ignored him, speaking to Sofia. "You were concerned about someone else entirely," said Jack, "weren't you?"

"Who?" said Demetri. "Who else knows? Sofia, did you tell someone else?"

Jack softened his tone a bit, but he stayed with Sofia, ignoring Demetri.

"What was it that finally convinced you so many years later, Sofia? Was it DNA? Was it the birthmark on his forehead? Or was it the same thing I saw when I met you face-to-face—the way he has your eyes, your mouth, your entire persona, really."

Demetri was suddenly silent, stunned, it seemed, that Jack knew.

Sofia said, "Does it really matter?"

"No," said Jack. "All that really matters is what you did after you figured out the truth. Demetri used it to make a buck. But you went completely the other way. You handled it only the way a mother would handle it. A birth mother who discovered that the child she had brought into the world was—"

"The son of rapists," said Demetri.

Sofia was sobbing on the line. "I'm so sorry, Demetri."

"It's not your fault. You were raped."

Sofia said, "You tell him, Jack."

"I don't have to," said Jack. "She already told you, Demetri. There was no rape."

"Then why did you say there was?"

"Don't you see?" said Sofia, a hint of anger in her cracking voice. "They threw you off a building for stealing fifty dollars a week. Do you think I wanted to raise a son to grow up in that world? I told you that I was raped so that my baby could have a chance. So you would *want* to give him up for adoption. I was so depressed, pregnant with you in the hospital. Who knows if I would have made the same decision if I had to do it all over again? But that's what I did. I'm sorry. And I'm not sorry. Look what he grew up to become."

Demetri stepped away, muttering in disbelief. "I blackmailed my own son."

Jack could see him slipping. He needed to reel Demetri in.

"You had no idea he was your child," said Jack.

"I sold his secret. I made him a puppet to Big Joe Dinitalia. I told the fucking mob that he was born in Cyprus. Do you know what that means? Swyteck, you're a lawyer. Do you know?"

Jack didn't answer.

"Tell them!" he shouted, gesturing to the camera. "Tell the idiots at home what it means if the president of the United States was born in Cyprus."

"He can't be president," said Jack. "He's not a natural-born citizen."

"*My son,*" said Demetri, his face ashen. "I took this away from my own son. This can't be happening."

"Demetri, it's over," said Jack.

"That cannot be my child."

"He is," said Sofia, "I'm sorry."

"No, *no!*" he said, screaming at the top of his voice. He threw a desk chair across the set, then another. The second one flew all the way to the weather set and knocked down the green screen.

"You bitch! How could you do that to me, trick me into giving away my own flesh and blood?"

He went to the news desk, grabbed the handwritten will, and tore it into pieces.

"This changes everything! You hear me? *Everything!*"

He walked around to the front of the news desk. Shannon cowered, thinking he was looking to take it out on a woman—any woman. But he pulled Jack to his feet.

Jack made fists to conceal the nail file, but Demetri noticed the blood.

"What you got in your hand?" he said.

Jack didn't answer.

"Open 'em," said Demetri.

Jack obeyed, and the nail file dropped to the floor.

Jack braced himself for the kind of beating Pedro had gotten earlier, but Demetri restrained himself.

"You're lucky I need you," he said coldly. "Or I'd kill you right now."

Demetri rummaged through the first-aid kit on the news desk and grabbed a roll of white medical tape. Then he pushed Jack forward to face the camera and came up behind him. He put the pistol to his head, pressed the sticky end of the tape to his gun hand, and started unrolling.

"Don't try this at home, folks," he said.

The tape went around Jack's head, and covered his mouth, and then it wrapped back around Demetri's gun hand. He continued the same motion over again, securing his wrist to the gun, and the gun to Jack's head.

"Do you see what I'm doing here, Henning?"

"This is a big mistake," said Andie.

Jack clenched the tape in his mouth like a bit, tasting the adhesive. Demetri kept unrolling it, this time going up around Jack's forehead, then wrapping it back around his gun hand. He continued the same motion over and over again, alternating between the mouth and forehead, securing his wrist to the gun, and the gun to Jack's head. When he'd finished, the gun was fixed in position and aimed at the back of Jack's head.

"Perfect," said Demetri, as he tossed what remained of the roll onto the desk. "We're like Siamese twins now."

Jack started gnawing at the tape in his mouth, grinding his teeth back and forth.

"Henning, listen to me good," said Demetri, his voice rising. "I'm walking out that door right now, and I'm leaving this building. Maybe some trigger-happy SWAT guy thinks he can get a shot at me, but take a good look at what I've rigged up here. If a sniper drops me, this pistol is going off, and Swyteck loses the top of his head. You see that?"

"I see."

Jack kept gnawing at the tape.

"Good. Here's the deal. Have a car waiting in the parking lot with a full tank of gas. If it's not there when I walk out, Swyteck dies. And remember this: I don't care about anyone or anything no more. Not the money, not the hostages, not even you, Sofia. *Especially* not you.

"Come on, Swyteck, you're my ticket out of this—"

Demetri stopped himself, then checked the tape. Jack could feel the wiggle room in Demetri's contraption.

"Damn you! You bit clean through it!"

Andie said, "I don't like what I'm seeing, Demetri."

"Too bad," he said as he reached for the roll of tape.

"I really don't like what I'm seeing," she said.

"I really don't care."

Jack glanced at the television. Demetri was assessing the damage that Jack's teeth had done to his gun rig, and he seemed to be trying to figure out how to repair it with the small amount of remaining tape.

"I see this as a big problem," said Andie.

"For you it is," said Demetri.

"Yes, I see everything clearly now. I see we are going to have to do something quick. Very quick. I can see that."

As Demetri struggled with the tape, Jack suddenly realized that Andie was speaking to him, not Demetri.

"I can see it all," said Andie.

She's definitely talking to me, thought Jack.

He checked the television monitor again. With only one free hand, Demetri was having trouble getting the tape started. Jack still felt plenty of give in the lower half of the rig around his head.

"Now!" Andie shouted.

The next few seconds should have been a complete blur, yet they unfolded for Jack like a slow-motion re-play. The television screen went black. Jack dropped to his knees. His head jerked out from under Demetri's contraption of white tape.

And the crack of gunfire in the studio reverberated like a cannon in a cave.

Chapter 59

At first Jack thought Demetri's pistol had discharged, and the hot spray of blood across his back and neck made him wonder if he'd been hit. Then Demetri collapsed on top of him, knocking Jack forward, and the two men landed side by side on the floor. The gaping wound in the top of Demetri's head told Jack that the blood, bits of bone, and gray matter on their clothes, on the floor, and all around them was not his own.

The Greek was gone.

The doors to the newsroom flew open, Demetri's makeshift barricade of stacked office furnishings toppled over, and FBI SWAT rushed in.

"Fan out, fan out!" the leader shouted, and the team scattered.

Two men dressed in full tactical gear went to Demetri. Three more went to Jack and the other hostages. The rest of the team swept through the newsroom to check for booby traps or other dangers.

"Are you hurt?" one of the SWAT agents said.

Jack sat up slowly, not really sure.

Andie rushed onto the set with a team of paramedics, and they started toward him.

"Help the cameraman," said Jack.

The paramedics went to Pedro. Andie came straight to Jack and knelt beside him on the floor, her tone beyond urgent.

"Are you all right?" she said.

"I think so."

She held him tight, ignoring the blood on his clothes, and kissed him. "You scared me to death when you ducked down before the shot."

"I thought that was what you were trying to tell me to do."

"No, I was coordinating the kill of the broadcast with the shot from the sniper. We had to make sure it wasn't on the air."

The television on the news set suddenly resumed playing, but Jack was not on the screen. *Action News* had shifted to the presidential motorcade.

"Where's my father?"

"He's on his way here with the president."

"I need to call him."

"Sure," she said, handing him her cell. "But we need you to keep it short."

"Why?"

Her gaze drifted toward the presidential motorcade on the television screen. "You'll see."

Harry took the call in the back of the limousine. It was hard to keep his emotions in check, but he, too, knew that the phone conversation had to be brief.

Harry and President Keyes had watched the final moments of the standoff unfold on television. Harry's pulse was still pounding. At one point, he'd honestly believed he was on the verge of cardiac arrest. He couldn't bear to watch, but he couldn't tear himself away from the television screen. He'd literally yelped when the broadcast went black, and he could hardly breathe again until the call from the CIRG leader confirmed that the mission had succeeded and that Jack was unharmed. Even so, his voice shook throughout the conversation with Jack.

"You're sure you're okay?" said Harry.

"Really, Dad. Other than a jab in the wrist from a nail file, I'm fine."

"I can't wait to see you. I'll be there in fifteen minutes."

Harry ended the call and tucked the phone into his pocket.

Seated across from him, President Keyes was wrapping up a phone call of his own. He hung up and peered out the window, so preoccupied that he didn't even ask Harry about his son.

"Jack sounds just fine," said Harry.

"What? Oh, God, I'm sorry."

"It's all right. That was quite a final performance by Demetri. I'm sure you have plenty on your mind."

Keyes was suddenly defensive. "None of it's true. You realize that, don't you?"

Harry said nothing.

"I mean, I've never even been to Cyprus. I was born in Pennsylvania. It says so right on my birth certificate."

Harry said, "I wouldn't put one ounce of blame on your adoptive parents for doing that."

"Blame them for doing what?"

"It's perfectly understandable that they would have falsified a birth certificate to keep you or someone else from finding out that your biological father was the man who raped your birth mother."

"I'm *not* the son of a rapist."

"But maybe your adoptive parents thought you were. Just as Demetri did all these years."

The president fell silent, staring blankly out the window at the painted traffic lines on the interstate.

"My father must be turning in his grave," he said.

Harry felt a little sorry for him, having just had his moment with his own son. But he stayed focused.

"You weren't born in this country, were you?"

The president didn't answer right away. Finally, he shook his head.

"I was two months old when I came here. A nice young couple who couldn't get pregnant adopted me. I've never known another country or another culture. I never even traveled outside the United States until I was in college." He gave Harry a sobering look and said, "But I can't be president."

"A dumb rule, I suppose," said Harry.

"But it's in our Constitution. Article II, clause five."

"I'm just amazed that your adoption was able to be kept secret all these years."

"It was never an issue. Not even when I announced my candidacy for president did people have any reason to question my birthplace."

"Funny," said Harry. "In this world of information overload, we think we know everything about our leaders. But still we don't *know* them."

"You're talking as if this is an obvious thing. It's not. Do your homework. Before the laws changed in 1961, you could even do an adoption by proxy from places like Cyprus. International adoptions in this country were a mess."

"Was yours one of the messy ones?"

"It was 1960, Harry. Imagine a woman knows her life would be better without the man she's married to, but she doesn't have the courage to leave him. She tells her husband that the father of their child was the man who raped her, but she wants to keep the baby anyway. What do you think she expects a thug like Demetri to do?"

"Leave, I'm sure."

"But maybe he surprises her. Maybe he loves her so much in his own twisted and controlling way that he thinks he can fix things—if he can just get rid of the kid. So he convinces Cypriot officials to look the other way as the child is smuggled out of the country, no paper trail. The baby is sold on the black market to an unmarried woman in Philadelphia who, for a fee, falsifies the birth records and pretends that the baby is hers. A nice couple then makes a perfectly legal adoption, knowing nothing about the smuggling or supposed rape that took place halfway around the world."

"Are you saying that's what happened?"

The ensuing silence was profound, not even the drone of rubber tires on the interstate audible in the fortified limousine.

"What are you going to do now?" said Harry.

He shot Harry a puzzled look. "You said it yourself, this natural-born-citizen rule is just plain dumb. I'm going to fight it."

"How?"

"With guns blazing. You have to stay with me on this."

"What do you mean?"

The president leaned forward, suddenly energized. "Stick with the plan, Harry. Be my vice president."

"And do what? Pretend I don't know your situation?"

"You don't know it."

"You just told me."

"Forget what I just told you."

"You can't hide this," said Harry. "They'll do DNA tests on you, Sofia, and Demetri."

"My lawyers can tie that up."

"Somebody is probably pulling copies of your phony birth certificate even as we speak."

"The birth certificate says I was born at home to an unmarried woman in Philadelphia who died thirty years ago. Both my adoptive parents are deceased. Demetri's dead. To this day, Sofia doesn't want to say or do anything to hurt her son. Who's to say that the fingerprints and footprints on the birth certificate were made when I was eight weeks instead of eight hours old? I've had a social security number since I was three months old. There's no paper trail back to Cyprus, and the records here are airtight."

"You can't keep this up forever."

"I don't have to. There are only two years left on my term. You step in as my vice president now, and you're the heir apparent to the Oval Office."

"I can't do that," said Harry.

"Sure you can."

"No. I really can't."

"You're being a fool."

"Maybe I am."

"Do you realize that if I'm forced to resign before you're confirmed, you'll never be vice president?"

"I do understand that."

"Your only way to the White House is through the vice presidency—through *me*."

"That looks like a pretty tough road right now, Mr. President."

"Harry, get a grip. You're not negotiating from a position of power."

"Negotiating?"

"Listen to what I'm saying. Either you stand behind me, or I'm pulling your nomination."

"Do what you have to do, sir."

"Are you crazy?" he said, his voice turning shrill. "What's wrong with you? You have nothing right now, do you understand? You have no power over me. You are not the sitting vice president. You do not rise to the presidency if I'm forced out. You are *not* Phil Grayson!"

A chilling silence filled the vehicle. Their eyes locked, as if neither man could believe what President Keyes had just said.

Harry turned very serious. "Phil knew your secret, didn't he?"

"From a little whore named Chloe Sparks."

"You gave Madera the green light to eliminate him."

"I offered Phil the same deal I just offered you. Phil had to be a pain in the ass, wanted to be president right now."

"You killed him."

"I told Frank to deal with it. I didn't think he'd pump him so full of ED medication that he'd literally explode."

The limo stopped. Harry checked out the window. They were still on the interstate, at least a mile away from the *Action News* studio.

"Why are we stopping?" said the president, though the question wasn't really addressed to Harry.

His door opened.

"What's going on?"

Agent Schwartz was standing outside the limousine. He flashed his badge, his demeanor all business.

"Sir, could you please step out of the vehicle."

"I beg your pardon."

"Sir, don't make this worse than it already is. Please step out of the vehicle."

The president chuckled nervously, but he was the only one laughing.

"Harry, do you know anything about this?"

Harry didn't answer.

Agent Schwartz said, "Sir, could you please—"

"Yes, yes," he said as he climbed out of the limousine. "But this is totally outrageous and insulting beyond belief. In fact, it's inexcusable. I want your badge number."

Schwartz showed him his shield. "You have the right to remain silent. Everything you say can and will be used against you in a court of law."

"Surely you jest," said the president.

"You have the right to an attorney . . ."

"I don't need to hear this," he said. But the recitation of his rights continued, and the president only became more agitated. Two other agents from the motorcade approached the limousine, one of them with handcuffs.

The president was red in the face with anger. Media helicopters were hovering overhead.

"Do you actually think you can arrest me?"

"Can I have your wrists, sir?" said Schwartz.

"I won't stand for this."

"Sir, your wrists."

"Is this some kind of political power play? This is—"

He stopped himself, turned, and peered into the backseat of the limo. The door was still open, and Harry looked back at him.

"You're wired, aren't you?" said the president.

Harry said nothing.

"You sneaky son of a bitch. You're wearing a wire!"

Harry drew on his oldest roots—those of a Miami cop—and forced himself to show no sign of enjoyment or satisfaction. In fact, he watched without any reaction at all as Agent Schwartz drew the president's wrists behind his back and slapped on the handcuffs. But self-restraint had its limits. As the president stood outside his presidential limousine, glaring at the vice presidential nominee in disbelief, Harry couldn't resist one parting shot—if not for himself, then for Phil Grayson.

"How do you like those beans, Mr. President?" he said.

Chapter 60

Jack locked up his law office at 3:00 P.M. on December 22. The move to the new building on Main Highway was a success, at least according to Theo, who had quickly pointed out that the reception area was the perfect size for an air hockey table. "Situation normal" had returned to Jack's life, just in time to be screwed up by the holidays.

President Keyes had resigned from office on the day of his arrest, the first U.S. president ever to do so from a prison cell. With no sitting vice president, the Speaker of the House was sworn in as president, and he promptly nominated former U.S. attorney general Allison Leahy as his vice president. Harry Swyteck was out, just as Keyes had predicted. Jack had actually dreamt that he represented Sofia at her congressional confirmation hearing for the number two spot, but in reality she was happy to return to New York and pour what remained of her heart and soul into the bakery that she and her late husband Angelo had created.

Predictably, the media—especially the talk shows—continued to feast on the White House scandal 24/7. Rumors were rampant, but there were some credible leaks. The last Jack had heard, Keyes might even identify a certain mobster who controlled him and Frank Madera, but only if the prosecution would cut him a deal on the conspiracy-to-commit-murder charge. Jack suspected there would be no deals if Elizabeth and Marilyn Grayson had anything to say about it.

"Jack, hey, I'm glad I caught you."

Jack turned to see his father hurrying up the sidewalk. His Lincoln was at the curb outside Jack's office with the motor running.

"Mr. almost-vice-president, how are you, sir?"

"Very funny."

"I thought you were leaving for Colorado today," said Jack.

"We're off to the airport as soon as I pick up Agnes. But there was something I wanted to tell you before I go."

Jack knew what a nervous flyer his father was. "Dad, we have this same conversation every time you and Agnes fly together. I know where you keep the key to the safe deposit box."

"It's not that. Before everything went crazy in Washington, there were more than a few jokes made about the fact that I fired you as my lawyer. The damn gossip papers even picked it up. I'm sure you realize what that was all about, but I feel like something needs to be said between us."

"I understand completely," said Jack. "You were working with the FBI, and one member of the Swyteck family at risk was enough."

"That's part of it," said Harry.

Jack flashed a hint of concern. "What's the other part?"

"I just want you to have the total picture. Yes, I fired you to keep you out of danger. But if this whole thing had turned out differently—if I had become vice president—it would have been a dream come true to have my son working in Washington with me."

Jack smiled, even though years of sad history lay between the lines. During Governor Swyteck's first term, the problems had run much deeper than the obvious fact that Jack worked for the Freedom Institute and defended death row inmates, while his father was signing more death warrants than any governor in Florida history. The rocky history dated back to Jack's childhood, and politics had made their disagreement so public that the two men didn't even speak to each other.

"Chief Justice Jack Swyteck," said Jack. "Could have had a nice ring to it."

"Let's not get crazy in hindsight, all right?"

Jack stepped toward him, and they embraced.

"Oh, one other thing," said Harry. "I've completely run out of time with the holiday crunch. Can you stop by Carroll's Jewelers and pick up Agnes's Christmas present? It's an antique, I guess you'd say. Make sure it's cleaned up all pretty and overnight it to me."

"Sure thing. Have a great time in Beaver Creek."

Harry thanked him and went to his car.

Carroll's Jewelers on Miracle Mile wasn't exactly on Jack's way home, and the last-minute shoppers made getting there a bit like sneaking into the Super Bowl. Fortunately, the jeweler recognized him when he entered, and she brought the box to the counter straightaway and opened it for him.

"What do you think?" she said.

Jack slipped the ring onto the tip of his pinky and examined it beneath the spotlight.

"It looks like my mother's engagement ring," he said, puzzled.

"It is," said the jeweler. "It cleaned up nicely, don't you think?"

Precious few family heirlooms had been passed down through Jack's maternal family. His mother had come to Miami from Cuba as a teenager with little more than a suitcase in hand. The Castro regime didn't let her mother leave for another forty years, long after Anna Maria Fuentes had married Harry Swyteck and died giving birth to a son. The modest, round diamond in a traditional Tiffany setting was about what one would have expected from a recent college graduate in the mid-1960s. Jack had never asked for it, but he assumed it would be his someday—passed directly from his father.

"He's giving it to Agnes?"

The jeweler seemed confused by the question.

Jack said, "My father asked me to come by and pick up his Christmas present to her."

The jeweler smiled, as if suddenly realizing what was going on. "Same old Harry the jokester," she said, shaking her head. "I think you'd better read the card."

Jack took the envelope and tore it open. *"I'm not good at surprises,"* the card read, *"but I think I got you this time. Give this ring to someone you love as much as I loved your mother. Happy 40th birthday."*

Jack felt tingles, even if his fortieth had passed two weeks earlier. Still, it was an incredibly sentimental, un-Swyteck gesture coming from his father. A little pushy too, actually. Jack and Andie hadn't even broached the subject of marriage, but it seemed that Harry was weighing in with his two cents: *Approved.*

The jeweler put the ring back inside the box, no charge for the cleaning. Jack thanked her, went to the sorry rental car that had replaced another polished old gem—his 1968 Mustang, now junk—and headed for Coconut Grove to meet Andie.

Maybe it had been Harry's plan, or maybe it was the thought of being forty, but the ring got Jack to thinking. Andie Henning was unlike any other woman he'd known, a self-assured thrill seeker who liked to push life to the edge and lean over. Jack loved that she wasn't afraid to cave dive in Florida's aquifer, that in her training at the FBI Academy she'd nailed a perfect score on one of the toughest shooting ranges in the world, that as a teenager she'd been a Junior Olympic mogul skier—something Jack didn't even know about her until she rolled him out of bed one hot August morning and said, "Let's go skiing in Argentina." He loved the green eyes she'd gotten from her father, the raven-black hair from her mother—and he loved that beneath the outward beauty, there was an intelligent and intriguing half–Native American who had been adopted into a totally Anglo world and who was as thirsty for knowledge about her own cultural identity as Jack was about his half-Latin heritage.

His cell rang. It was Andie.

"Change of plans," she said. "Meet me at Cy's."

Cy's Place was special in Jack's book, and the grand opening had proved to be the night that everything clicked for Jack and Andie. The two of them had talked and laughed till 2:00 A.M., listening to Theo's uncle Cy give them a taste of Miami's old Overtown Village through his saxophone.

"See you in five minutes," Jack told her.

He arrived even sooner, but it took another five minutes in the parking lot to decide what to do with the diamond ring—hide it in the car or bring it inside with him. Car break-ins were rampant around the holidays, and the thought of his mother's engagement ring ending up in some pawnshop was too much to stomach. The box was too big for his pocket, so he removed the ring and put it in his pocket—promising himself that, no matter how much tequila he drank, the ring would not see the light of Cy's Place. Jack took the rear entrance through the kitchen and continued into the bar, where he was immediately greeted by a roaring "Surprise!"

Andie threw her arms around his neck and kissed him.

"Happy birthday, old man," she said.

Jack smiled, but he wasn't really surprised, even if it was more than two weeks after his actual birthday. Telling Andie *not* to throw him a party had been the surest way to get one. It was wall-to-wall memories as Jack embraced one old friend after another—Theo, who gave him a spine-cracking hug; Uncle Cy, dressed in his vintage natty tweeds; Neil Goderich, his first boss at the Freedom Institute; and on and on.

The longest hug, however, was for *Abuela*.

She tried to whisper something to him, but the emotions choked her. As much as Jack resembled his mother, his fortieth-birthday celebration was at least on some level a tough reminder of how long it had been since *Abuela* and her daughter had said good-bye.

"Drinks are on Jack!" shouted Theo.

Cocktails were flowing all around the big U-shaped bar, and Cy's Place was oozing that certain vibe of a jazz-loving crowd. Creaky wood floors, redbrick walls, and high ceilings were the perfect bones for Theo's club. Art nouveau chandeliers cast just the right mood lighting. Crowded café tables fronted a small stage for live music. The hand-painted banner hanging from the ceiling, however, was a bit puzzling:

HAPPY SECOND ANNIVERSARY!

"Second anniversary of what?" said Jack.

"Your thirty-ninth birthday," said Theo as he filled two shot glasses with his best *tequila añejo*. "Cheers, dude."

Jack belted back one with him, and then Andie intervened, promising to make it well worth his while if he remained conscious tonight. Theo talked him into one more when Andie wasn't looking, but Mexican brain-blaster number two put Jack in a serious, reflective mood.

"What are you thinking?" said Andie, as she returned to the bar stool beside him.

"Forty has been a pretty wild ride so far."

"You can say that again."

Theo came over in need of quarters for the pool table. "Dude, got any coin?"

Jack glanced at the cash register behind Theo's bar, but the point seemed too obvious to make. He emptied his pockets onto the bar top. The engagement ring poured out with his loose change, the diamond sparkling beneath the white LED lights. The sight of it nearly stopped Jack's heart, and he snatched it up. Theo grabbed the coins and, as he walked away, Jack buried the ring back in his pocket.

"What was that?" said Andie.

"What was what?"

She smiled. "That sparkly thing you just shoved back into your pocket."

"I didn't just shove any sparkly thing back into my pocket."

Her smile turned seductive, and with an inquisitive tilt of her head a wisp of long dark hair fell into her eyes the way Jack found irresistible.

"Jack?"

"Yeah?"

"Can I see it?"

"Nothing to see. Really."

"I want to see."

She reached for his pocket.

He grabbed her wrist.

She grabbed his elbow. "Jack?"

"Yeah?"

"Are you going to let me see? Or am I going to have to break your arm?"

"I—uhm . . ."

A saxophone bellowed, and Jack turned to see Theo coming toward him, his uncle's old Buescher 400 in hand. A jazz solo quickly morphed into his rendition of "Happy Birthday." The crowd began to sing, and suddenly Andie was leading Jack around the bar to a big cake with forty blazing candles.

" . . . *happy birthday, dear Ja-ack . . .*"

Andie came close and put her lips to his ear. "Come on, Swyteck. Just let me see it."

"*Happy birthday to youuuu!*"

Acknowledgments

"I've been orphaned," I said to myself as I hung up the telephone. I had one published novel to my credit, and my editor had called to tell me that he was leaving HarperCollins.

An hour later, the phone rang again. It was my agent, Artie Pine.

"You're going to get a call from Carolyn Marino. She's a big fan of yours. You're gonna like her."

That fan was my new editor. Over the next twelve years, Carolyn would guide me through fourteen novels of suspense. One of our most recent, and I think one of Carolyn's favorites (she loved Uncle Cy), was *Last Call*. The title now seems prophetic.

Amid the flurry of six Grippando novels in the span of three years, something happened on a less public level—the announced retirement of an outstanding editor at HarperCollins. She'd served the company brilliantly for eighteen years. More important (at least from my perspective), she groomed her stable of authors the way editors supposedly don't anymore. Many she discovered as newbies. Others were household names. All are better writers today, thanks to Carolyn Marino.

Carolyn is at least a foot shorter than my first editor at HarperCollins, probably less than half his weight. She's thoughtful and soft spoken. Her range of knowledge is astounding. (Can *you*, in the same breath, debate the legal niceties of bonding out a criminal defendant and then tell me when Prada shoes became generally available in the United States?) Her manners are impeccable. Thank-you notes are always handwritten—never e-mailed—and I've never heard her cuss. If you didn't know her, you might expect her to shush you at the library. You might even think the corporate world would eat her alive.

You'd be dead wrong.

"She's good," Artie's son Richard had warned me. "And she'll bust your chops."

She did, of course. Many times. But always *politely.*

Carolyn loves books. That may seem like an obvious and unnecessary thing to say about an editor. Carolyn's love is pure, however, and never cynical. Everything mattered—because everything could be made better. If it was time to start a new series, we talked about it. If my Russian mobster sounded too American, she'd tell me about it. If that scene with the python went a little too far, I'd hear about that, too. Her gift was in knowing when it was just right, whether it was the plot, a character, a sentence, or a word. Case in point: *Intent to Kill* (coming summer 2009). The first draft had my lead character take to the bottle after the tragic death of his wife. I thought I was creating the most engaging flawed protagonist since Paul Newman in *The Verdict*. "He's passed out drunk with his six-year-old daughter upstairs," said Carolyn. "I don't like him." He's now a lovable insomniac in the best father-daughter scenes I've ever written.

Sometimes Carolyn would tell me why a change was needed. Sometimes not. She just knew, even if she couldn't put it into words. That bothered me at first. I was a lawyer before I was a writer. Reasons were important. As a writer, however, you soon learn that only the weak and insecure feel a need to explain every editorial decision in terms of right and wrong or good and bad. The best editors aren't the ones who think their every hunch or impulse can be empirically justified. What you want is an editor who knows your body of work as well as you do, and who knows your audience

THE NEW LUXURY IN READING

We hope you enjoyed reading
our new, comfortable print size and found it
an experience you would like to repeat.

Well – you're in luck!

HarperLuxe offers the finest in fiction and
nonfiction books in this same larger print size and
paperback format. Light and easy to read, HarperLuxe
paperbacks are for book lovers who want to see
what they are reading without the strain.

For a full listing of titles and
new releases to come, please visit our website:

www.HarperLuxe.com